I0547603

THE JUDGE MERIT GOLFING CLUB

MATT HARGROVE

STRETCH RUN Publishing

Dallas

The Judge Merit Golfing Club is a work of fiction. Names, characters, places, occurrences, and incidents either are the product of the author's imagination or are used fictitiously. Any resemblance to actual persons, living or dead, events, or locales is entirely coincidental fiction.

Copyright © 2019 by Matt Hargrove

All rights reserved

Published in the United States of America by STRETCH RUN Publishing Company

ISBN: 978-1-7339331-0-0

eBook ISBN: 978-1-7339331-1-7

www.stretchrunpublishing.com

Illustrated by Jay Cantrell

TO

My Mother and Father

My Father taught me lessons, skills, and the things that are most important in sports. More importantly, the same in life. My Mother… the manners, the math, and much of all and everything beyond that. They are the best team I've ever witnessed in the definition of such.

THE JUDGE MERIT GOLFING CLUB

CHAPTER 1

The prairie, unbroken and slightly sloping downward toward nothing in the south, laid blanketed with a stretch of knee high sour green grass that went on as far as eyes could see. Off to the north was a short stint of the same, though gently rising to a ridge that ranged the landscape into the distant west. The open terrain was split in two by a new section of railroad track being placed by Hunt Railway & Navigation Company, albeit construction ceased last fall and work was moved to advance the northern part of the loop up near Whitewright. This pleasant morning in early spring found the stretch of fresh steel serving as the footpath for one westbound pilgrim, which was Sam. Along the rail line, to his left, was a rutted wagon trail and to his right, the Peltry River. Shallow and barely flowing in spots, the river resembled more of a proper creek. Scattered along the banks were gigantic elms with bustling undergrowth rising from the steep mud on either side, the only trees around besides a dozen clusters of oaks along the route or out in the fields. Spring rains had shown their grace a time or so and though leaving nothing yet in bloom, a new freshness was beginning to break in the land.

Sam, no doubt, felt a freshness looming in his own body and mind. Trouble had put him on the move for over two years and only in the last weeks had he began to feel somewhat comfortable with the expanding distance from the matter. Weary of living as a transient, he'd decided stopping time was coming. Two years going, plus a fair amount of time spent pretty much wandering prior to his imposition, was turning rough on the young fellow.

The first time he set out alone it was decided that going back north to try finding family was pointless, and that premise was followed upon embarking on this latest quest. This time Sam thought about heading to all sorts of different places, each an unknown destination in the disappearing act he was in the process of performing. Anything west of the Mississippi was a game option, until realizing the miles ahead were getting tougher. The young traveler quickly ruled out stretching the distance to the limit and going all the way west. The weather was reportedly ideal but the longer journey placed the Pacific as a last resort. Reeling back, the Rocky Mountains had his eye until he thought seriously about the cold and snow ruining so much playing time. After crossing the Mississippi, anything north was ruled out for the same reason. South, to the coast, was a dead end and probably crawling with friends and acquaintances of the problematic matter at hand. Making off in a sinuous and undulating direction toward nowhere particular, impulses were sworn off in deciding when and if a time and place were right. Anxiousness pricked deep though found itself fended off at the crossroads in numerous cities and towns. Mississippi, Arkansas, Louisiana. More distance was often the justification for moving on, and he did. Sam kept going, pondering his surroundings, and searching for a feeling. There wasn't exactly a finely tuned agenda, other than to stay unwavering in his plan.

Making his way down the tracks, steps were quick and landed longer than normal as the young and seasoned legs stretched to meet every other tie. Engulfing him at that moment was the feeling a horse gets when headed back to the barn after a long day out, eagerness sprung the hastened steps. Sam had faith that a blessing lay ahead in the unknown and his quickened pace was indication that the kid was ready for something positive to show itself.

Just ahead, the line ended with a painted wooden sign declaring so. He left his morning pathway and stepped outside the rails for the first time since sun up, veering down the slope at the spot where the river curves north toward the ridge. Sam walked under the shade of a group of elms to a small patch of loose black dirt amongst the weeds. Bending down, he placed on the ground a small wooden trunk with leather straps followed by a floppy leather satchel. A golf bag slung from his bony right shoulder. The bag was made of goat skin, about a hand length around by waist high, and stood erect with the help of a few yardsticks that were tied in place at the top and bottom of its interior. There was a tin coffee can, J.A. Folgers brand, lining the bottom of the bag and a double thickness of canvas reinforcing the top. Woven rope served as the shoulder strap and was affixed at each end with steel rings. A damp and dirty white cotton rag was knotted to the top ring. At the time, Sam carried only one golf club; the one he called the broadstick. A jewel of a tool when in the young hands.

Reaching to the ground, he snatched up a tattered leather golf ball that had been stitched together with horse hair and stuffed with boiled chicken feathers. Grimacing after a hard look at the expired orb and its busted condition, Sam untied a pocket on the side of his golf bag and swapped the used-up ball for a paper pouch of tobacco. He didn't much care for it, but the habit was recently taken up along the journey. The main idea was that smoking made him seem older, then it came to be an aid in passing time. One could suppose it helped to ease the nervousness, too.

A calmer mind grew at every footstep and even more so on each of the long train rides away from the quandary, along with a makeshift plan for what to do with himself. The feeling of a chase coming from behind was beginning to lessen, however, Sam had a lot of negative thoughts stuck as certain fact about the situation. He supposed wanted bills were up all over the south. All over the east coast, too. A poster, describing his height, weight, build, and a list of who-knows-what fabricated crimes was liable to be made available to people by the thousands. They probably even had an artist to sketch a likeness of his description.

Sam reckoned there was a small gang scouting around and spreading the word, plus any number of renegade bounty hunters out looking to make a nice chunk of change by securing his capture. He was cognizant to the likelihood of an intense manhunt and often wondered about the exact extent of all that. Making light in the situation, sometimes he'd make jokes to himself about the possible amount of the bounty they had advertised. Likely, it wouldn't have been less than twenty-thousand dollars. That's what he walked with, and those well-to-do Georgia boys were pretty ticked off suckers after getting taken on so many golf holes in a row.

Placing himself states away from the matter helped, but then again, they might always be on his trail. Surely, they were looking out west. All outlaws head west. No matter how far, Sam would always be mindful of the matter, as a bad reputation was indeed sticking around behind the hunt. Always wondering what's behind you is no way to live, and he was not one to go through his days in that manner. After time, he mostly subdued the 'what if' from being a bother, but always carried hints of uneasiness about the ordeal. He'd feel all right about things, then have a bad day and consider otherwise. The early days of the ordeal saw his ways quickly change and the young man started going around looking over his shoulder, if not, his head was down and hidden under a hat. One thing for sure, the end of the face of the earth would not turn him in the opposite direction.

Staring south into the mute landscape, rather than watching his hands work, Sam rolled a perfect smoke and tossed it to his mouth. Idle time had provided plenty of practice for perfecting the task. The cigarette dangled from his lips as he squatted and opened the trunk for a match and a freshly cleaned and folded white collared shirt. Sam nearly always wore a white collared shirt, sleeves rolled up, and navy-blue trousers. Always had his straw fedora on or, if not, handy nearby. Same thing every single day, though once in a while you'd catch him working in a pair of overalls. Still wore the white shirt with sleeves rolled. He was about average height for his age, trim. A handsome, well kept, young fellow. His looks most definitely had to of come from his mother. After tucking in his shirt tail, rolling his sleeves, and straightening his collar, Sam grabbed hold of a tin canteen and enjoyed a long and welcome guzzle of water. The young man doused his hand and rubbed it over his buzzed hair, then had a seat on his trunk to finish up the smoke and the gander into the southern prairie.

Milder weather, the pristine land, and the lack of people encountered over the last days had first brought about the idea. Perhaps there was some good ol' springtime motivation spawning his thoughts. Beginning to conceive that the distance was aplenty had made settling enter as a reality, rather than left standing as an out-of-the-question dream. The craving for what was around the next corner held strong desire to carry on living out of his suitcase, though a sensible brain was suggesting that it wasn't a brilliant plan to be galivanting in and around all the different cities and towns. Sooner or later he'd wind up at the wrong place in front of the wrong person, leading to trouble. Word can get around in a flash. Fact of the matter, he didn't know who all might be trying to sniff out his trail nor how close they might be. A nice out-of-the-way nook was the wise choice if he was going to settle and situating himself in a small town, a place that would be lasting, was certainly far more appealing to the laidback Sam than spending his days bouncing around dealing with the uncertainties that go along with rambling. In his current place, for whatever reasons, all was seeming to fit. Hope was at an all-time high.

Peering west through the tips of the grass, he could make out six structures showing themselves against the pearly blue horizon. Squinting to tell more, Sam stood and pulled his hat further down his forehead, gathered up his load, and then walked over the last section of rail. After hopping down the embankment, he stood still for a moment, eyed his path, and stared anxiously ahead toward nothing familiar.

Breathing slow, his vision rolled into a daze as he considered the big things that had transpired, thus ending him up at that locale in the world. The times, good and bad and bad more than good, flickered on and off in his temporary daze. The scatteredness happened often and the thoughts became haunting in the times when they dragged on. Questioning some of his past choices issued serious fret over decisions ahead. Hills to climb before him, the kid would get himself all worked up and really labor over this or that. Not this time, not any longer. There wasn't going to be any more questioning himself. And, no more doubt. In this moment, he left a lot behind and moved forward with prayer for a needed blessing.

After an uplifted head, came about an intense focus backed by the lad's will and determination. Despite any odds, he was always striving to play things smart and this was going to be one of those critical times when he needed to do just that. The focus was sorely needed and it rooted from his discipline in the game, though any and all thoughts about golf had filtered out of his head for the moment. There was a long last drag from his cigarette and Sam snapped from the blur, then set forth at a regular pace down the middle of the wagon trail.

The dried mud in the ruts was black and cracked. Other than grasshoppers, there had been little sign of life since walking away from the near abandoned train station several hours ago. Sam arrived at a wooden post that carried a sign distinguishing his pathway, to that point, as Katy Trail East. Another sign on the post labeled a smoothed black dirt road as Main Street, which only made a jog south, then ran all the way due north and straight up to the ridge. Three buildings, each right beside another, were on the north side of the wagon trail and three just the same to the south. All were on the west side of Main, and each was built with freshly cut and whitewashed lumber. Four were one-story and the two on the corners of the intersection were two-story. The architectural detail and fine craftsmanship of the structures was very notable and like nothing Sam had ever seen. And, he'd been to all the big cities on the east coast and across the south. Nice buildings, but not much to call a town. There was also the much larger structure, surrounded with stacks of lumber and tin, that was situated further down Katy Trail. A skeleton, very much still under construction. Not one home or cabin around and none of the buildings appeared to even be occupied. There were no other signs displayed and not a single hint of a human being anywhere. No noise except for an occasional squeak from a sputtering windmill off to the south. Not a horse, nor even a wagon around in the motionless town.

Stalled for the moment, Sam pondered his best back story. There were a wide variety that had been passed off to strangers, only when asked. Along his way he'd mostly managed to side-step the routine and meddlesome questions from those trying to drum up conversation by asking who he was, where he was from, or where he was headed. When cornered by some old joe that was poking and prodding, his answers and stories were impromptu and quickly forgotten. The journey had provided ample time for conjuring up his best tale, but he'd yet to put in the effort. The fly by night answers to get through the short term had come easy. A realistic and admirable reputation did not. Sam knew his next conversation was right around the corner and it would be the most important one to date. Rolling on with the plan was dependent on the first impression that he was about to make. If things didn't go well, this time would be considered practice and, again, he'd move along. Quickly, so as to leave any knowledge or evidence of his appearance in the dust.

Whomever Sam ended up talking to here at town would most certainly inquire for details, and he knew there best be satisfactory answers and explanations for any chance of a welcome coming forth. Sam felt he didn't have the life of a person that someone would want to have around, as such, he had always kept his business behind a wall. His whole situation led to an inward soul and it was hard for most to see any further past a drifting, likely troublesome, teenager. Over the last two years, his eye contact with others had been very minimal. Unless some sort of supply was needed, Sam's trail bypassed the populations and, in town or not, his eyes stayed hidden underneath the hat as he stuck to his business and put down the miles. Although he easily could, a lone Sam was not going to produce a series of tales to forge an undetectable past. Fibbing, before too long, would definitely lead to being forced to move on or worse. The kid had always been honest, at least where it mattered. The truth tarnished only by the white lies that were necessary in his certainly justified elusiveness. This time, telling his tale mattered more than anything. At that moment though, the mind was still made up that he could not lead on to his plight.

The glass paneled door opened at the building on the northern corner and a tall, slender, gentleman in black pants and a black vest stepped into view. Darkened above his knees in shadow, the man tugged at his bow-tie with both hands, then reached out making an upward swoop of the hand. The middle-aged fellow was now standing at the edge of the porch with his hands propped at the hips. He was glaring out of the top of his eyes and a dark hairy chin was angled down, both telling that an acute inspection was underway.

Pulling the trunk back to his hip and shrugging the golf bag further over his shoulder, Sam began walking, head now down, across the smooth dirt road. The walk was short in distance, though long in its moments. He looked up and felt like a hole was shot through his lonesome heart as he stepped off the smooth dirt surface of Main Street and into a narrow easement that was spotted with smashed, dead grass. All of the sudden, the man was right there and the presence was large. The feeling of standing in the spotlight shown down and into the soul of Sam. The kid's stomach was rumbling and had a bad, ailing feeling as though his last meal, a hard-boiled egg, was going to be relinquished.

"Son." The black beard bobbed a tick downward and the stare drew more intense as it ran to each end of Sam's being.

"Hidey, sir." Sam looked down then back up from the dusty earth, "Sam Stallings." he spoke up as he removed the fedora and squished the name into one word. His voice was still pretty high-pitched at the time, though gritty and clogged up from having not spoken aloud in a day or so. His youth stuck out like

9

a sore thumb, mostly given away in his frame and the fact that the fresh face certainly wasn't sporting any whiskers.

The traveling boots came right up to the front steps. Trunk and satchel were set to the side, then Sam leaned his golf bag against the edge of the porch. Cold and hard eyes watched his every move from high above and half-way through an awkward and extended moment of silence, now standing up straight, Sam knew the man was trying to figure out what the hell this strange kid was wandering into town for.

The breezy hum of silence was drowned by the deep voice, "Sam, you say?" the gentleman asked in a stern and direct tone that was meant to sound halfway like he cared and halfway like he didn't.

The cooled off and refreshed kid was now all of the sudden sweating, again. Nerves were throbbing and words needed were thankfully routine. Thankful, because all others and anything else worth saying would have been hard to come by. He rubbed his damp palm against his pant leg and looked up, "Yes, sir. Sam." he said, thinking better, abruptly stalling, and choosing to leave out the last name this time.

"Sam, L.T. Murchison." Slowly and lowly graveled the man. The two characters shared a brief handshake, quickly cut off by the lengthy arm that was extending out from wise and dithering eyes. Sam was sure that Murchison wasn't going to stand there for any small talk or other kind of bull and the man was towering, six feet and four or five inches tall. Height included, he also looked and dressed exactly like former President Abraham Lincoln. No stovepipe hat, though same beard and his hanging jowls accentuated its thickness. He was dressed as though, and coming off like, he was in the thick of a busy business day, even as there were no apparent affairs taking place in this small town. The man's temperament was leaning toward needing to get on with something more important and matched with the outfit. Murchison gave his attention, yet it was clearly occupied with something else and seemed to be dangling only briefly before Sam. His hair was slicked over and thinning with only a dab of black left on top. L.T. Murchison's look and presentation bled experience and demanded respect. A kind man. Fairness was apparent and in sensing that, Sam relaxed only a tick. Murchison began to speak on, though his voice chugged like an old engine trying to start. Contemplating the dusty leather boots standing before him, he coughed and swallowed hard, then the rusty pipes growled, "Pardon, I haven't spoken a word all day." He cleared his throat, solving the issue and speaking clearer, "You said Stalling?"

"Stallings." Sam replied, as he nodded once and gave a long hiss of the 's' at the end, "Yes, sir."

Murchison was the first person to hear Sam's last name in quite some time. Coming in contact with people in towns and along the railroads, along the trails, here and there, most inquirers had never even heard him so much as divulge his first name. Rather he'd spout out any old made up one, and never the same one twice. The iota of folks that had heard the kid introduce himself as Sam, most certainly caught a fake last name and that only when he was pressed. Most often, the pressing was from old-timers or immigrants seeking to make a connection to any relative on any branch of the family tree, or an acquaintance of. The timid young soul finally took a big step away from the shadows by speaking his true and full name out loud.

"Stallings, Stallings, Stallings, Stallings." Each call of the name faded more than the last and the next one would have been too loud, "I don't believe there are any Stallings in the area." Murchison spoke up.

11

Sam didn't know if anyone else was around or not and he didn't look to see, but his ears were cringing. He was adamant about keeping the name out of his own mouth, so it was a devastating surprise to hear it caroled about from someone else. His years of staying the course in the background seemed like they were gone to ruin and there was only solace in that this was a well thought about and expected hump. Justification set in abruptly and Sam was reeling himself back in. Murchison spoke out, "You a transient? A juvenile hobo off the railroad, carrying that odd bag and such?" His last words were lengthened with a thick southern accent.

In Sam's mind, Murchison spoke like those people around New Orleans or like a politician. In more ways than one, the man quickly came off as an old stubborn diplomat of some sort. Sam felt he was on the bad side already, though held his composure. Judgement was coming fast, if not, about to set in. The young looked the old in the eye and vice versa. An up-to-no-good named Stallings that was run out of town was not what the boy needed, but things could quickly turn that way and then he'd be suspect in any and all mischief throughout five counties. The young man knew right off he had his work cut out if he was going to make a positive impression, one that would gain any kind of decent ground for an outsider. And, he also knew the work, the act, the ploy, the plea, the words, whatever he was going to do, better start fast. He stood still, silent, and feeling the blood rush in and out of his extremities as his mind and mouth scrambled for a response.

Having visited, extensively, each and every one of the small towns in the surrounding area, Murchison was certain that he had never laid eyes on Sam, nor seen anyone that looked possibly akin, nor heard of anyone named Stallings. After all, there was not too much of a population anywhere in the region. Those that were around, were known, and likely betting on a potential spurt of growth and opportunity in the area. Strangers and wanderers were rare in these parts, if not, non-existent. The middle-aged man stood with his hands pressed back on his hips as he rocked up on his tip toes, stuck out his chest a bit more, and twisted enough so that Sam couldn't help but catch an eye-opening glimpse of a pistol hanging from atop the long right leg. A shiny new Colt Single Action revolver in a black holster. And, one couldn't help but to also notice the polished brass buckle holding the leather belt in place. In an instant, the already thick frog in Sam's throat almost leapt out as his eyes met back with the piercing glare.

Murchison was leery of roguery and presumptively analyzing everything that had come into town. And, at the same, time sizing up the work potential of the hand before him. There was a lot to be done before the upcoming auction and the town keeper was desperate for the help. Hopes were high and enthusiasm bustling when he first advertised the new settlement and available land, last spring. All and everyone, everywhere, were no-shows for it. Hopes dashed and as beat as cornbread batter, Murchison gave up on establishing the town, and spent the better part of the year in a depression-filled funk. In the last weeks, with a springtime aura in the air he had begun to climb from his dark times and decided to give an auction another chance. Much had been accomplished by himself, but much was still desired for the place to attract anyone. Once in a while, there was manual labor help from a couple of out-of-town boys, a preacher's son, Ross MacLean, and a barkeeps son, Otis Shelby. The young men were from over near Leonard and would make the trek for work randomly at Murchison's special request, and usually for only a day and a half on those rare occasions. The most progress was made when Murchison had their help for a three week stretch, right before the failed auction. After talking up the auction so much, a touch of embarrassment had kept Murchison from venturing into the surrounding areas and, as so, the boys hadn't been over to help out since.

Despite days of hard work on his own, things were running behind in preparing for a better auction and a better town. There were also intentions of making the price of land a little more attractive. Sam probably walked into town at exactly the right time. Murchison's determination was running strong and he knew he needed help. Actually, the man was likely quite excited to see anyone at all coming through. Big plans were quickly in mind and Murchison was taking his thoughts through his to-do-list. Though he wasn't totally sure, with the kid's small and skinny frame, that he'd be worth a lick. Sam's clothes were too new for someone that'd be out roaming, looking for work. However, there was no one else around to help, so Murchison had to give it a shot.

Sam was about to offer up a vague explanation of who he was and what it was that he was there for.

"You need work?" Murchison finally rescued the stunned and shy young lad from feeling the need to answer all or any of the prior questions.

"No, sir." Sam replied, then swallowed hard and, again, cut his reply short after recalling the aim to keep words as few as possible. Murchison shot his eyes at Sam's belongings and darted them amongst each one. The young eyes dropped downward, then fixated on his golf bag, too. In an odd silence Sam readied for what was coming next.

"Well, that's not making my day." Murchison slowly spoke the words, and it appeared as though he was in the midst of deciding if his determination was going to double up or if the door was going to be shut and the roamer sent on his way. Hopes were dashed and he was probably near cussing about the answer, though the response did pluck curiosity. "What's your business out this way then, young

Sam Stallings?" Passing through and needing help, or direction, was the next thought with a raised eyebrow. Then, Murchison started making assumptions. Perhaps the kid was going to pitch a story and beg for money or food. Sam was young, but still, too old for a runaway. Could be on the run or hiding was a thought. Perhaps having that trunk, he was a salesman. Murchison was an instant away from issuing a dismissal, no matter the answer. His eyes dropped left to see where his feet should step and the shoulders were on the verge of following that way, to the door, as well.

"At the station back yonder, there was an advertisement for land out this way." Sam got to the point with a slight southern drawl in his voice, more than normal. He did have a bit of an accent, but so slight no one could ever place it to anywhere particular. He wasn't from the south. He'd just been there.

Murchison hesitated. His head and eyes turned back and the shoulders twitched back to their spot. He appeared shocked, stunned, and speechless, until there was a gulp when his words were ready. "There is an auction taking place. Nearly every inch of land within eyeshot is available." he stated in a more friendly and business-like tone, proud in saying it. The glare had left and then was right back. "What's a young fellow like you want with a land auction?" Murchison queried, sounding like he may have been teetering back to the bothered side.

Sam's young age begged the question and brought about the suspicion. He was around fifteen or sixteen, but certainly didn't look it. Maybe thirteen or fourteen, tops. If he was out on his own at that age, it wasn't likely he'd be affording land.

"I'd like to purchase a lot." Sam stood still as a stone. His statement felt, and sounded, like he was asking permission.

"You here for your mama and daddy?" Murchison asked.

"No, sir. Just me." Sam replied.

Murchison took a moment in quiet thought as he once again looked the stranger over from head to toe, belongings too. He wasn't sure if he was wanting to take Sam seriously, or not, and then he started in, "Just you. Well, what are you looking for? A lot of what?"

"A lot of land, sir." Sam replied on-point, looking humble, feeling confused, and back to his nervousness which was about tilting toward that of a skulk of foxes on the run from a pack of hounds.

"How much is a lot?" Murchison immediately chimed back.

"I figured you'd tell me that, sir." Sam countered back after a long moment, dumbfounded but not showing the expression.

"Tell you what?" the deep voice cascaded down and made Sam feel like any kind of deal was on its way out the window.

"How much a lot is, sir."

"Common sense tells that a lot is more than a little." Murchison let the southern accent loose with a small grin at the end.

Feeling some frustration, yet stern in the plan, an eager Sam got down to business and slapped his front pocket, "Well, Mr. Murchison, I've got more than a little for a lot."

"A whole lot?" Murchison was cracked up with laughter on the inside and so was Sam. Murchison was on the verge of showing it, Sam would have never been the first one to do so and was as serious as a young man could be.

"Yes, sir. A whole lot." Sam said, as he nodded with a proud, but small smile.

"Good. Because I ain't selling half lots." Murchison gave a light chuckle, "How much, son, are you expecting to spend for a whole lot?" Murchison's scowl was back, but Sam knew right off that the look was presented sarcastically.

"Only a little." Sam said. They both smiled big and let loose chuckles of laughter, Murchison first.

Relaxing more than he had in years, the laugh made the youngster feel a sense of welcome. In that instant, the man gave Sam a small slice of home, something that was sorely craved. Murchison, laughing longer than Sam, moved to have a seat on the step and was now a smidge below eye level with the lad. Sam had a slight smile to cover his nervousness as he now inhaled what couldn't have been anything other than straight whiskey from the man's breath.

The deep laugh ceased and a serious look was in full fruition, not a scowl though. Sam's small grin left in an instant and he intently looked Murchison in the eyes. Murchison hesitated, then spoke. "I'll tell you what. I'll sell you a piece of land. There's plenty around." His volume went down, "To be straight, the auction is still a week away. Next Sunday." Murchison gave Sam a hard looking at, head to toe, golf bag again, and other belongings too. "I need a little help here and there to get ready. You help me out and I'll cut you a fair price on a couple of acres."

The sound of silence rang in Sam's ears as each man waited on the other to speak.

There was only a small amount of contemplation to finally come up with the correct words. Nonetheless, there he stood timid to say it. Sam knew what he was after and he also knew that if he was going to reach his big-time goal, that he best go after a place that was going to be proper. "Mr. Murchison," Sam said, softly. Although clearly not, he had the feeling that he was interrupting and began to speak with a stutter, "I… I'd be glad to help you out in any way I can. Though, I'd like to get a hold of more than a couple acres."

"I see." Murchison said, keeping any solution hidden and nodding a time or so. Then the man stayed quiet and kept his chin raised, waiting on Sam until it was clear that there was going to be nothing spoken. "The lots for auction are along Main here, two acres each. Though I suppose if you want more, there is farmland here to the south. I suppose I could, perhaps, spare you a chunk. How much property are you talking, young Sam?" Murchison seemed kindly interested in fitting the young man's needs, yet was likely standing with no hesitation of creeping back toward the unsure side of the fence. A smaller lot, maybe. One of the bigger plots hadn't even been considered. The larger chunks were going to pull in the big money, eventually. In his pause atop the fence, Murchison was thinking and wondering even more about what Sam was up to, especially, what he was going to be up to with this land.

"I have two one-hundred-dollar notes stuck right here. What'll that get me?" Sam said with a tone that begged for a bargain. The young man knew the average cost of land from looking over flyers posted here or there, at rail stations and advertised on town bulletins, though he was shooting high with his offer.

"Two hundred dollars." Murchison paused for a moment, nodded his head, and gave no expression as he looked Sam in the eyes. "If I might ask, where does a lad your age get two-hundred dollars? And, two-hundred dollars to buy land with?" Murchison had his volume and politician accent going at full tilt, "You can guess my imagination might run wild. Rob a bank? A train or somebody in one of these other towns? You understand why I'd ask, Sam. It's not every day you see a young man skipping around with two hundred dollars cash in his pocket. That's a lot of money, and even more for one your age."

"Yes, sir. I understand your questions. I would say, worked hard, lived smart, saved up, and here I am. Might as well spend the money on something worthwhile. A nice investment. Better than spending it in a saloon or someplace like that." Sam said, free as can be at what is possibly the most likely age for a renegade to develop. He had never set foot in any type of said place nor even had one sip of alcohol. Mostly, because of the lectures and learning that came from what rearing there had been. It was a rule he had for himself and wouldn't even consider galivanting around such establishments. Pushing open the doors of any social joint would be stepping into enemy territory, asking to be found out. Saloons and public houses were probably the first place they hung the wanted posters.

Murchison respected the answer and liked the mention of the purchase as an investment but was a hint exasperated as he thought about all the dollars he'd thrown down in bars. Then he went back to his efforts to get to the bottom of what Sam was up to.

Like anyone would be, the man was leery of a kid coming up out of nowhere to buy land. Albeit, settlers were passing through from all over. And, in the aftermaths spread throughout the country, youngsters were left in all types of tough situations to dig their way out of. Anyhow, a sale was a sale. The town wasn't going to spring up by turning customers away. Though, an easy sell wasn't going to keep Murchison from assuring himself that Sam wasn't some con. "I don't mean to be prying Sam, but you spend two-hundred dollars on land, does that leave you sitting high and dry?" the businessman in Murchison asked. His intentions were to ensure all would be stable in the future, though he was hoping Sam would divulge more history and more clues about any plans for the future.

Deep down, Sam was leery of everyone, but could tell Murchison was an honest and respectable man. The youngster was nervous but comfortable. Whatever they were, there were affirmations in his soul that settling here was a suitable idea and going to be all right. "No, sir. No problem with you asking. I appreciate and understand the concern, but I'll be fine. Two-hundred is exactly what I set aside for a piece of property." Sam said nervously, as he knew that he was levying himself deep in to the decision of a lifetime.

Murchison waited. Sam continued to hold his poker face. Murchison looked into the distance, then stared down at the trunk, floppy satchel, and golf bag. He did take note of the shiny hammer-like thing protruding from the bag, which received second and third looks. Sam's eyes watched his eyes. Murchison's eyes were filling his brain in wonder as they shifted between the objects, then back to Sam's frozen gaze. He looked down at the white cotton rag, smudged with dirt and sweat as it was. Then he eyed, again, the iron of the broadstick, then the boy. The hairy chin raised and there was a hint of a nod north with the eyes, up Main Street. The man was contemplating something and Sam stood crisp and numb in the standstill.

After tense moments of silence, moments of obvious reflection, a small smile showed and Murchison budged, "Okay. Sounds like you are a man that wants to get a hold of some acreage. I have a piece in mind that, I believe, will sit at just under fair market value for your two-hundred dollars. Best I can do. It's about forty acres, give or take. Your two hundred-dollar notes in exchange, and I'd sure appreciate a little help on top of the transaction. All needs to be ready for the auction, this coming Sunday."

Again, there was silence as Sam stood in deep contemplation. While not letting go of his plain expression, he waited for more information. Murchison, for the first time, had the feeling that he needed to work to close the deal. This sell would be a start. "I offer the acreage, Sam, because there is a section back over the hill that I think will fit you fine. Probably suit you and your priorities better than any other place." Murchison looked at the golf bag, then at Sam and sized up the lanky arms. Then he went back to sizing up the character and took a long pause, though it was clear that there was more he was going to say.

"Like I said, I think it will be a nice place for you. Besides, if you take that piece, it would keep me from going ahead and cutting into sections of land across the trail here." Murchison explained as he pointed to the south to the open landscape.

"Deal." Sam said as he stuck out his hand, anxious and borderline cramped at the thought of letting an opportunity slip by.

Murchison chuckled his way into words, "I think you should go see it first. Make sure it's to your liking. If so, come on back down and we'll prepare a deed." Murchison instructed, and then had another looking over of Sam, "Does that sound like a deal?"

"Yes, sir." Sam replied. He was grinning ear to ear and stepping toward his belongings, until Murchison began to speak.

"Listen here." Murchison said, "Go up over Dead Horse Hill." The man arranged his finger and thumb like a pistol and popped it up Main Street to the top of the ridge, "Your place will be on this side of the road. There's a red flag over the other side of the hill which notes the start. The flag is your southeast corner with your southern boundary running parallel along the other side of that ridge. What's left of Main Street is your eastern border. West and northern property lines are Brown Cat Thicket, right up along the tree line. Put simply, it's all trees over on that side of the hill. Your property is the clearing. Rectangular lot with a big oak tree in the field. You'll know the place when you see it."

CHAPTER 2

A dozen lots lined each side of Main Street between the intersection and Dead Horse Hill, with the boundaries of each marked at the corners by wooden posts with a tied-on strip of red fabric. Not recently, but the sour green grass of each property had been trimmed and was a foot and a half shorter than everywhere else. Thick and lush. Too tall for golfing. Though, like most all the land Sam had seen in the area, it was only a good chopping away from a playable lie. Trees had become absent from the landscape, other than those still lining the river, which now ran beyond the lots on the east side of the road. The properties on the west side backed up to row after row of a plowed up black field, hundreds of acres apparently set aside for farming. The intimidating thought of who in the world might, one day, occupy the empty spaces crept up as Sam passed each one of the twenty-four lots. Thoughts of the auction and a potentially crowded town brought up doubt about settling. Strength in his will dismissed the notion and aimed the focus back toward what was ahead.

As the steep incline of the hill began, the smoothed dirt surface of Main gave way to two wagon ruts which continued over the top. To Sam's right, the ridge was killed off by the river and then continued on eastward from a sheer cliff on the other side. Perhaps a twenty- or twenty-five-foot drop from the ledge to mostly dried up bed. Between the ruts and halfway up Dead Horse Hill, he looked back toward town and now appeared a wooden barn situated behind Murchison's place. Straining his eyes, he made out two mules and a wagon. This brought underlying thoughts to light and answered, yet still, created questions. Where was anyone else? Did Murchison have any family around? Exactly what was his story and who else was in it? Sam wondered, though it wasn't something that was eating at him. All seemed dandy with Murchison. It was the unknown others that brought the doubt, and from that Sam momentarily hesitated on succumbing to any feelings of finality about purchasing the lot. All was seeming too well, and too quiet. Buyers would most certainly have to be traveling in for the auction, as there was nobody around for miles. Who knew who all might show up? The town was plum in the middle of nowhere and surrounded by nothing. Surely, Murchison was not foolish in his thinking that a community would blossom like a wildflower. With all due respect, Sam was comfortable with the chance of a successful auction sitting at slim. The town suited him in a much finer fashion the way it was.

These thoughts about the other ones that might be around somewhere, or those that might be coming around, brought back moments of that nervous anxiety that Sam ran from. All of it derived from a day and a half of golf against the wrong crowd. The happenings of the past had greatly dictated his actions, likely not for the better. All said and done, Sam did no wrong. Not guilty. The scoundrels that got whipped in the run of golf rounds were out to get their revenge on the kid. Ever since, that weekend had torn at his mind yet made him that much more precise and stubborn in his play and in his living. Worked up and considering that he might need to keep on going and keep on going forever, he calmed himself with a reminder that not everyone was going to be out for the throat. One could not be on the run all of their life. And, Sam vowed that the threat would go no further. There between those ruts, looking to the marvelous southern landscape and the luscious big and blue sky, feeling the epitome of springtime beginnings, the decision was made that the running was over no matter what was on the other side. In that instant, the unwanted nonsense of trouble in his rearview seemed to cease like it was never there.

Thoughts clear and out of the past, a rough estimation of the walk up Main figured at a half mile. Not that it would play into any decision on purchasing the land, but it pleased Sam. Over the hill, far enough away to be out of the buzz of town, if there was one, and the noise of the railroad, if there was one. He had the feeling that he was on to something. There for the beginnings of a place that would provide a wealth of goodness, like a gold prospector coming to rest and knowing himself to be the first to stake claim in a promising valley. Pivoting his head back north during the final steps to the summit, Sam raised his chin and looked out of the bottom of his eyes so as to catch each new inch of earth as it was presented from the other side. Below, in the distance harshly interrupting the beauty of the sky, a dense and dark forest surrounded an open and grassy parcel. Before the young man, sat a serene lot that appeared at a size that would have to be forty acres or darn near it.

The encompassing land was a mess full of mesquite trees and cedar trees, hackberries and junipers about, and who knows what else. From the top of the ridge, Sam awed at the dark and dead land extending beyond sight to the north, east, and west. The murky tangle of trees appeared as a different world and was in sharp contrast to the fresh openness of the prairie, and the boxed in forty acres. Across Main, the elms were still lining the river, though only the budding green tops could be seen rising above the dullness of the boscage. Not the least bit inviting, the blockade that was Brown Cat Thicket seemed to hold all sorts of creepy stirrings. The name, Brown Cat, sure spoke to some kind of lurking critter. Sam kept his shoulders square and his head ready to swivel, ready to pounce, as he surveyed the immediate grounds of the wooded jumble. The wagon trail cut its way into the woods and soon thereafter disappeared, as did the river and everything else once yards into the rough and tangled mess.

Sam paused his walk and started an intense investigation off the toe of his boots. Running his eyes down the northern pitch of the hill, about halfway down, he found the red marker Murchison had described. Another twenty yards down, the land flattened into the wide-open space, again filled with knee-high grass that stretched lushly across the tract and right up to the thicket. The land sat lower than on the other side and the grass was shades darker. Smack dab in the middle of the property was a tremendous, matriarch of an oak tree, the Jackson Oak as it would come to be known. At the time, the trunk was close to ten feet around and the two big, long branches started at about twelve feet up and extended like bent arms down to shoulder height. One pointed west and the other swung around to the south. Near the opposite corner was a small dried up slough that exited from a shallow opening in the trees and stuck out as the only bare earth on the place. The instant Sam's eyes saw the tree and then bounced around the land, he knew without a doubt it would be his paradise. The spot was perfect, the deal seemed even better. The kid was feeling cozy. Like at home, already. What became of the town, he was thinking he could deal with. If a bunch of people moved in that needed shying away from, Sam would be satisfied keeping to himself and golfing those grounds as a horded-up hermit.

Confusion tried its best to breeze in and was bested by a thought of hope that he was looking at the chunk of land that Murchison was referring to. Sam looked around for any another place that could be the one. As described, there was nothing but the thicket strangling all land north of the hill. His eyes shot immediately back up for another look, this time with a smile rather than an open mouth as he knew that it must be the place. He likely got stubborn about it all of the sudden, as beautiful as the lot was. And, spring hadn't even set in yet. When everything greened up, the place would look that much grander. The forty acres fit an image from his dreams so closely that he quickly bullied up the notion that it'd take hell or high water to keep him from having his hands on the place.

Sam stepped to the red marker and placed his wooden trunk and satchel on the ground, then slung the golf bag from his shoulder. Standing on one foot with the other leg kicked out behind him, he bent and snagged the busted golf ball from its pouch and then pinched out pieces of fractured stitch and tossed them to the wind. There was a look over his shoulder, as far up over the hill as he could make, to ensure no one was around. He turned his ear up, was still, listened for a moment, and then turned all attention to the work before him.

As he'd done so many times before, he unbuckled and flipped open the trunk to pull out a needle and a small piece of leather with a strand of horse hair wound around it. Hands were shaking from the sheer energy of the day as he had a seat on the trunk and began trying to thread the needle, which was always a chore. The whole task had become monotonous and he was pretty fed up about not having a decent ball, nor proper materials to produce one that was truly worth a lick. Since making his first one, dozens of ideas about a best ball were floating around in his brain and he always had an eye out for anything that could be used to make one. Rocks, wood, yarn, even used animal bones that had been scavenged. Often, any kind of scrap anything was turned in to a makeshift ball for as long as it would last or until something else that was as good, or better, came along.

A wisp of air blew from his mouth and, with eyes wide, the fingers gave looping the needle and thread another try. Then he greased the horse hair in his lips and tried again. There was another look over the shoulder. He alertly watched and listened for anything. Squeezing the needle tightly in his right and the hair in his left hand, he reached out his arms and shook them rapidly. Exhaling, he stared intently at the task and tried again.

After four or five more tries, Sam reached in the pouch on his golf bag and pulled out the tobacco. He rolled a smoke, licked it, lit it, and stood as he deeply inhaled and exhaled the first drag. It's near guaranteed there were curse words that flew during the break from the golf ball and its needed process. After even more attempts at threading the needle, he was ready and set to sew. The needle used was a very small one with a smaller eyelet and the horse hair thick and course. This made for a tough task that was near trying to put a square peg in a round hole. Sam insisted that was the best way to make a golf ball at the time. Keep the holes as small as possible and use the strongest hair possible, to make it last as long as possible. He was certainly not a fan of those old bean bags, which is what they were. Another look over the shoulder, this time a brief glance, then he turned his full attention back to the golf ball.

After three new and near perfect stitches, the leftover bits of dust from what had been a small burlap sack full of chicken feathers were squeezed in to tighten up the ball. Leather stretches easily, always busts at the seams, and causes golf shots to be squirmy as all get out when wet with the morning dew. These facts, among others regarding performance, had revealed to Sam that the breed did not make for any kind of decent-performing golf ball. He knew there was better, but simply couldn't get his hands on much else. Sam sucked on what was left of the smoke as he meticulously crafted one last stitch and looped the end back under twice. The work was sub-par that of a seamstress, but it'd do. Only a week old and the thing had quickly become a soft piece of patchwork and needed to go anyway.

After shoving the ready-to-go ball into his back pocket, there was another look over the shoulder. This one a long scanning look while standing tall and stretching taller. Sam reached in the trunk and grasped a glass jar, then shook it vigorously, eyeballed it, and then shook it again. He lifted the pint-sized container to the light of the sun and examined it like a laboratory scientist anxiously evaluating a new discovery. Inside was a host of different seeds collected along his journeys. Most were from along the south and picked up while the journeyman was walking various backlands.

Sam pulled a sharp knife from his trunk and twisted the tip into the tin lid of the jar. He pulled out a strip of cord, covered the pierced lid with a cloth, and wrapped the cord several times around the glass neck. The cord was then tied, jar hanging upside down, to his back belt loop. Sam also pulled out a small, folded over piece of paper which held seeds from the famed Mr. Ellis Fair's garden. They were planted by Mr. Fair, with Sam's help, prior to the gentleman's tragic death. The odd-looking seeds were picked up after floating to the surface during a vicious rainstorm on the dark and dreary day of the funeral. Sam held on to the dozen or so nuggets for quite some time and had always told himself that they would one day be planted in memory of the revered man. This is what started the whole seed collecting hobby and there became purposeful intentions behind the stock pile. Withdrawing from the moments of his dreamy pause, Sam pulled the broadstick out from the golf bag and started walking down the sloped trail. Gazing into the beautiful plot, Sam was near overcome with an array of emotions. All of them, top to bottom feelings and everything in between, all at once, and he was at a place like no other that he had ever been.

Life had been pretty rough on Sam, with a tough stack of odds to overcome. He grew up fast, even for youngsters at that time. Couldn't see trading nothing for anything, was a fact in his feelings though. Looking at him, you could tell he was as smart as a whip. A polite young man. He spoke generally proper English, knew his arithmetic, and a lot about the sciences and geography. A whiz kid when it came to anything having to do with geography, especially in the south. Knew all the lakes, rivers, creeks, crossings, mountains, small towns, big towns, rail lines, and backwood trails. Might not have known each by name but he recalled many a visit to many a landmark. Though there were only a handful at the time, Sam, like the back of his hand, knew every golf hole in the south and the way to each. He might not have played on all of them, but he scoped each one out. Along the latter part of the journey, the young man was invited to a small selection of different golfing grounds when the broadstick or bag were noticed. Attention had been most often called to the rare, and chance, encounters by old timers that were sitting on a porch or at a train station. And throughout, he snuck on and played too many grounds, fields, pasture, plots, and etc. for counting. Sam never received too much of a formal education, in fact, you could say he was more of an all-around, self-taught, renaissance man. That mostly true in the last two years. When he learned about the game of golf, you could say that the desire to learn anything else went out the window. There were certainly street smarts functioning within and they were, indeed, fine-tuned during his first golfing experiences.

Growing up, Sam made his way without much family to speak of. Around age four or so, he was traveling with his mother, father, and a number of brothers and sisters. He didn't know how many siblings, maybe five or six. Remembering time on a large boat, Sam held the belief that they had all arrived to America from Europe. While waiting on the crowded platform of a large station in one of the big cities up in the northeast, the child all of the sudden stepped up onto a train car that was beginning to roll out. Said he remembers doing it and the next thing he knew, he was gone in an instant on a steam locomotive that was bound in another direction. There is not an inkling of a notion as to any such rescue or search attempts. Sam said he remembers hiding at first, then going from car to car clutching his leather satchel along the way. Over the next days, he was off and back on trains likely searching for someone. Young Sam would poke around, then get scared and go back aboard to hide. Remembered a flood of tears shed during the adventure. Never had anything to eat or drink for almost a week and was near done for, if an accident or something else didn't get the loose child first.

On a cold winter morning during a stop at a rural depot, a young street magician, Ellis Fair, jumped onto the box car where Sam was hiding. Into that leg of the excursion, the desperate young child peeked out from behind a stash of boxes and saw the man asleep at the opposite end. Sam Stallings was printed on the tag attached to his satchel and aside from that there was not much else that was known, or learned. The child was overcome with a shocked, and mostly mute, shyness. The words he did speak had a hint of a British accent, which he lost altogether.

The two rail riders beat it on down the line headed south, off and on more trains. At one point during the adventure they were caught by a brakeman and booted, Mr. Fair narrowly avoiding arrest and a trip to jail. Claiming to be a single parent of Sam, he was let go. Mr. Fair, a transient himself, knew from his own experience that the kid would likely end up on an orphan train if turned over to an authority. Therefore, he chose to hold on to Sam until he arrived at his planned destination, his older sister's place in Washington D.C.

During the months before connecting with his sister, a school teacher, Miss Annette Fair, the two former train hoppers survived on the streets of D.C. during brutal winter storms. Sam was often kept entertained with playing cards and other sorts of magic while huddled around a fire, and was soon put to use in the act. Busking on E Street, Mr. Fair, in performing the grand finale of his show, would have himself secured inside a large wooden trunk with a big brass lock on the front. He would then wait patiently. After minutes had gone by, he would begin calling out as though he was struggling and having a troublesome issue. He was milking the audience and he would keep on with it, shaking and rattling the trunk and pretending he couldn't escape, until a commotion could be heard from a gathering. Then, in a big thump, the lock would pop, the lid would fly open, and young Sam would stand and appear from the box. The boy would then hop out and go around collecting cash and coins in that fedora. Then Sam would get back in the trunk and close himself up. After several random rattles, the lid would fly back open and the great Mr. Ellis Fair would appear and then go around soliciting more money in the hat. A back-to-back pair of performances that drew generous audiences afforded enough funds to rent out a bunk house until the sister was located.

Nearly a year after meeting up and then moving in with Miss Fair, Mr. Fair died while performing a stunt during a show along the Delaware River. Sam was present, there for his role in the swap trick but could only faintly recall the events. A big brass band played over an enormous congregation on the western bank and there was even a large party watching from across the water. Sam remembered the performance taking place on a makeshift dock and that night was the first time he had ever seen fireworks light up the sky. Mostly engrained in the young boy was the roar and tremendous applause that exploded from the crowd when the trunk opened and he was revealed in Mr. Fair's place. That loud cheer, as he raised his hands like in victory, was certainly never forgotten. In the back of his mind, it was something that he longed to hear again. A moving moment, even for a child, and it had been since those days that Sam was last around a group any larger than a dozen. Maybe there had been more passengers than that on one of the later train rides into Texas, but certainly not on the car where he was sitting.

The next part of the show, the feature, required a large crate to be suspended above the river. Mr. Fair was locked inside and attempting to escape while the rope that was hoisting the crate burned in the dark star-spangled sky. Something with the stunt went awry, there was a large gasp from the onlookers, and then a hectic rush ensued as a rescue was attempted. The box had fallen into the river and was floating down with the current when the child was whisked away from the chaotic scene. Sam learned of the death shortly before the funeral, which was also attended by a very large mass of people.

Miss Ann, as she was called, took in Sam and raised the boy on her own, providing a nurtured upbringing and solid formidable schooling. When Sam was about the age of ten or so, she decided to move South to the Carolinas. The two loaded up a wagon and set forth, with two mules, on the journey from Washington D.C. Three months into the trip and just having left Virginia, Miss Annette Fair fell ill with pneumonia and, as a result, passed away in an infirmary at age 29. Sam was living in the wagon outside of the hospital during the week she was being tended to, then left out on his own consequent to her death.

The kid drove the wagon on south and managed to make do for himself along the way. Rough terrain was navigated carefully and, ultimately, skillfully. Camps were always off the beaten path, set up late, then broken down quickly before sunrise as the boy never found much that was interesting and kept moving on. Cooking wasn't his thing and he got by keeping it to a minimum. Rabbits for protein and any fruits or vegetables that he could get his hands on. Warm meals from friendly encounters came at the right times, though Sam wasn't yearning to take on too much help. There were occasions of people trying to take him in or have him hauled in, simply for being a young wandering kid. Gentle politeness went a long way in holding up through rough months.

Around the age of twelve or so, Sam stumbled down to Georgia. The wanderer milled around trying to find his way, already adhering to the shadows and behaving in endless efforts to stay out of any kind of trouble. Mostly because he was terrified of what lie ahead. Brave, but terrified. The youngin' didn't much know what to do with himself and had somewhat come to a standstill. Loitering around different places hoping for a job didn't bring more than an hour or two, maybe a day, of work here or there. Nothing he much cared for, anyway. Now, it didn't take too long for Sam to become barely afloat. Giving up was on the mind and he was on the verge of surrendering himself for help.

Journeying along one day and not sure where to go, he found a big oak tree that offered needed shade and comfort. He made the space his temporary home and would sit under that tree dreaming away the boredom. He was dreaming of what to dream about, just not knowing what to do. A plan loomed to somehow get himself back north to search for mother, father, brothers, sisters. Success there felt doubtful at best, it had been too many years. He wondered and tried to think out a pathway to a decent profession, how you become a train engineer and what do you do to be a doctor. He considered building and selling wagons, he'd repaired Ms. Ann's carriage numerous times. About the only entertainment there was, throwing a knot in a string that had a small washer tied around one end. After he mastered one knot, he went to a double knot, then to untying it. All by giving the free end of that string a flip of his wrist. Still, boredom ran deep and the energetic child looked out for anything to grab his attention. Early one morning while snagging a peach from nobody's land, from across a pasture out there east of Atlanta, Sam Stallings first bore witness to the game of golf when he heard the loud crack of iron meeting a wooden golf ball.

From afar and then closer and closer in the days following his first observance, Sam watched while hiding behind weeds and trees so as not to be found out. The enamored kid soaked in all he could while observing the sometimes two, sometimes four men, knocking balls around the grounds that were up the trail from his camp. Now, surrounded by a wealth of action and activity, the camp quickly became more than a temporary home.

The gist of the game materialized quite quickly in Sam. Late in the evening on day two, while walking back to his tree, he paused in the weeds, squared up, and took his first swing at the air with an imaginary golf stick. Steps further, there was another one, and another, and dozens more in the pitch dark once back at camp. He was like a cat with a ball of yarn. There was a lot of thinking, wondering, figuring, and wishing.

Within earshot on day three, he figured out plenty to have a general idea of what was going on rule wise. Day four, Sam went back to keeping his distance, sitting under an oak and watching that morning's game in the shade as he chewed down a juicy peach for breakfast. After closely observing the early play on day five, he was walking to a market in the nearby town. A hungry Sam was hoping to fetch some kind of golf-like stick and an adequate ball, maybe food, when the man rode up and started asking questions of the youngster. After a free lunch, Sam had a job maintaining the grass for a fellow named Plemmons out at the local golfing holes. Five cents a day.

Sam did a lot of studying while he worked and never once had any kind of fundamental golf instruction from Plemmons, who was the outright best in his regular foursome. The three others players were always the same gentlemen and their skills lacked a shine. They were casual golfers, at best. The men enjoyed playing the game and, even more so enjoyed playing the game with whiskey in their hip pockets. Perhaps even more than playing, drunk or not, they enjoyed wagering on the outcomes.

The end of the first month found Sam with a borrowed golf stick in hand and an allowance to hit a bucketful of shots in the evening time, wooden balls. It wasn't another month before the kid was on top of Plemmons and his pals, showing them a thing or two about golf. Once that happened, the men, soaked with whiskey, began to play less and marvel more at the youngster's golf artistry. Plemmons and company had never seen a golfer that was even half as talented as Sam. Even though Sam skills were superseding, each evening found at least a couple of the men sitting in rocking chairs on the back porch barking out free advice. And, they would always want to issue a challenge or two while they were at it, betting that the youngster couldn't perform some type of inconceivable or bizarre feat with a golf ball. Nine times out of ten, Sam would pull off the provocations, including the time he downed a buzzard. Plemmons had just put out some hog guts after a slaughter and from that smell, one of the scavengers began circling overhead. Sam was all set for a golf shot when Plemmons called out, "Damn buzzards!" The ball flew, and that bird swooped down to meet the drive head-on. All were shocked, mostly Sam, and money changed over to Plemmons hand. One of the favorites of the men involved the target of an old moldboard plow, with wagers generally placed on either an odd or even numbered streak of striking it from across the pasture. Sam never was in on money changing hands during those instances, only Plemmons and company.

And, to wrap things up and run Sam out of that place, it would take another month for Plemmons to drum up the match against a tight-knit group of three local young men that were likely some of the roughest around. The real smart-mouthed one that lost the most money, Ripley Dukes, proclaimed to be the best in the south upon arriving at the pasture. Plemmons and his partners egged it all on like they were ringmasters showing off some sideshow with Sam. The opposing Georgia boys were decent players with deep pockets before the two-day match, mad and broke afterwards. They couldn't live on the gambling philosophy of 'quit while you are ahead', because they were never ahead. Dukes resentfully, and in protest, quit the competition after sixty-one holes and after Plemmons took his last dollars. Then, the three degenerates took a turn to pugilism at the least. Thank goodness for Plemmons and his pistol warning them off Sam, for the time being. That Sunday, the day Sam would leave all of his belongings under the oak tree and scatter off in his escape, those lowdown sore losers couldn't figure out that they were never going to swing things back to even, much less win a single hole. Sam left at Plemmons advisement, those boys and their daddies were likely going to be out for blood. Weeks later and just into Alabama, Sam came across a wanted poster pertaining to Ripley Dukes. A five-hundred-dollar reward was offered for the capture of the man responsible in the beating of Odell Plemmons.

Back on the remains of Main Street, Sam reached the northeast corner of the property and trained one eye on the darkness looming about in Brown Cat Thicket. The trail turned even more rough as it sank down into the dark land and then the ruts disappeared into the tree tops. Across the way a pair of mockingbirds were bickering about, the first beating hearts around, besides Murchison. Sam was shrewdly keyed in on who might be around, anyone and any critter. Below the jammed web of mostly bare tree limbs, the forest floor was riddled with dead leaves and branches, brush, briars, and all other sorts of thorny vine-like rubbish. Poison ivy or poison oak, one, could be seen littered about. Sam wasn't going to take the time to look close enough to figure out which of the two. Brown Cat was altogether unsightly and very unwelcoming. The lot was like a chunk of gold in the mud. A turn and a look over the smoothness of the forty acres and in his mind, it was only by grace that such a beautiful place was situated as so.

There was a short squint at the sun as it made itself known in dropping to the west side of overhead. He acknowledged the shower of gold filling the air, which was outshined by the blinding white radiance gleaming from the object clutched in the young right hand. A chunk of iron had been obtained from a scrap pile at a foundry near Atlanta and was shaped to Sam's liking by a local blacksmith. The work was completed in exchange for a day's worth of labor. The shaft was made from hickory wood and had formerly served as a walking cane. Certain possessions were left to Sam after the deaths of Mr. Fair and Miss Ann, though most everything was sold or traded off in order for the youngster to make do during the time after her passing. The cane and also that wooden trunk belonged to Mr. Fair, as did the straw fedora. Sam had whittled, filed, and sanded at the cane until it reached perfection for use as his tool of the game. Then, he attached the hickory stick to the hosel part of the iron using a pair of horseshoe nails that were in turn clipped off. A sturdy piece of wire was wound about a dozen times over the connection for support and then coiled with fine twine. Soft cowhide was used for the grip and made tight with multifarious crisscrosses of thread. He was hesitant to make the thing and carry it around so brazenly after being run off by the Georgia boys, but the game was calling. Once made, he kept it hidden for many of the first miles. He'd shove it down his pant leg and walk with a straight-legged limp, a part of his disguise in the early days. Once out of Georgia, the broadstick became a staple in his hands. By far the most unparalleled and sturdiest golf stick that Sam ever made, it knocked golf balls many more miles than any of the others he eventually used. You'd hardly see him without it. And not just golfing, he'd use it for all sorts of things. It certainly knocked many a peach free from trees.

Like a bold knight exhibiting a sword, Sam grabbed the iron head of the broadstick from the belt loop on his right hip and pulled it to the sky until the handle unthreaded from its holster. As a seasoned farmer would check soil, the tip of the grip was jabbed into the earth. After pokes here and there, the ground below the thick and near emerald green grass was found to be not hard and not soft, but just right. The plane of knee-high grass held amazing and calming beauty, as well as great promise for great golfing. There would be a vast amount of work ahead. Sam didn't necessarily have a green thumb, but he knew what would work in regard to a decent playing surface for the game. He wasn't stubborn at all. For Sam, what worked was any kind of earth. Certainly, too tall, the grass would first off require an even taller order of a major cutting. After dethatching and a good clearing, and with the new spring growth filling the sparseness between blades, the playing surface would be not too far away from absolutely ideal.

The creating of a masterpiece and the keeping of the grounds was one of those long-term projects that he was looking forward to in addition to the game itself. He believed working the grounds and learning the lay of the land enriched a player's game. Though he most often didn't have to worry about any place other than exactly where he wanted the golf ball to go, on every single shot, he studied the desired parts of the holes and the trouble spots that were lingering just alike. Besides, Sam wanted it all looking fantastic. The beautiful landscapes that he had played over his travels were peaceful, challenging, and inspiring. In that sense, he was spoiled, and wanted the same for his own grounds.

Steps down the northern property line, Sam grasped the glass jar, ripped off the cloth, and then left the container to hang from its noose. He waded on through the grass mostly watching his footsteps, though often shifting his eyes to size up small changes in elevation across the place, which for the most part could be called flat. Still, there were cautious looks into the dark thicket. With each gaze, his attention would be drawn from looking out for any potential trouble, to that of wonderment and curiosity as his eyes got lost in the dead busyness that went on and on and grew more forbidding as it did.

Nearing the northwest corner of the property his eyes fixated on the only unsightly part of the pristine land, the small slough. The main part of the collection hole was a pond-sized bare spot of dried and cracked mud, near egg-shaped. The earth on the banks was grayer, while that of the bed was the blackest mud there could possibly be. The chute part ran into a hollow on the northern side of the property line, curving out of sight and into the black woods. Sam wanted to walk back and investigate the past source of the abandoned reservoir, but that could wait. Besides, he didn't want to be causing trouble by trespassing. The newcomer didn't know a thing about the neighboring property. Some mean old man was liable to own Brown Cat and the young man was still hell-bent on keeping his nose clean.

Sam moseyed around the slough and paused in the corner. A look back across the place filled the heart with a deep admiration and appreciation of the peacefulness that came with the secluded lot. Just looking over the grounds and knowing there was the chance that he could be playing golf, things felt different. Typically, his views were accompanied by the sound of footsteps. He would have soaked in more, but for his brain really ticking. Many ideas were sprouting on their venture toward a big genesis. He kneeled with one leg up, an elbow on the knee, chin in his palm, and had a long look over everything. The body was absent from the land as his mind viewed the grounds before him from all angles. It was a blank canvas he had hoped for, though the feeling had become that any place would do. There was a nod back east and a look at the ground in front of him. A nod over to the right, a nod there, another there. A tee here, a green there. The fairway will shoot right up along this way. Ideas were rolling on, and on…

A crack from the thicket, finally, drew Sam from his knee and from the figuring and totaling that was going on. Still as a dead man, his eyes checked as much of the scramble as they could. Nothing drew his suspicion and he tried to slide back into his thinking. He dropped back to a knee half hidden, half still taking in the grounds, and half keeping an eye on the woods. The heartbeat began to slow and an alert Sam continued to remain still, waiting for the bout of fear and nervousness to flutter away.

Walking south along the western property line, the eyes aimed only at the grounds. Sam would look at one spot, then imagine a decent golf shot off in one direction, then another shot on over to a green. Then he would look at the first shot going in a different direction two, and so on from there. Satisfied or not with the sequence, he would think about another layout and thus he milled all about the acreage. His feet were lifted high as he strode paths all through the tall grass. Using the broadstick, he'd whack at weeds when he needed to and, once in a while, there would be more jabs into the earth with the handle. Following more walking around, he ended up in the southwest corner, again, on a knee eyeballing it all. There was slope going down toward the oak in that corner, not much but a little. He walked on, jabbing at more ground as the jar continued to dangle. Sam would pick it up and shake it when the holes were clogged and hold it upright to stop any flow as he crossed an area or alleyway that could potentially be used for golfing. He about covered it all. No ant hills, mole holes, fox holes, rabbit holes, or snake dens. All were likely at home in the thicket.

The jar emptied and the paces along the southern border were spent staring that twenty feet up to the ridgeline. The lot on the other side held the same easement, likely meaning the ridge was set aside for public right of way or some other purpose. Sam considered offering more money to procure the slope all the way to the top, but then decided it would be best not to press things right away with Murchison. Having made the perimeter of the property and arriving back at his trunk, there was a sip from the canteen, another smoke, and more contemplation. The burn from the hot last drag of the smoke stirred the occupied mind and Sam set out inside the shallow ditch between the property and the remains of Main Street for one more trip through.

In the dead middle of the eastern boundary line, his boots made a bee-line toward the oak tree. Once near the mammoth trunk, the sun became hidden from view by the bountiful umbrella. The tree was solid, strong, and in it's prime. Coming from an awestruck state of mind, Sam stepped slowly over the shadow line and set foot into a room of darkness. The grass beneath was shorter and sparse and a patch or two of bare ground occurred where the sunlight had no chance of ever reaching. A half-dozen roots reached from the earth and back to, stunting any chance of grass germinating in their path. Outside the line of the shadow, the blanket of knee-high lushness shone ever brighter. Shades of green and freckled specks of old yellow were showing in the intense light and an occasional breeze from over the ridge would bend the grass and, in the push, reveal even fairer colors. The land resembled that which would have been owned by the finest of farmers, if the fellow was cultivating the finest of golfing grasses. The best Sam had ever laid his eyes on.

A dwarfed Sam, swollen in wonder, circled beneath the big oak and glanced back down only when his neck began to stiffen from the long gander at the magnificent canopy. A hand rested on one of the large limbs, and the look around the lot from under the ample shade sold him on the place- as if he was not already. Imagine standing in a dark room and peering outside to a bright and sunny day. The tree was a place to cool off on a break, take a relaxing nap, use for cover from any spring rains, and also maybe the perfect spot for a picnic. A rusty shovel was discovered laying mostly covered by leaves, the wooden handle partially sunk into the earth. Sam tried to compose a story but could not justify its being. Someone had left the tool. Perhaps it belonged to Murchison and was used when installing all of the posts. The shovel appeared to have been there quite a while, maybe left by settlers making camp years ago. Dead Horse Hill didn't leave much to the imagination, perhaps the thing was left behind when the horse was buried. There was a cringe at the thought of the place serving as an equine graveyard. It sure appeared that somebody had been digging in the area. Murchison would know and disclose more history about the place in a bit.

Sam left the shovel be and pointed his walk back around the slough, to the small northwest corner section that was guarded on one side by black mud and on two sides by the thicket. After rounding the mudhole, he measured by paces the twenty feet by twenty feet square. The patch was a tad elevated and covered in tall grass like the rest of the land. Sam stood smack dab in the middle of that section, unhooked the jar from his hip, and unscrewed the lid. He put the lid in his back pocket, got down on one knee, and after pulling away some handfuls of tall grass, gouged his fingernails into the black earth hidden below. He placed the jar down in a hole, filled in around the sides, and used his boot to make sure the top was flush with the ground. Then, using gentle fingertips and extreme care, the edges were lightly smoothed. He raised his head and gave a long look over his shoulder and over the tips of the grass at the stretch between the hole and Main. All thinking was settled, he was itching and ready. An effort to see the top of the hill was shunned by the big oak.

After making his way back around the slough, Sam headed straight toward Main Street with a profoundly purposeful stride. Once at the edge of the road, he strolled back north for a short stint, then walked off into the tall grass. His eyes looked over the immediate area and, with a quick thought, he decided on the exact location that the house would go, some day. He took in the grandeur and stood enamored in the place that would become the screened back porch and the most comfortable sleeping spot he'd ever had. There was a long and thoughtful gaze straight down to the glass jar at N°· 1 which lasted beyond that of any others in memory.

Sam reached deep into his front pocket and carefully pinched out the seeds, the ones retrieved from Mr. Fair's garden. He held the dozen or so hopefuls in his palm and, waiting for one of the rare breezes to come through, scanned the edges of the property. When the grass in the south bent and gusting air barreled on like a charging army, with eyes closed, Sam gave the pieces a light toss. After the bountiful blow of wind ceased, smiling a smile of fond memories and dreaming of glory days to come, Sam walked the jaunt north and picked up his hat from atop the tall grass. The hat went on his head and then Sam wiped his right hand on his right hip followed by the left on the other side. His mind was back to real business.

In that spot, where the hat had blown, forty paces north of the back steps, Sam Stallings pulled more tall grass and tossed it aside. He then pulled a golf ball from his back pocket and let it drop to the ground before him. The fedora was cinched down on his forehead. When the hat was snug and comfortable, eyes shifted from behind his palm to peek back at the hole. Holding the broadstick in his right hand and giving a tug on the right sleeve, he then switched the golf club to the left hand and gave a better tuck to the left sleeve. Rolling up the sleeves was one knack that was acquired from Mr. Fair, who would always put the cuffs up when doing any tricks so as to convey to the audience that he was not hiding anything. Sam just didn't want the cuffs in the way of his magic. The sleeves were set although there was not an ounce of thought to it. The world stopped, as Sam stepped around to the right and about-faced to the gleaming bead of light reflecting off the distant rim of the glass jar. It would later be figured that the distance he was intently looking at was exactly 180 yards.

Hips cocked to the south, the right foot was slightly in front of his left and supported less weight. The shaft of the broadstick hovered above his right collarbone and the relaxed grip rested on his chest, below the chin. Looking down at the ball, which was hugged snugly by the grass, Sam kept his head still as he raised his eyes to begin an in-depth, impassioned, and very perceptive study that would spark millions of synapses in his adolescent brain. Reminiscing each footstep from his time meandering in the targeted space, as well as considering all that was such with the lie below, the sporadic and mostly feeble breezes, and that potentially calamitous golf ball, Sam rightly figured a near impossible order was before him. Aside from going over the patch and into the thicket, the muddy mess of the slough stuck out as the prominent obstacle. The mudhole was guaranteed likely to eat up any shot that wasn't more intelligently left shy.

Sam twisted over, several times, the handle of the broadstick in his right hand as he stepped back left, then mightily assumed his routine and bold statue of a golf stance. His movements were slowed, but steady and with purpose. A warrior on the cusp of battle. Calm, under immense self-control, and ready to fiercely slay the task at hand. He placed his left foot a tick ahead of the right and just in front of the ball. The golfer stood tall with a slight bend at the knee, the left one a tad bit more than the right. An easy lean forward at the waist, the back was straight and head was aligned perfectly with his trunk. Chin was dropped

47

and eyes both looked left with an intense, undistracted, piercing stare that was dead on with the middle front part of the twenty by twenty patch. To any observer, the focused and undistracted eyes, the smooth and well-practiced body movements, the very semblance of his being at that moment in time, cast a dauntless look that spoke to the becoming of a grand act. When Sam commenced with his golf game and the aura was fully displayed, it'd make your mouth open, just a bit, and would cause your breathing to slow while in wonderment of what you were about to witness.

The broadstick was clutched with hands that were away from the body and below his waist, arms extended. Left hand on top, right on bottom, and about an inch of space in between. Firm, but relaxed. Steadily, he placed the iron head beside the rejuvenated golf ball. For a slight moment, Sam lifted his head and, again, sized up the space past the slough. Eyes were working with eagle-like ability, then fell quickly back to the ball. There was now an automatic feeling deep in his muscles and bones, which were now unconsciously controlled. Sam inhaled a slight, last dose of spring air through his nose and then breathing stopped.

A hint toward looser with his grip, the head of the broadstick retreated as Sam's chin rose a very small tick to his right. The right elbow bent and the left stayed straight, crossing his torso until the latter shoulder met chin height. The wooden shaft reached parallel to the tips of grass with the iron now placed off his left side and reaching toward the promised land. Like in sleight-of-hand magic, the golf club appeared from a blur and hovered above his bony shoulders. At a moment of complete stillness, with every muscle in his body acutely enacted in a symphonic mission, Sam knew nothing besides a keen awareness of the necessary and unknown path that would lead to a miraculous destiny. All might was present in, and flowing rapidly through, each system of the body as all necessary components of the great game of golf stood ready to fly toward glory.

Abruptly yet smoothly, motion shifted in the opposite direction beginning with a slight jig forward at the hips. The old cane returned into its magical blur and the iron launched, in controlled chaos and appearing as though fresh out of forging, into an orbit around the soul of the master at hand. In an instant the air before his body rushed to find space. A whoosh led to the thwack and a sizzle began as the jolted ball sprung from the grass with the speed and trajectory of a slightly upward bullet. Sam's body twisted, left hurling into the effects and aftermath of the act, then effortlessly slowed to a pause near its moveable limits. Now at ease physically, the mind had just begun its emotion-filled journey from that of a landscaper to a weatherman, a mathematician, a commanding general, likely a reverend, and ultimately a hopeful bystander.

The sizzle faded and the ball grew darker and smaller as it rose toward the western white clouds. Eyesight struggled to keep track of the retired old thing as the mighty soar faded toward the origin of the shining bead of gold. Head held high with eyes scouting across the picturesque land, Sam held confidence in the powers that be. The broadstick had dropped and rested on his left shoulder. The toe of his right boot was twisted into the black earth as he stared into the distance and had no thoughts about anything. Not the past, not the future, not the trouble behind him, not where he was at, and certainly not his next destination.

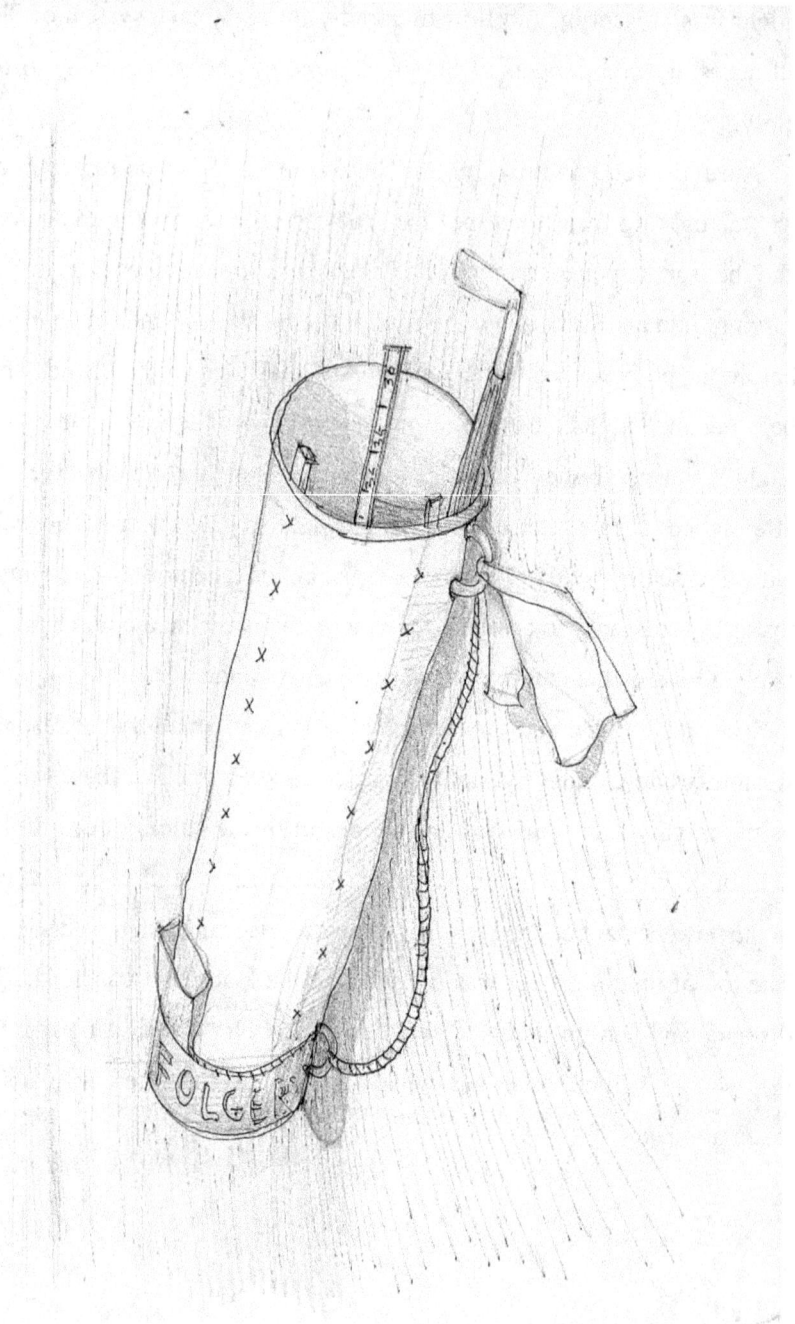

CHAPTER 3

A slim stream of smoke was rising from the back of Murchison's place when Sam finally, and reluctantly, reached the top of the ridge. Most of the straight line, half-mile walk was spent in deep thought and with dazed eyes staring to the white and gray curl spawning from the fire as it lashed up to the sky. Both, nervous as a tick and excited like a child, Sam mulled through potential questions and debated over if they should be asked. The Katy Trail intersection arrived quickly and in much the same manner, the rumbling arrived deep in his belly. Breakfast was rumbling, again. There was no lunch, as it was skipped in favor of keeping his streak alive of knocking the golf ball down the middle of those railroad tracks. After placing all belongings on the front porch, he straightened his collar and pulled the fedora back down. As he stepped to the door, Miss Ann's lessons on manners jumped to mind and he tossed the hat on the trunk. Sam hadn't made a habit of walking into too many buildings over the last years.

A light double knock with his knuckle caused the glass-paned door to creak open and Murchison, sitting at a large roll-top desk near the back door, turned to look over the top of a pair of gold wire-rimmed bifocals, "Sam, come in here." Murchison's gun and holster were hanging from the inside door knob and there was a deaf and still quiet after the door closed shut, "Have a seat." the gravelly voice offered at a volume level that indicated a concentrated effort was taking place. Sam moved slowly and stepped lightly across the glossy oak floor and sat down in a wooden chair that flanked Murchison, who had kept his attention at the desk top. Despite the efforts, the door, the footsteps, and the scrape of the sliding chair wrecked the silence and echoed throughout the loft of the mostly empty, two-story building. Sam tried walking on glass, but nonetheless Murchison still had his full attention on the paperwork when he reached to dot a feather pen in a small jar of black ink. "Thoughts on the place?" the man said as he glanced at Sam and pushed up on his glasses, then continued writing.

"I'll take it." Sam said, with a down-to-business nod that Murchison never saw. Hesitating one moment, the kid reached to his pocket and slapped two one-hundred-dollar notes on the desk. He was anxious. The bills were brand new, stuck together, and ironically contained the portrait of President Abraham Lincoln. Sam had a kick out of the coincidence from the get go, and not wanting to call the striking similarity to attention, erred on the side of caution by placing the bills face down. Sam knew of Lincoln, but the only picture of the man he'd ever seen was that which appeared on the bills he was carrying. Murchison did not utter a word, nodded, continued writing, and never looked at the cash.

After more quiet moments, the writing was finally completed. Murchison scooted his chair to the side, squaring up to Sam. Using his fingertips, he turned the long piece of paper diagonally on the desk so it was now also squared up to Sam. The young man leaned forward in great anticipation. Murchison removed his glasses, looked directly at the lad, and said, "Put your money back in your pocket." The tall and wretched frame then stood and began walking away. The young man hesitated and did nothing, except lose his steady poker face when both his eyes and mouth rose open. In an instant, hopes sank with the notion that he might not end up with the land. Something was astir. Heartbeat accelerated, Sam felt the blood rushing into his head along with all the possibilities of what Murchison might be up to. The young one leaned more toward bad news coming than he did in the direction of good. Perhaps that was not the deed on the desk and the purchase was not as close as thought. Sam was about to hit the floor when he realized that he needed to muster up the will to stand. He then received a smile affirming all seemed well, as Murchison turned and said, "Let's see what we have for supper."

The two new acquaintances spent the next hour, shoulder to shoulder, slicing vegetables, chopping beef, and chewing the fat. Murchison had yet to disclose anything about himself and throughout his line of questioning was afforded a wealth of information about Sam. The train incident, Mr. Fair and his tragic demise, Sam's school days, and the journey from the Carolinas. Tangents sprung in the conversation regarding various landmarks and towns along the way, as the elder probed with direct and indirect questions in an effort to verify Sam's past whereabouts. Murchison did hear relatively everything, though Sam kept the story short when it came to Georgia. Murchison seemed like he was a churchgoing man and any disclosure of playing a game for money could portray a sinful disposition, thus bringing about a final strike. All of the past was nobody's business, anyhow, and talking about it wasn't going to help today or tomorrow.

It's fair to say that Murchison came out of the conversation with a fond liking of Sam, most would. When asked how he ended up in Texas, Sam recited a quote that was written by a hero frontiersman, the great Davy Crockett. Crockett wrote of Texas, that it was "the garden spot in the world," with the "best land and best prospects for health I ever saw."

"The words aren't up to snuff with the description of the eternal biblical garden, but sounds like a wonderful place to be. And, I'm not sure about the health bit, but the surroundings sure bring a blessing to the soul." Sam expressed.

The two jabbered on about different places while the ingredients for the stew were tossed together and then placed to cook on the fire out back. Based on the given statements, Murchison seemed convinced that Sam was a wholesome and legitimate human being. Since arriving back at town there really had not been any talk about the property, which had the kid worked up, anxious, and kicking himself for tossing those seeds about. Sam, nigh to let slip questions about the land, was figuring the best course was to let it come without any prodding as such. As hard as it was, he kept a patient display and promised himself, if he had to, he'd go out on his hands and knees to pick up every one of those seeds.

"Let's go back in and pour up a whiskey." Murchison unexpectedly suggested to Sam.

"Yes, sir. I suppose I could manage one." A shocked, surprised, and half-scared Sam said, as he started following Murchison, who was already making quick work of the walk to the back door.

"Let me tell you one thing. You can stop with the sir business." Murchison demanded, as he stopped Sam in the doorway.

"Yes, sir. Mr. Murchison." Sam said, out of habit, and then had a quick chuckle, "It's a habit."

"Not a bad habit to have." There was a pause. They looked eye to eye and Murchison gained a grin, "Around me, none of that mister stuff either." he added.

"What'll you have me call you by?"

"Murchison. Everyone calls me Murchison."

Sam thought to himself, who was everyone?

Beside the roll-top desk, Murchison opened the doors to a handmade liquor cabinet and pulled one of a dozen bottles of the same brand of whiskey, Old Overholt.

"Got a brand of whiskey you like, Sam?" Murchison queried as he set two tin cups on the bar top.

In silence, Sam was struck. He was under the impression that whiskey was whiskey. "I suppose whatever there is."

Murchison jarred down the bottle on the marble bar top and stood up straight while caught with a cough during a chuckle. "There is no bad whiskey." he said with another chuckle.

Sam stood still, not the least bit collected, and the two shared a smile. The drinks were poured deep. Murchison's, two fingers more than Sam's. The wrinkling hands plugged the bottle, which was then pointed directly at Sam's chest. Murchison's blue eyes and the bottle then both aimed toward the desk, "Dab that feather pen and scribble your Sam Hancock on the line. We'll figure a price later."

Sam grabbed the pen. The last time he'd held one was during his last school lesson with Miss Ann, years ago. His lips parted as he began to silently read from the top of the handwritten document.

Land Deed

6th of March, 1892
Merit Settlement, State of Texas

Certified: L.T. Murchison
To
Owner: _____

Lot 25: 40 Acres, north of Dead Horse Hill, east of Main Street

"Merit Settlement?" Sam said in the appropriate tone to pose a question.

"For temporary and official purposes. Truthfully, there is not a name of the town. It's yet to be decided. I suppose those that live here should have that say and nobody's ever lived here, except me. You, Sam, are the first official citizen." Murchison declared, "There is a story behind the name Merit, I'll fill you in." Murchison motioned for Sam to return his attention back to the deed.

Being marked as the first resident had Sam giddy, but he didn't know what to make of it. Good or bad. If the title was any sort of merit badge, it would simply go into the back pocket. He turned back to the paper, dabbed the pen without looking at the ink jar, then leaned his left elbow on the desk top. Slowly and delicately, the youngster penned his signature and became a land owner. The only place he'd ever seen his name written so neatly was on the luggage tag that had traveled by his side for so many miles, roads, and rails. A never-felt-before easiness rushed over his body and mind as he exhaled. In signing, Sam tried to insist that Murchison take his money, but it was, again, refused. "We'll work it out." Murchison assured. Sam, still in the process of setting the pen down, turned to find Murchison's outstretched arm and a glass of whiskey.

"Cheers to Sam, the young man with a lot." Murchison exclaimed.

Sam mirrored Murchison, raised his glass, and grinning ear to ear, said, "I'm not sure what to say. All of my gratitude for you and your generous act in granting the deal. Thanks a lot." Sam professed, and they both chuckled.

The tin cups came together. Murchison's entire drink went down in one gulp and then, bottle still grasped in hand, he poured another one. Sam caught a whiff while the concoction was on the way to his mouth and relented to wetting his lips. Then the kid bucked up and went in for as much as he could muster, which was less than half of what was poured. The first timer would end up sipping on the rest, and never made it to the bottom. Not so with the veteran, as he used up his drinks much quicker than what was normal pace.

"We'll talk about what you can do to help me out, then figure a price." Murchison said, as he reached to shake Sam's hand.

"Yes, sir."

"Watch it now." Murchison winked and firmly gripped Sam's hand, then rattled it to and fro. They both had a notion that the other was now beginning to be a pal of sorts, though Sam continued to hold the man as a high authority figure.

Stew simmering, the sun had fallen, and in one rocking chair on the back porch, whiskey went down. The other rocked and sat by. The bottle, carried outside, was half gone when Murchison began diving into his story. The adolescent ears were tuned in although the money situation, the story about the town and its name, the questions he had about the property, and the alcohol left Sam sitting with a short attention span. During any spare moments of thought, Sam was hard up not to be drifting and dreaming about that land and the golf shots that would be all over it. The kid listened patiently and the vague story became more detailed and interesting.

The son of a minister, Murchison was raised down near Jasper, Texas in an area that was consumed by activity during the Civil War. At the age of sixteen, on his father's insistence and dime, he enrolled at a small private college in town to study mathematics. He did not graduate and, before he was nineteen, in an effort to find greater prosperity Murchison ventured out on his own. Times were tough for a year or so. After bouncing between jobs that allowed him to scrape by, a promising offer carried him to north Texas.

The reminiscing man advanced through the first years without many details, appearing to be in deep reflection of the moments that were recalled. Tangents that didn't much matter began showing up in his talk. As slow as Murchison was to divulge a tale, Sam reckoned the whiskey was fogging not only the drunken man's speech but his recollecting capabilities as well. After a minute of silent staring into the fire, in which it was clear that the tale was not yet told, Murchison soberly sat forward in his chair and rested elbows on his knees. The glazy eyes met with Sam's, who tuned in from the fire as well.

In the Fall of 1870, Murchison was hired by Judge Jackson Merit, of Tarrant County to manage a side business, a small general store. Not long into employment the young worker had shown enough promise to take on the most trusted of duties and became the judge's right-hand man when a bank and another general store were opened. Murchison oversaw all three businesses.

About the only thing a sharp and loyal Murchison didn't oversee was Mrs. Mary Merit's weekly offering to the Fourth Street Methodist Episcopal Church.

During his years on the bench, the judge entered into numerous land deals and raked in a hefty chunk of money reselling the property in smaller and pricier lots. Murchison received generous compensation, as he had advised on, and managed, each and every one of the deals. They lived high on the hog for a stretch, even in a state that was going through reconstruction, and despite most of the region suffering in hard times. Judge Merit and Murchison, were near exhausted in their efforts toward reconstructing or helping to establish the government and overall standing of Tarrant and other smaller counties in the area. There was a wealth of donations, straight from the judge's pocket, that helped spur the flailing economy for quite an expansive area. It was Murchison's job to oversee that the judge's appropriations were spent on the best of good will. Creating jobs, establishing schools, funding hospitals, and providing for injured soldiers stayed the primary focal point of the Merits' charity, though the generosity went to many more causes than so-called normal philanthropy.

On a December morning, Judge Jackson Merit suddenly announced his retirement and ordered Murchison to begin selling off all businesses. He had picked up knowledge that the railroad would be coming through a beautiful area that he was quite fond of from his boyhood days. The judge had always hoped to relocate there and disclosed that he had purchased sixty thousand acres deemed on paperwork as The Merit Settlement. Murchison was charged with developing a plan for establishing the new town, as the judge was counting on taking full advantage of the initial business opportunities. Once the basics were in place, Judge and Mary Merit would be settling into a peaceful retirement. The change was less about business and more about making a charming place to live.

Murchison, indeed because of good pay, was going along and would need an office on Main Street to handle the new affairs. Judge would become entirely hands-off after the move and promised Murchison the schedule would become more easily managed. "Once we're going, the last thing else I'll command you to do is execute my will." Judge would kid, "Ain't going to be some low-down lawyer doing it."

A date was set and before sun up, Murchison and Judge Merit set out on the first trip to the settlement for a survey of the land. Time on the wagon was spent planning and organizing a timeline. The best carpenters in Texas, Sullivan & Sons, would be hired for the brunt of the construction. First a barn to house the workers and materials, then Murchison's office building, with living quarters above. As the overseer, Murchison would be the first one to officially make the move. A lumber yard, was to be the first business constructed. The best workers on site, and only the finest, would be dedicated to constructing an extremely large house for the Merits somewhere on a fine piece of land, away from the bustle of town. A general store, a gristmill, and a new bank branch would follow. These businesses, once established, would be sold off at fair pricing to locals that were looking to make a sound investment.

Old friends of Judge Merit, the Bateson Brothers Construction Company, owed favors and would be constructing a cotton gin for a discounted fee. There was the impression that the railroad would be up and running in the next year, and the gin needed to begin producing simultaneously. The gin would be sold off as well but would be a big attraction to the area for farmers and workers. Judge Merit would also send word to another old school mate, Cleve Solomon. Cleve and his team of world-class mules would be tasked with plowing up hundreds of acres of prairie land for planting cotton.

Murchison and Judge Merit stayed a night along the trail and arrived to the settlement late morning of the next day. Supply notes were taken and stakes were placed for buildings and for Main Street, laborers would be starting the following Monday. After a long day and evening of business, there was a brandy toast to the new place and the two men stayed the night by the river, under the navy sky which was spotted by too many stars to count in a lifetime. Before sun up, they began the journey home. Judge was expected to return before church on Sunday. Both of the men continually spoke for days about how serene and beautiful the land was, and how much they were looking forward to the new place. As the dear friends and colleagues contemplated life in the new town, Judge Merit promised indefinite good and prosperous times ahead for everyone.

A second trip over to the settlement, to check up on construction, was to take place a month later. Murchison was fighting a bad cold and did not go, at Judge Merit's insistence. The judge opted to make the trip by himself, arriving to the settlement at sundown on the next to last day of July, 1889. He spent the two days looking over things and firing out instructions about details of the buildings, which were beginning to take shape. He ordered the road cut another ten feet wider and improvements to Katy Trail for five hundred yards in either direction. Plans were also laid out for the cotton gin and it was commanded to the Bateson brothers, who made a day trip from Anna for the meeting, that work be started before fall.

Early morning of the third day, Judge Merit hooked his mules to the wagon and informed the foreman, L. J. Sullivan, that he was heading out for a closer look into the thicket, going to do some scouting around, and would return by lunchtime. The judge did not arrive back at town until the work day was finishing up. Sullivan later told that Judge Merit was sweating and looking flush when he returned. He cooled down with a glass of water and attributed the overheating to a hike through the rough terrain of the thicket. The judge then told a story of two different sightings of big brown cats lurking in the dense forest. The first instance was a pair. The second, about an hour later, was a solo and older-looking male. He was not talking bobcat, nor ocelot. The judge said they looked like stout pumas.

Sullivan and the workers were paid their monthly due in crisp cash and two bottles of fine brandy were opened while the sun was still up. At supper, Judge Merit declared to the foreman that he and Mary would reside in the clearing over the ridge, with the big oak tree in the middle. The land was to be cleared of any debris and he'd be back with plans for the house in another month. Clean up the edges and straighten out the property lines, too. Also ordered, was to go ahead and smooth the road over the hill and all the way to the tree line. The judge advised Sullivan that Murchison would be back in two weeks' time with more instructions, then polished off his drink and laid down to sleep in the back of his wagon. Judge Merit was long gone before the sun rose. The laborers, sleeping in the barn, never heard a peep from his leaving.

The judge was due back in Tarrant County early the next Saturday. By afternoon, Mrs. Merit was concerned, though there was no real alarm. She assumed the judge might have gotten a late start or was handling matters in town and would be out to the place before sunset, as usual. At nightfall, with the matter too bothersome, she saddled up a horse and rode in to Murchison's place, above the bank. Murchison did not find any alarm in the matter and assured Mary that the judge would be home later that night, or early the next morning before church. "Who knows what kind of business he might be drumming up." Murchison told the concerned wife, who had become like his mother.

Beginning with the congregation, word of something askew spread quickly when the judge did not show for church. A group of men skipped service and set out on horseback but were back by nightfall having scoured the eastbound trail until it split with no sighting of Judge Merit.

Monday morning, Murchison, along with Sheriff Holden Cole and Deputy O.H. Black, set out east toward the settlement. Murchison driving his wagon with supplies and the law men on horseback, were figuring the worst. It was hard to come by, but Murchison had the notion that the judge simply stayed extra days to get business situated. If that was the case, the judge would be mad as hell about this whole search party ordeal. It wasn't like him though, Murchison was always kept abreast of plans, to a 'T'. The thing that kept lingering in the worried and weary man's head was that there were all sorts of vandals and outlaws about Texas. The Indian Territory was not too far north. Judge Merit should have been able to protect himself as he was always carrying a gun, a Colt Single Action revolver with the initials JM scrawled on the butt. Often carried a musket too, which he most certainly carried for the journey. Things had become safer in the last years, but the open range was still dangerous. Sheriff Cole had been up through those parts the year before and was lucky to manage himself to the better side of an encounter with a small group of braves, Comanches.

The first day was spent barreling down the trail as fast as the wagon would allow. Murchison would keep rolling as Sheriff Cole stopped and questioned any passersby, which there were no sightings or clues of any kind that were revealed. Sheriff Cole rode ahead and to the south toward Dallas, considering the judge might have chosen an alternate route. He had old colleagues that worked out of Dallas. Murchison and Black headed up through Collin County. Authorities in both places were alerted to the situation and search parties went out in and around each jurisdiction. Judge Merit's old law buddies hadn't seen nor heard from the man. U.S. Marshalls were notified in Dallas and a posse set out headed north up the Texas & Pacific Railroad. Meanwhile, Sheriff Cole turned around and, double timing it on a short cut, joined back with Murchison and Black at the head of Katy Trail where they made camp for the night.

Early into the next morning's outing, a scene prevailed ahead of the men on the tree-lined trail. Not a word was said as they all slowed and assessments of the situation totaled in. A hundred or more yards away, Murchison knew something was badly wrong. The very concerned and shaken man kept the wagon rolling until Sheriff Cole called all to a stop. Murchison paused, briefly, but kept on against the sheriff's wishes. The judge's mules, still hooked to the wagon, were off to the side of the trail grazing on leaves in the trees. All supplies were missing, along with the trunk that was nailed down on the back. Sheriff Cole spotted dried blood on the cab floor and driving seat. Deputy Black noticed the whip laying in the trail about twenty yards further up. Feet past the whip, there was a scattered set of footprints that led to the north side of the trail then disappeared. They were definitely the judges prints, Murchison had followed the shoes too many times. Deputy Black headed into the woods, seeking more tracks and any possible clues. As Murchison and Cole were departing for the settlement, the U.S. Marshalls joined and they fanned out north behind the deputy.

Sullivan came down off the roof of Murchison's new place when he saw the cloud of dust racing down the trail. He gave his account of the judge's trip and then gathered the laborers to join in the search. Murchison, going off Sullivan's story, saddled up and took off north on Main Street and over the ridge to have a look at what the judge might have been up to on his morning outing. The acreage with the big oak tree was identified and shortly thereafter, Murchison dismounted his horse as the woods became too dense. He searched on foot well into the thicket looking for a sign of some sort, anything, though returned to town at sunset with nothing. The Marshalls, Sheriff Cole, Deputy Black, Murchison, and the sheriff from Hunt County, Dane Van Zandt, all met in Murchison's would-be office that evening. A plan was discussed, and the following day, before sunrise, the law men launched an all-out search to the north. Murchison returned to Tarrant county to share the devastating news.

Numerous waves of efforts to locate the judge, or his remains, were made by a wealth of individuals and surrounding law enforcement agencies over the next months. Murchison insisted that work on the new settlement continue, although the dream slowly waned and any progress had been abandoned by the end of winter. In February, Mary Merit required Murchison to sell all land and absolve the remaining business interests, as she was moving south to be with family. The man who had been so dedicated throughout the years was left unemployed and received the single last remaining investment, the land and assets of the Merit Settlement, as a severance package. By summer, he was living all alone in the town that was quite shy of being a town. Even for the times, you could say the place was primitive at best.

Murchison was slouched in his chair when the story ended. His speech had gradually become more drawn out and slurred over the course of the hour and the final words were mumbled with eyes all but closed. It was abundantly clear that there were earlier pulls from the bottle. Sam, done drinking after one, did not remark to the story and allowed Murchison to fade asleep. After quietly easing up and stirring the stew, he then pulled the iron pot from the fire and helped himself to a bowl full, figuring Murchison might awaken in the meantime.

Planning was interrupted by more perplexing thoughts about Judge Merit, about Murchison, and about his place in the middle of all this. Sam was sitting with big boys and definitely had the notion that he better sit up straight and keep his elbows off the table. He exhaled a last white cloud of smoke that hovered undisturbed in the stillness of the night. The distant black trees faded behind the engulfment as his thoughts went up Main Street and over the hill to the empty lot, occupied only by the awe-inspiring oak tree. The beautiful plot was one of the last places Judge Merit stepped foot. The man must have certainly dreamed hopeful thoughts of a new homestead, much the way Sam was feeling right then. The young mind wondered many things about the judge and what had transpired in his days. He thought about what Judge Merit would think of his place being sold off to a drifting young kid and turned in to what some, at the time, might have referred to as a playground. There was a vow, a commitment, a promise to establish and sustain the grounds in a way the founding fathers would appreciate and admire. Sam was out for a lasting place that would long stand over those forty acres, perhaps outlive the big oak tree.

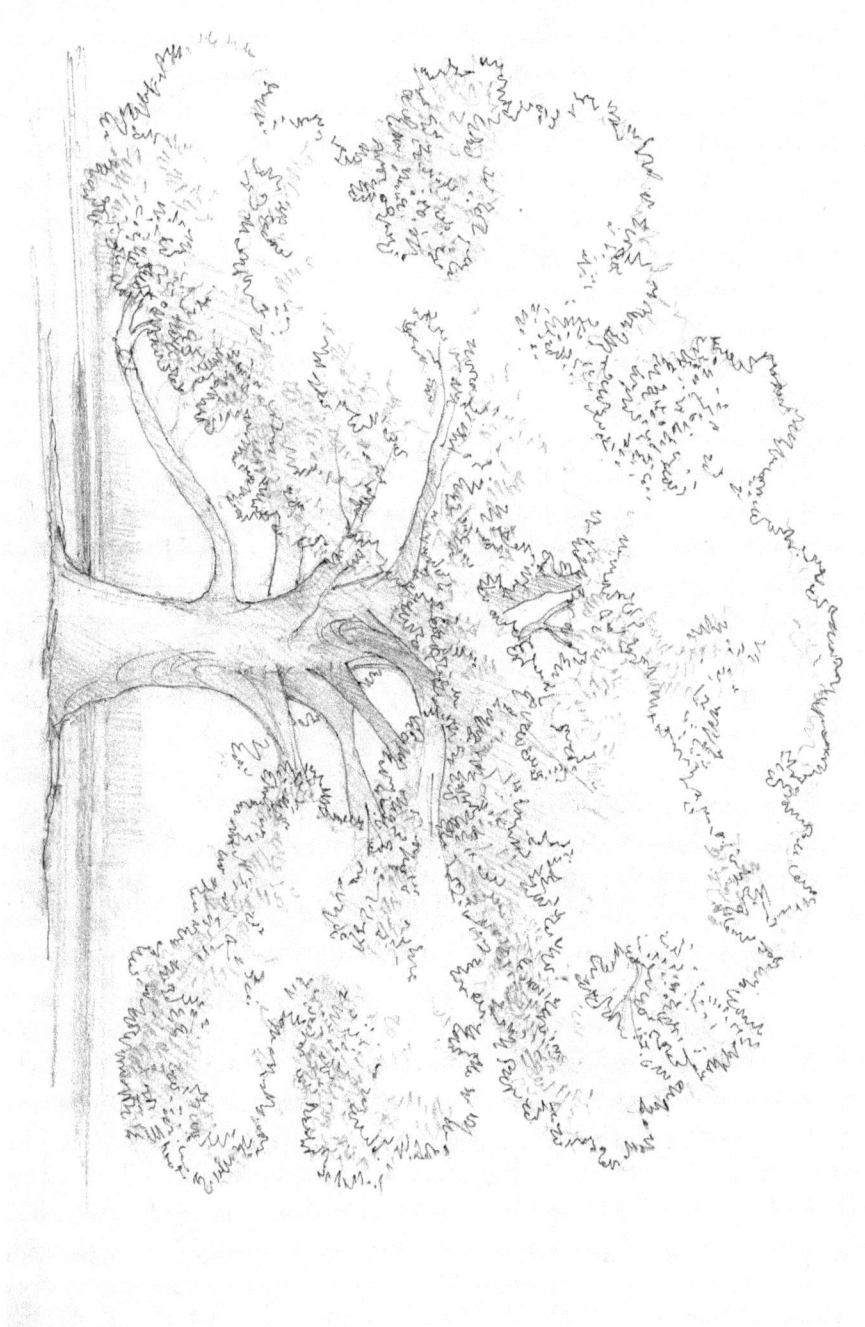

CHAPTER 4

A cold chill flushed through the air when Monday's sun first cracked upon
Sam's closed eyes. Despite all on the mind, his tired bones slept well with
head on the golf bag, feet propped up on the front steps, and straw fedora tipped
over his face. Likely, just the most comfortable place he could find. It was quite
normal to sleep under a tree, in weeds, at a train station, or any other place
besides a bed. Even with his name on the paperwork, he awakened not feeling
much like a landowner, and still waited patiently for an opportunity to query
Murchison about some details. In Sam's mind the first order of business was to
get the property paid for or worked off, either one. Clouding things, was
uncertainty about how much work was expected and exactly what kind of a final
deal would be had once all shook out. There were plans and things to do, and an
urgent desire was busting at the seams. Out of character, for the first time in a
long time, presumptions were to the positive.

There was a deep aching to do one single thing. Each and every morning, he
had an up and at 'em attitude because of what was soon coming. Golf was to
Sam like brushing your teeth is to most people and he had to resist the routine

on that day. The antsy kid knew citizenship was in line before a game. Paying the full amount for the lot, or not, he needed to help Murchison out. It was the kind thing to do despite any discount. The work and the wait had a monumental amount of promise, so Sam gritted it out. New and pretty much ignorant to any type of market or real estate know-how, and for that matter to all of life's big decisions, he was timid about everything that was going on. To Sam, the sale should have been as simple as buying a piece of bubble gum. Here's my money, now let me chew. The smallest of wrong acts, words, jerks, nods, or winks could possibly wreck the deal and he was ever-so-mindful of that. All in all, he wasn't exactly himself at the moment, as the kid felt like he was still on thin ice.

It was early and a quick trip to the new property was still forcefully tugging. Sam was a moment away from heading up Main Street, but Murchison moving around caused the begging desire to cease. Anyway, there was work to be done and the help was making certain there was a prompt display of readiness. Sam stayed put. Boots were on, sleeves were rolled, and he was sitting on the steps, with an elbow on his knee and chin in his palm when Murchison stepped out to speak morning greetings.

Conversation did not dominate over a bowl of oats and a cup of J.A. Folgers coffee, Sam's first-ever cup of the familiar brand. Murchison asked where Sam laid his head for the night, then went on to a few lines about the day's weather, that was about it as far as any talk around the table. The oats went to long gone and Sam's cup held one last cold swallow. In the bored silence, he stared at the inside rim of the white cup and let go more daydreams about knocking shots around the new place, where all his heart, mind, and body were desiring to be. Stirred from golf land, he told himself to stay patient when Murchison pulled out what appeared to be a page long to-do-list. In a slight, unnoticeable, exasperated huff, Sam would have probably rather pay the two hundred for the land and be off and going with his own work.

The coffee did the trick and the youngster, sitting perfectly still in his chair, was jittering with an underlying twitch to get going with something. As he sat tight, the caffeine sparked a desire to talk. He was ready to finally speak out with questions but Murchison didn't appear up for it. The man was focused on the day ahead, as he silently reviewed the list from over the top of his glasses. Finally, at the very tail end of his breakfast, the boss man began listing out a plan for the workday. The new employee was careful to sit up and take note of every detail.

The last cold sip of coffee briefly swished in his mouth before he mustered the swallow, then Sam followed Murchison through the front door. The first stop was the structure furthest south, where the two stepped into a large room filled with boxes upon boxes and four or five large crates. By the time the sun was dipping that Tuesday evening the place was set up as if it were ready for business, except for a sign on the store front. Supplies of all sorts were stocked neatly on shelves throughout. Grocery, hardware, basic dry goods. The shop had nearly all the essentials one needed during the times. A long counter, with glass top, ran the length of the place, holding all sorts of needs and wants. Belt buckles and bolos, handmade holsters, sewing supplies, varying lengths of knives, different wooden and tin toys, and even a small variety of timepieces, among other knick-knacks. At the back were sacks of flour, wheat, corn, beans, sugar, and oats. Fresh fruits and vegetables would be delivered weekly from Greenville starting on the first of next month.

Tobacco products and spirits had their place behind the counter and next to that were the medical supplies. A nice collection of brand-new fishing rods stood in one front window, with nets, tackle, and accessories on a rack below. Sam found this odd, as he hadn't seen a hint of a decent fishing hole around. This obviously begged a question in addition to the other ones, but still there were none asked. He just worked away. The other window area was kept vacant except for a map of the settlement, lots marked, hanging on the adjacent wall and a cabinet of mailboxes arranged below. In that nook, on the side counter, sat a wooden cash box with an open slot on top. The store would operate on the honor system. After lunch on Tuesday, Murchison scribbled 'Stallings' on the map inside of the big lot north of Dead Horse Hill and assigned Sam to Box N$^{o.}$ 1. This brought a needed dose of solace to Sam's worries and more of a decent night's sleep back on the front porch.

Sounds from the far-off thicket during the late darkness of Wednesday morning helped bring needed sleep, but it didn't come until later than what was normally rising time. Sam, given a cot after politely refusing the barn for the stars, was awoken by the slam of the front door closing. He was right to work, no breakfast, with the days major task of dusting, mopping, and cleaning the inside of the other two southern buildings and the one furthest north. In their uninhabited state over the last years, the structures had become quite grimy. Spiders, mice, and all that comes with them. Murchison mostly stayed in his place, only stopping in a couple of times to point and holler from afar as he kept his distance from the work. By late afternoon, all three places were spotless, shining, and ready for lease. Sam licked his chops thinking he'd made quick enough work to leave time for a trip over the hill before sundown. A mind, preoccupied with golf, set foot outside the two-story building and Murchison showed to lay down another assignment.

Sam spent the next hours on the backside of the store constructing a new public outhouse. He dug the hole, then hauled over lumber from the cotton gin and built the thing. Murchison, again, kept his distance from the work. The tall man did make the trip over to the gin, and while there offered a heck of a deal on a batch of fine lumber that had been set aside for the judge's home. Told Sam it belonged out at the forty acres. After the outhouse, Sam took on the uphill task of transporting the wood over the ridge and to the new property. During those times over Dead Horse Hill, it was like a kid looking through a candy jar as Sam lauded the lot. After the arduous and grunt-filled trips, a mile long each, Sam was near as worn out as the mules. The lumber purchase, as well not yet paid for, brought more affirmation that the land deal was a lock. Sam was still holding an air of hesitation about something being too good to be true. Murchison hadn't been seen since before sunset and was passed out in the rocking chair, empty glass in hand, when Sam arrived to tie the mules up for the night.

Thursday, the two were up and at it painting signs on the front porch of the store. A large black one with white letters for Murchison's General Mercantile, a large white one with red letters for the auction, and three smaller advertisements, left natural, that read 'For Rent' in red paint. Murchison was quite the stenographer when it came to the detail. Each letter of his name was painted in thick, black, and perfect cursive letters that were outlined with a pinstripe. Printed below, also perfectly, in black and bold capital letters, a description of the business. Sam filled in between the lines while learning as much as he wanted to know about paint, painting, proper cursive letters, advertising, running a store, and so on.

Waiting for the paint to dry, the work was plucking stray weeds from around the intersection. Murchison stayed inside doing paperwork and pricing until lunch time and then, after chewing on chunks of salted ham, the two went at a project together. Sam found himself in quite a precarious position hoisting the large wooden sign above the mercantile, as Murchison hollered from across Main Street to get it centered. The other signs were hung in their respective places and before putting the white paint away, Sam did some touching up around the front of the buildings. Then, it was back to pulling weeds until there was not one that was littering town. The brush pile burned orange in the dark blue sky behind Murchison's place while the day was finished up sweeping the porches and raking the black dirt of the easements. Murchison had the stew warmed up and waiting but was passed out in his rocking chair. Sam partook of the supper alone and then faded to sleep while staring up Main Street.

The tired young man slept in and awoke Friday when the bright sun struck his face, realizing why Murchison stayed his nights on the back porch. While in his golf bag to fetch a morning smoke, he realized Murchison wasn't up and going and therefore found a moment to get a new ball in the works. There was hope that one would be needed sooner rather than later. It had been five days since the last shot and the week dragged. After digging items out of the trunk, he went to it with a scrap piece of leather and made quick work of the unadoring task. The ball lacked a little more stuffing and stiches to close it up when Murchison finally hollered. After a late and quick bite of biscuits and coffee, they walked through a doorway in Murchison's small kitchen area and into the building next door. Oak planks were turned into a decent looking handcrafted bar and three shelves were erected against the wall behind. Murchison would pick up trim on his next trip to Greenville.

The elder one performed a first-witnessed act of manual labor and swept up after the project. Sam carried in from the barn, four empty barrels and more than two dozen barstools. He oddly smirked at times during the work, as he was helping to create the kind of place that he was not too fond of. Miss Ann had warned of saloons and all. One thing he was not going to do was lose the land because of not partaking in a drink. The young adult had been making his own decisions for some time. A long time. Being all-the-time lonesome, he considered that this social roundtable could be an all right place depending on who filled the seats.

At times that day, the opportunity to ask his questions seemed present but Sam hesitated. All focus was kept on the work. The understandably timid new resident decided it was best to let the subject of the money and property, and whoever else was around or on their way, come up in Murchison's words. A population seemingly on its way to town, found Sam wondering and worried about who all he would encounter. He was all ears and wanting to know any information that would be willingly divulged in regard to the coming days in the settlement, but zilch was voluntarily disclosed.

The time passed easier that day as there was more than a fair share of bar jokes, including one about the farmer's daughter stepping on grapes and coming up with blue feet and beer. And, there were select stories straight from the bench of Judge Merit, from which lessons and reminders prevailed in Sam. Some stories were a guilty verdict on the smallest of mischievous misgivings and some brought forth determination to stand just. Some brought to light struggles to overcome and some set free bindings from years past. Sam wrestled between the good times and the bad times, shying away and making his way, the welcome and the unwanted, going for it or not, jumping or not, a yes or a no. He never talked about that stuff, most always keeping it inside. You could see it flare up in his golf from time to time, but for the most part he stayed cool as a cucumber when playing the game. Playing golf was the time of his life, every day. It's when he felt best and had no worries in the world, except for the shot that lay before him. He did ask one question that day, and like the town, for now there would be no sign out in front of the bar until a suitable name was decided.

Two large mirrors were carefully carried in and precisely held in place while Murchison secured them on the wall above the shelves, between remained a near three-foot void. Below the mirrors, on the top shelf, a load and a half of liquor was stocked bottle by bottle. You name the make, it was there. Gin, tequila, rum, moonshine, brandy, and of course whiskey, the most prominent selection. A case of Old Overholt, minus one, had its special place underneath the cash drawer on the bottom shelf. The bar establishment would not be running on the honor system. After more tidying here and there, Murchison brought in boxes of crystal glasses, a brass spittoon, and a very elegantly framed portrait of Judge Jackson Merit, which was carefully laid atop the new bar. The painting was done in oil by renowned artist and violin maker H. E. Fain. Judge Merit hated the thing and had stashed it away with a mountain of other junk in the back of the barn. There was a hope that it would never see the light of day, and if so, that would be posthumously.

An end of the work day drawn to at Murchison's saying so, Sam stood silently posted up against the bar with the past spurting into thoughts of the future as he watched himself peering back in the mirror. Besides a reflection in a train window, a fair amount of time had passed since the maturing lad was face to face with himself. There had been deep reflection at each of those sightings, but here and now, he was too anxious to consider anything besides silent prayer in hopes that the deal could be settled and he could then be on his way with golfing. Murchison was still rummaging about behind the bar and drew Sam's attention when he hammered a nail into the wall at the precise center of the vacant spot, eye level to the tall man.

"The old judge was a great one." Murchison called out. Quiet stillness filled the bar room. Murchison stared his late mentor and pal in the eyes, likely recalling cherished memories that were countered by tragic mystery-filled nightmares. Sam watched Murchison's silhouette and still perceived the clear and apparent despair that slowly turned to a hesitant and condoling smile. The silent buzz dissipated when Murchison grabbed hold of the picture, then angled it to the dropping sunlight coming inside from the opened back door. "You know it, Sam?"

"Sure sounds like it." Sam said, as he laid an eye on the judge's likeness for the first time. A smart-looking and stout older gentleman with shaggy gray hair that was combed back on top. Baggy, worrisome, blue eyes covered by a pair of gold rimmed bifocals. A gentleman, even in his portrait, that came off as wise as old Solomon. A gentleman that carried a demand for respect, and it seemed likely that in person his presence would make any plaintiff, guilty or not, stand up straight and at full attention.

In a reflex, Sam was drawn deep into the portrait of the man, whom appeared as an important type of historical figure. A far away fictitious character. If one likened Murchison to a young Lincoln, they'd have to liken Judge Merit to George Washington in his prime. The fact grew to be astonishing and incomprehensible to Sam, that he was settling a deal on the old judge's land. The retirement paradise for a noble life. The prestige of the plot and its presentation had been graded high by Judge Merit when the place was decided as the new location for living. That's what was known through Sullivan's words, who said the judge rambled on and on about the plot and the plans. The forty acres of declared personal property and its potential took up the brunt of the conversation over brandy that evening before the fateful trip out of the settlement. The area was dear, the acreage must have struck deeper chords. Dreams and wishes. Hope for the best of life as the end drew nearer. The desire to be surrounded by grace and beauty and looking at your own aweing piece of creation.

After hanging the picture perfectly straight and giving Judge Merit an approving nod, Murchison grabbed a crystal decanter of brandy and a pair of glasses. "That's all for now. However, this occasion requires a drink." he said.

Sam was following the barkeep's working hands and offered nothing in response, having already quickly learned that no matter what, a drink was coming his way. The two glasses were turned upright. "This one's for Judge." Murchison exclaimed, honoring his old friend and boss. The drinks of brandy were poured, Murchison's again a couple of fingers taller than Sam's.

"You appear as a law-abiding citizen, Sam. Would you say it to be so?" Murchison asked, as he moved the short glass away. Sam readied himself for something along the lines of a lecture on upstanding behavior around town or a warning on riffraffing. Perhaps conditions on the property were coming.

Sam nodded one time in agreement, "Always have been, except for when I hopped that train. I'm pretty sure I wasn't supposed to do that." Sam winked and there were slight and all-knowing smiles from both sides of the bar. Murchison looked away and to the opened back door in decision but stopped short of any comment on Sam's adventure.

"Sit there glad you'll never be required to set foot in Judge Merit's courtroom, tough as nails." Murchison turned back to Sam and claimed, "'Tough, but fair."

There was a quiet pause in obvious respectful memory as Murchison stepped back and leaned to rest his elbows. To the other side, Sam was adrift, drumming up images, notions, thoughts, and perhaps a lesson with the words.

"Judge Merit was honorable as a good old dog. Loyal as one, too." Murchison added. "If he were here, he'd likely say, pour that kid more in there." Murchison gave a short laugh as he snatched Sam's glass, filled it on up, and then passed it back. He then reached for a new glass. "Judge would also be pissed off that I didn't pour him a swallow. In memory." Murchison gave a one-huff-of-air laugh.

Sam imagined the two old friends sitting around doing exactly what was about to commence, and was also feeling that Murchison sorely missed having a faithful drinking pal to shoot the bull with. Sam was familiar with feelings along those lines, though never had a pal to miss. The two glasses clanked on the half full one that was sitting on the bar, Murchison's first. Then the two full glasses clanked against each other. Murchison let out a sigh as he quenched his thirst. Sam sipped at first, then had a heavy taste that caused a slight cringe to come forth.

"I appreciate all of the help." Murchison said, then finished off his brandy with a big swallow and directed his eyes over to Sam, "What do I owe you?"

Sam stuttered, "You… Sir, you are welcome to the help, anytime. You, you don't owe…" He began to launch into an on-the-spot explanation, antsy and craving finality to the purchase. There was a long and silent scowl from Murchison, and the scowl went on. Murchison's chin dropped and the harshening look stayed stuck to Sam's watery eyes.

"My apologies." Sam smiled with the words. The smile and the scowl left slowly and the expressions changed to friendly, sincere, and serious. Murchison first.

"You were taught right and there shouldn't be any apologizing for that. It is well preferred that you leave out the sirs and misters with me. I don't need to be made to feel any older than I'm gettin'." Murchison said, "I reckon you making your way to owning a piece of land, puts you as an adult. Same as me. We'll speak gentleman to gentleman." Murchison, looking Sam dead in the eye, winked, and then the glasses, Murchison's empty, clanked again. Sam cringed another drink and Murchison poured himself another, this time Old Overholt. Before plugging the bottle of brandy, he even topped off Sam's glass.

"Tell me, Sam Stallings. What is it you're going to be doing with that land? Start a living off the place? Raise livestock? Crops?" Murchison asked, then took back to his whiskey.

Sam had stomached the swallow and it near came to spewing. His Adam's apple bobbed in shock and, without hesitation, he made a quick decision that the truth was getting told. If it came to where he was losing the place over golf, then so be it. The liquor perhaps already did its trick as truth serum, as he had considered otherwise of being so forthcoming about his project. Sam was way more than hesitantly worried that Murchison would scoff, likely cuss, the idea of dedicating the land to some feckless golf holes. He looked directly back at the man, with a seriousness that had never come over the young face. A burning desire to fulfill a dream was showing strong, despite his guilty fear.

"I'm going to make it into golfing grounds."

"Inform me as to what the hell are goffing grounds?" Murchison bellowed and let the F's hang, as he swirled the last sip of whiskey around in his glass, then downed it.

"Golf, with an L. A gentleman's game. Swing a stick, striking a small ball down range to a small hole in the ground." Sam swung his left arm into a shortened golf swing motion, then still leaning against the bar on his long side pointed with his index finger and let it fall back to the bar. "Cover the distance and get the ball in the hole with as few swings possible."

"Yes." Murchison replied, "I suppose I've before caught wind of it. Game played over in Scotland or England, Europe, somewhere over there." Murchison looked up to the rafters in recollection for a brief moment and then back to Sam. "Never seen it." Murchison was not akin to many things at all outside of work and business, which had taken up nearly every minute, except for sleep, of his entire adult life.

"Join me for a round of holes and I'll show you sometime. Careful though, it'll grab hold of your legs and pull you in. A man knocks one good golf shot, he'll gain a new love forever. Some catch a fever, like me." Sam proudly said, and received back no response to any such potential happenings.

"So, you are buying land for a game?" Murchison asked sharply, with what was perhaps an interested look. Sam didn't know if the look, or the question, was good or bad. Promising toward a blessing or promising toward a yanked deed, and at the least a changeover to another section of land elsewhere.

"A game, though much more than a game. In my brain, bones, and heart it's life. Nothing else I'd rather be doing."

"I don't know that golf is any smart way to make a living. I hope you know that. Two-hundred dollars to have a chunk of land for a game sounds like a waste of land and money. I don't see why you wouldn't farm the place and knock your ball somewhere else. Down the trails or wherever. Knock you a ball on up Main to the sign post. Then knock you another one down to the bend of the river. Play you another one back to the cotton gin. There's all the world to swing at golf balls. Why do you use a perfectly decent piece of property for something of a game?" Murchison's words seemed fierce, though Sam felt he was searching for understanding.

"There's a lot of trail golf to be played all over the earth, or wherever one may roam. Nature itself is as much a part of the challenges as some old golf ball or a tough opponent. The way I see it, you might as well make it all take place on well-shaped grounds. Beautiful, challenging, meant for and dedicated to the game. A fine backdrop makes for a fine display of talent and creates an exciting, challenging, and meaningful stage for a participant. Not to mention, more of a spectacle for any willing spectators. Like the finest of artistic sets for a big play or like the ornate coliseum poised to host the fiercest of gladiators before a jubilant crowd. A place that allows a player to thrive and keeps them humble at the same time." Sam had way overstepped his normal boundaries for spelling out something that was on his mind, but before today's judge he felt a well-pleaded case was necessary. Just off and rolling with a buzzed spout into the glory of golf, Sam closed his mouth and turned nervous as a tick between dog teeth when Murchison interrupted.

"Are you suggesting that people are going to line up to watch, as you knock a rock through your pasture? Fill your coliseum, your play house?" Murchison asked, in a practically argumentative and dramatic tone.

Sam filled up with regret for showing the passion, then quickly tossed the feelings aside and polished off his drink while Murchison waited.

"I don't know that they will ever line up around here to see me play." Sam gave an honest and humble smile, "Though, if luck has it and the grounds are good enough, maybe one day they will line up to shoot a round themselves."

Murchison was taken with a gut full of understanding from the sharp reply that sounded rehearsed, and probably was. "If that's your dream, no one is to say if it's a better or worse dream than any other. That is what Judge Merit would rule." Murchison paused briefly and the moment settled, "I'm not trying to be hardnosed. Nor am I prodding. I want you to be certain of what you are doing here, Sam. Make sure you and the place, together, will last. I do think the idea is near hairbrained, though if that is your prerogative then wring that chicken's neck."

"I've never been more certain of anything and I've made it this far going along with the breeze. I suspect I'll be even better once planted." Sam replied.

Murchison started to speak, then paused, and began with different words, "I'll tell you and I want you to know, Judge Merit would much appreciate you making a golfing place out there on his old property. He sure enjoyed leisure time or a contest. Fishing a pond. Gambling. He was one heck of a card player. Hell of a bluffer." Murchison said, with a chuckle at the end. "On Sundays, at the fellowship suppers after church, Judge was a guarantee to be in the money, no matter his draw in a game of horseshoes." Murchison was smiling more than he had since Sam arrived in town, "He would much appreciate it and I think it would suit him fine, what you are going to do. Hell, what do I know? Your place may one day be a draw itself to the town. In fact, I will be writing Mrs. Mary Merit to inform her of the plans. I'll tell her we're going to have golfing grounds here in the settlement. I think it might offer some sort of consolation."

Sam was emotionally moved and stood as humble as ever, soaking in the blessing. His body and his gaze were as usual, though everything else was raging with full confidence. Now, with Murchison's support, Sam was swollen with enough motivation to top the biggest of dreams. Probably, that imperious swagger began to evolve as he didn't care much about anything else.

"I'll do you and the Merits proud." Sam said.

"Well, I know you will."

Murchison then stopped and contemplated pouring another drink, before plugging the bottles. "Now listen, I believe tomorrow once daybreak hits, we will begin seeing folks rolling in for Sunday's auction. I have high hopes it'll be a big day, along with a heap of office work before then. I imagine you are about ready to get to your own work, to your golf grounds. You have your deed. You've worked off the price of the land, and for the lumber I might call on you for help another time. Deal?" Murchison nodded and opened his eyes wide at Sam.

"Now, I'm going to pay you a fair price for that land and lumber!"

"Sam Stallings, you are not. I insist, and do so, because I am quite sure that you will be worth your weight in gold around here. Like I said, I may call on you for help here or there, and other than that there will be no more discussion of the matter." Murchison ordered with his elder command.

"Without arguing, there is not much I can say. You won't regret it. Call on me anytime. Try to avoid the hours directly after sunup and directly before sundown. I'll be golfing." Sam smiled just thinking about it, and also to let Murchison know he was only kidding around.

"I'll get you during the heat of the day." Murchison said, then gave a big laugh as he stepped around the bar to shake Sam's hand. "Anything you need to be situated for the night?" he asked.

"I don't believe so. I'll keep those cats at bay with my golfing stick." Sam said.

"Are you carrying a firearm?" Murchison asked.

"My old broadstick and a golf ball work dang fine. I've never needed more."

"Well, I have a spare pistol next door. Take it with you, in case." Murchison offered.

"I appreciate you looking out, but I'll be fine." Sam said, with the utmost confidence as he stepped out of the door and onto the front porch. Murchison followed.

"Grab your things from next door and we'll see you tomorrow. The pistol is in the drawer of the white hutch if you want it."

"My aim would be better with the broadstick, so I'll decline the offer, but thank you." Sam said.

"Tomorrow evening, I'm hosting a cookout for those that have arrived to town. Come down and meet everyone, have supper."

Sam got an instant knot in his stomach, then gave a simple nod. "I appreciate everything, Murchison. Your generosity and hospitality have been a blessing that is second to none. I'm looking forward to living here, and to the indefinite good times there will be. Thank you for everything."

"You are welcome for everything, Sam. You are a hard-working hand at the least. It's a blessing to have you here." With that Murchison turned back inside and closed the door to the bar.

Sam stepped inside Murchison's front door and slung the golf bag over his bony shoulder, picked up the trunk with both hands, and then snagged the satchel with his index finger. After swinging the door shut with his foot, there was a pause on the porch and a brand-new Sam set out for home. The steps were oddly quick and landed longer than normal as, like a child leaving the school day, he threw the makings of a black dusty cloud with his fast footsteps up the west side of Main Street. Though he had been there once before, he was on the way to a new place. His place. His golf grounds. During the walk, the past was nonexistent and the future held everything. A half mile long list was piling up with things to do, while the question of where to start held firm at the forefront.

The moon was sliding in as Sam ducked under the outstretching limbs of the oak tree and arrived to the neat stack of lumber that he'd situated beneath. He sat atop the wood and the world, staring over his property with long looks into the darkness and the paler shaded field of grass that was barely waving. Late in the evening, the boots were slid off and his back laid against the oak. In the ringing silence spread across forty acres, the brain-engrained list grew longer and more detailed as the thoughts and dreams grew richer. Sometime after the moon was high and the stars were in their fullest form, Sam, laying on the wood pile breathing slow in infinite thought and imagination, drifted to sleep lost in a vison of his own slice of heaven on earth.

The welcome light of the morning came fast, though an air of reluctance lingered about the day. Property seekers were steam-rolling their way to town and, not only that, Sam had been asked to congregate with said folks. These situations brought about the dreaded task of having to speak out to a group that had previously been rambling amongst themselves, then suddenly put a cease fire to the talk and directed all their eyes and ears to the lone outsider. Somehow,

85

if he could help it or not, the conversation would always turn to golf and a round of obligatory questions. Hereafter, was usually an informal dismissal from any further social inclusion. This was welcome by Sam, as playing was much more desired than talking about golf or anything else.

The new leather golf ball was finished off during the morning smoke, then Sam spit-shined the broadstick. After a quick jaunt over to a running part of the river and a much-needed bath, he changed into his best pair of navy pants and his cleanest white shirt. Looming stout in his mind, was a calling to inspect the northwest corner for that golf ball he hit last Sunday. After mulling it over, he called it a truce and decided there wasn't any use looking for it. The things often didn't last a day, and this one was likely busted to shreds shy of the slough, or in it. Besides, Sam's nerves were figuring it best that he get going.

Sam was sitting on Murchison's front step, all belongings to the side, facing the dead-on rising sun when the door was pulled open.

"Back so soon? The cat's run you out or are you here for a refund?" Murchison graveled in a clogged voice.

The gaze that was stretching far east down Katy Trail and keeping watch for any sign of anything, zoomed back to the present. Sam stood and faced the man. "Morning." he said, "I want to let you know that I appreciate the invitation, but I will not be attending tonight's function. Leaving for the city to stock up on supplies, I need to."

"I understand." Murchison said, "Dallas is closest, and your best bet at a decent selection of anything you might need."

"I figured so. Spotted it on the map at the train station." Sam replied.

"West to the Texas and Pacific line, then south until you get there. Take you a day and a half. You'll make it before sundown tomorrow."

"Best of luck with the auction. I hope all goes well, and I'll look forward to coming back to the progress." Sam said, and then tugged down on the brim of the fedora. "Keep an eye on the place for me?" he added with a grin.

"Sure thing, good man." Murchison smiled back, turned, and then, once in the doorway, looked back to Sam with a down-to-business mug. "Keep an eye out yourself and be careful out there." he said, and then closed the door behind his back.

After replying with a nod and an assuring smile, Sam gathered his gear and hugged the trunk at his hip as he walked to the middle of the intersection of Main Street and Katy Trail. He freed his hands, then slung the golf bag from his bony shoulder and with a fist full of iron pulled the broadstick from its holster. Sam reached into his back pocket and, as he stared down the black trail below the baby blue western sky, before him was dropped a brand-new leather golf ball.

CHAPTER 5

The time having not yet reached noon on a fair-weather Monday found
Murchison sitting comfortably inebriated and drifting toward a midday
nap in a rocking chair on the front porch of the mercantile. Straight into his ears
and from out of the blue, a loud bolt of noise mobilized the buzzed man from
the stupor and caused his eyes to go wide. A gun shot, he thought in his muffled
mind as he twisted left to find the source. The blurry investigation reached a
dead end at the corner of the vacant two-story building and, one moment later,
a golf ball bounced to the exact center of the Main Street and Katy Trail
intersection. In his state of fogginess, Murchison had no idea what the shiny
white orb was. The thing was marveled at once it stopped, then the noise of
hooves clogging and wagon wheels rolling drew his attention away from the
confusion and alerted the daze back to the corner. Sitting up straight on the edge
of the chair, he gave a glance to the pistol on his hip and waited for a truly
necessary reason to draw. The tall man didn't stand at first sight of the two mules

walking side by side, but he sure did when he saw the brand-new driverless wagon and the bundle it was carrying.

Trailing behind the wagon was a big Billy goat and bringing up the very rear was the golfer. He was walking into town tall as ever. The fedora was pulled way down and the broadstick, with iron in hand, was being used like a cane. The trip to Dallas had been very fruitful as far as setting himself up for living. Surprisingly fruitful for golf, as well. Sam was stocked up with all of his needs and wants and, without command, every bit of it halted just shy of the bright and gleamy golf ball. On the porch, Murchison stood with hand on hips and closed his mouth to a speechless smile as he mulled over the wagon that was filled up well beyond the sideboards. Most of the load was boxes or crates. There were a few filled up burlap bags, a couple of rolled up cow hides, a credenza, bed posts and boards, as well as a shovel and a pair of rakes hitched to the side. The arrival back at town was greatly easing Sam's mind. He was as excited as anything to see Murchison, who was quickly and without thought situated on the father-figure side rather than the cold gentleman across the street or the wheeling and dealing land salesman. The sight of Murchison meant the land was a true and honored deal. The Merit Settlement and the forty acres had gone nowhere. Home, Sam was. The excitement likely came from the fact that the young man had never experienced the feeling of coming home to anyone, anywhere. At least, for some time now.

While Murchison made his way into the intersection, Sam stopped and took in a glancing three-hundred and sixty degree look around town. Everything seemed just about the same as when he had left, a month ago. There was one difference that immediately stuck out, a covered wagon and a single mule parked up on the east side of Main Street. Someone was in town and Sam was nervously wondering who. The near staggered stride carried Murchison to the golf ball and following warm greetings and a hand shake, Sam right off asked about the auction. The auction did not fare well and it was somewhat indicated in the man's demeanor. The first fact mentioned, with a sarcastic laugh, was that everyone that showed bought a lot. This provided a small amount of relief to Sam, yet only focused the wonder on the owner of the wagon up the street.

Duley Short, a young fellow for the first time out on his own, purchased Lot 4. In addition, he also bought the half-finished cotton gin for purposes of converting it to a hardware store and lumber yard. Duley was the youngest boy of Short and Sons Hardware, a staple for more than twenty years in Greenville. The Short family well knew the word in the area and their investment in the new settlement was a hopeful sign that others were coming. Sam was drawing conclusions from the camp when Murchison spoke that the two young men might get along well and end up as good friends. Sam shrugged off the supposition with a cold shoulder. He had his priorities and making pals was not on the list.

Another sale, a gentleman by the name of Finus Ryan purchased Lot 1. Upon returning in a months' time, he would again be in the market for another section of land on down Katy Trail. The second place would be for the purposes of his blacksmith shop. The mention of this news quite certainly perked Sam's interest, and his wheels were immediately turning. Mr. Ryan was bringing the right business to the right place, if Sam had an opinion on it. Finus was a salt of the earth elderly man that started his apprenticeship at age eleven. He knew his trade backwards and forwards and was probably one of the best in the business during his prime. Age and the hard nature of the labor had taken their toll in the last years and, though he couldn't do it like he used to, the tough old man was still hoping to garner upcoming railroad work. Murchison had plenty to say about Finus and it was clear that the blacksmith would be an asset to have around. After hearing the scoop, Sam was already fond of the man and could not wait for an introduction. Thinking back a moment, he considered that maybe the hardware kid could be of help in running down the appropriate attachments and ornaments needed to produce proper golf clubs.

Also, Arwin Rank, a younger fellow from down yonder south of town, signed an agreement to rent the two-story place opposite Murchison. Arwin and his wife would live upstairs and run a cafe downstairs. Murchison didn't know much about the Rank's, except her mother's cafe in the southern prairieland was quite a place to eat tasty frog legs. Sam had no appetizing thoughts about frog legs, though felt a place to eat in town would be a plus. A cafe just meant less time putting together meals and more time on the golfing grounds.

Murchison was filled in on the details of the new wagon, purchased at Montgomery Ward for a pretty penny. Then they talked about the mules, Shoe and Sock, purchased on the way into Dallas from a pig farmer named Owens that had a place on the edge of Collin County. Judge Merit had known the Owens Family, Murchison did not. There was a decent afternoon rain shower two days before and other than that, per the norm, no other action stewed around town. As he had done from day one, Murchison made sure Sam was situated food wise, of which he was. Probably wasn't going to gain any weight but he stocked up with staples along the trip. Sam smiled big and commented that life was nothing but better with fruits and vegetables, when it was mentioned that a variety of both were now stocked in the mercantile. A stop by tomorrow for a grocery basket was promised, and when Sam asked about the peaches one was retrieved and tossed his way. Murchison, again, granted Sam all the water he needed from the windmill and advised Sam on putting up his own at the forty acres. Sam was already planning on it, and asked Murchison to give word for the windmill man to come as soon as possible. Green grass certainly requires water, the windmill was going to be a necessity for golf and life. Conversation could have gone on and on, but there was a lifetime of work to get started with. There would be other opportunities, rounds of drinks, and more time to chit chat. After refusing one drink to celebrate his return, Sam snatched up his golf ball and called it farewell for now. Lastly, Murchison encouraged Sam to stop by on his way up Main Street and say hello to Duley Short.

A leery and shy Sam did not stop to say hello to the new resident and didn't even consider it. In fact, he discontinued his golfing for the rest of the way just to keep things quiet. He looked over the new camp, enjoyed the peach, and went right on by. Sam certainly wasn't going to get in anyone's business and he more than certainly didn't need anyone in his. The newest resident must have been shacked up in his wagon or else off somewhere because there wasn't a sign of anyone, anywhere, anyway. If a chap was around, the most he would have received for a greeting was the witnessing of a bite into a peach, a glance of a stare, a yank down on the fedora, and then a pop as Sam smacked the back of the wagon signaling the mules to hurry along. A hop, a skip, and a jump put the young man in the driver's seat having to really bare down on the mules to get the heavy load over Dead Horse Hill. The incline was accomplished when Shoe's backside met the leather handle of the broadstick. On the other side, the reins were pulled and the wagon slowed to a creep as Sam took in a close look, near and far, of the lush forty acres.

After the ride was parked along the rugged remains of Main Street, Sam leaped off the wagon and went right to work. The first order of business was to get some tall grass out of the way. The Billy goat, nameless, had tall orders and was led by six feet of rope to the exact spot where Sam had struck the first golf shot, then staked in place and left be. Numerous trips were made back and forth between the wagon and the oak tree, where most all items were stored for the time being. Once all was unloaded, Sam drove back south to the water source and filled up a barrel and a pail, then made his way back home. Along the way, thankfully no Duley Short and no Murchison, which was just as well. Sam turned the mules loose to graze with no worries about them running off, as the thicket was too dense to allow for an escape. And, besides that, the grass on that forty acres was too lush to walk away from.

Though golf was resisted upon the immediate return to the grounds, there wasn't anything else on Sam's mind. All the while he was situating the new possessions, there were long stares around the place. He talked out loud at times and would all of the sudden stop everything to walk here or there in order to exactly confirm distances, calculations, and visions. There had been a lot of figuring during the trip to Dallas, although being there at the forty acres in person was bringing in some second guessing.

During a brief break from the heat of the falling sun, a day-old biscuit and a chunk of ham were supper. While taking in the routine after-meal smoke, Sam went through a nightly inspection of the broadstick with a fine-tooth comb under fire light. His brain was still churning from the mention of a blacksmith coming to town. Though he would never abandon the broadstick and its magic, the golfer was ready for and needed other types of clubs. A long-distance driver, a short chipper, a putter for the greens, and maybe some others in between. The trusty golf stick was placed back in the bag for the night and, leaning against the oak tree, Sam's eyes grew heavy as one of the new shiny and smooth golf balls was rolled and rubbed around in his anxious fingers. Anxious, because tomorrow there would be golf.

The sun had no chance of beating Sam to the punch that Tuesday morning. In the cool spring darkness, the goat and a fresh pail of water were moved from the spot of the very first golf shot to the patch on the other side of the slough. The stake was placed off the old glass jar and the goat went to chewing. By this point, Sam knew that the one goat was not going to hack it. There was too much grass that was going to have to go. He needed a whole herd. Out of curiosity there was a peek down into the dark glass hole. Using the tips of his fingers, Sam gripped the jar and pulled it from the black earth to pour out about a quarter-inch worth of filthy rainwater and an old leather golf ball that was near busted to a shred. There was a spin with a 180-yard look of awe and wonderment back east to the first tee, now a perfect circle of low-lying grass beneath the knee-high plain. At the realization of the hole-in-one, Sam, with an ear-to-ear grin, was flabbergasted, floored, astonished, and near overcome with indescribable impulses running through his young body. The smile never left and a tear nearly fell. Neither the goat nor Sam needed any more motivation to go to work than what they already held. The glass jar was replaced and the remains of the old leather golf ball were nailed to the trunk of the oak tree. As the morning sun was beginning to peek, Sam dove into the work day.

The stash of lumber was carried over, stacked, and ready on location for the small house. The home would be a place for staying out of the cold and rain, nothing else. The young man was not completely capable of building something fancy, by no means a judge's home. There would probably be an ample supply of materials leftover. The wood was situated and out of the way. Building a home was on down the list. Anything with golfing was sitting at first priority and, besides, the weather was too nice to not sleep outside anyhow. The wagon was pulled by hand through the tall grass to the nearby home site and parked. This would mark the entrance into the golfing club, though at the time it was just considered as the short trailway to the homesite. A lean-to was constructed at the northeast corner of the property, in case storms were to brew. The shed is where all the supplies were stored out of the way, including the household items Sam gathered on the trip, the pieces of furniture, and the reserve of items that were for the game or the grounds. Personal belongings stayed under the oak tree with the rakes and shovels, he felt safer that way. The tools were there because they were going to be needed soon and often, and that's where the still story-less shovel lay. Sam wondered, again, about the abandoned spade and, with nothing, leaned it against the tree with the new ones. Supper was a peach, and the bushel was also kept handy under the oak tree.

Another item that stayed under the tree was a wooden box of gutty balls. Siblings to the bright and shiny one that had rolled into Murchison's dreams. The gutta-percha golf balls were made of special rubber and what the best players of the game were now using. Other than knowing they were way better than the leather ones, Sam didn't know much about the new balls. He was just glad to finally have his hands on some. These golf balls were smooth, not dimpled or nubbed, and were acquired during a chance encounter.

On the trip to Dallas, Sam was playing his normal run of trail golf along the west side of the Texas and Pacific Rail Line and had crossed Bullington Street. The new, beat-up leather golf ball lay in a small patch of short grass that was surrounded by a bunch of waist high weeds. Sam lined up behind the ball and picked out his target, the street sign one block up. This would be the last leg of golf for now, he was getting well into the city and didn't need to be drawing any attention. After lining up the shot, he lined himself up and let one go. The ball flapped and fluttered as it took forth and, per its director, had one short hop before coming to rest at the base of the sign post for Magnolia Street. Sam gathered his belongings and started walking up. A man out of nowhere, Jack Malley was headed in the opposite direction.

At sight of the busted ball, Mr. Malley struck up a conversation on golf and invited Sam over to his place for what turned into a long visit. He was an old-timer, a seasoned golfer that had known the game since boyhood. On up there in age, yet he still played reasonably well. His golf swing was relaxed to near lazy, though he was spot on in precision. Over from Ireland, the elderly man had a Leprechaun's bite in his voice and a shade of red tipping off the gray hair. Sorely missing time playing the links, he had laid out a golf hole that played over a shallow crick behind his house, which was blocks over and off Swiss Avenue. The hole was about one-hundred and twenty yards long from tee to green, prime range for the broadstick. The crick ran below a short downward plain of mostly Dallas grass, and the green was high on the other side with an unforgiving slope that came right back at the water. More than half of the putting surface was clouded over by an old cedar elm with an oblong and droopy crown. Putting surface and green only generally describe that part of the golf landscape, it was rough dirt. Old Mr. Malley and young Sam played the challenging hole again and again that afternoon and evening. There was finally a break for supper, Mrs. Martha Malley had cooked fish. Despite her calling, Sam and Jack had a cold meal. Turns were traded over and over, and not once did either man best a 3. Sam lipped a tee shot in and out of the hole and Jack rolled one over, but both of those ended up trickling back down toward the creek. Between each shot taken and during the back and forth, a new friendship was forged. Jack knew more stories about golf than he did where to get any equipment or supplies, but he's where Sam got the gutty balls. The young man fetched twenty out of the creek and paid a nickel a piece.

Listening to Jack's stories, Sam also picked up knowledge of the putter and the driver as well as helpful hints on his golf swing. Jack was truly and duly impressed with Sam's skills in the game, though talked up a young player from the west coast that was regarded as one of the best to come over to America. The Whammer they called him. Jack had caught wind of the renowned player via newspaper article and had a cousin that saw the phenom win a contest in the sand-surrounded green grasses of Arizona. Jack asked if Sam had encountered the man, which received a reply of the story about coming from the east. Hearing that a player, or the game, was newsworthy, made the young golfer as puzzled as he was proud. Sam stopped back by Jack's place on the way home and it was all 3's until the sun went down. Then, the young man put the last one in the hole before leaving out. More than anything, meeting Jack gave Sam a sense of normalcy. There had not been someone to share the pastime with for a long while. The meeting also gave Sam something to look forward to, as Jack had promised a visit out to the settlement once there had been time to get the grounds off and rolling.

A long wire was strung across the property, passing on the south side of the oak tree. There was no need in mixing the mules and golf, so each got half for the time being. The goat was staying hard at work shaping the N°· 1 green, while Sam situated items here and there until it all felt neat, organized, and cozy. The red flag from the property post was fetched and tied to a long, thin, stiff, and straight branch that had been located while in the city. Sam marched across the forty acres with the marker flying high overhead and made his way to the green and the glass jar. Once posted, the flagstick had a lean, but it would do. There was extra pulling and cleaning of grass that was done around both six-foot diameter circles and the broadstick was used to relocate some goat waste. The golf stick was immediately wiped clean. The goat was put over with the mules and then Sam changed into his navy-blue pants, white-collared shirt with sleeves rolled, and fedora.

With the first half of the day spent working hard and the noontime sun beginning to unleash its fury, Sam stepped under the shade of the oak tree to wet his whistle and enjoy a lunchtime peach. He then grabbed his golf bag and stuffed his pockets with a dozen gutty balls. At the first tee, the broadstick was pulled and the bag left to lay. Golf balls were hit down to that glass jar until sundown. Every single day over the next month he would play on that hole from sunup until he couldn't see anymore. There was only a sprinkle of shots that landed outside of that six-foot round circle, marked at 180 yards down and over the slough. A bulk of golf balls were pulled out of the jar and, a time or so, the darn thing was stacked full. Seven at a time would fit.

He did the necessary eating and sleeping. The river had picked up with a sprinkling of mild spring rains and, together with a bar of soap, it took care of necessary hygiene. The water level of the slough had risen, but only to not quite halfway. Grass was growing, but the goat wasn't necessarily needed. Sam was keeping the grass at the tee and green stomped down pretty good himself. The golfer had also worn down a clear route between the two. Down the left side, around the slough, and up to the circle. The pathway was becoming quite prominent from all the shagging of golf balls he was doing and, by the end of the first two weeks, the walking trail sat bare like it had been there for a month of Sundays.

There was a trip, or two, to town during that golf fueled time. Water, grocery items including more peaches, and iodine from behind the counter. Blisters were wearing on the hands, but even this did not slow the sunup to sundown pace. Murchison was doing well, hard at work trying to drum up lot buyers. On the way back home from the second trip, crossing over Dead Horse Hill, Sam noticed boot prints that did not originate from his soles. With a paper sack in his arm, curiosity investigated and found the trail coming up Main Street and stopping there where he stood. He peered off to either side of the trail, then down at the property to see no one in sight. The walk in was a crawling one, like an ambush from the tall grass or the thicket was almost expected. Groceries were put away under the oak tree, which now had a sort of gypsy-looking camp underneath it. Next, there were more cautious looks around as he shuffled items here and there while tidying up and making sure all was there and in place. The sight of the footprints had shaken Sam near to the core and left the startled soul wondering who the hell was poking around.

Nerves settled quickly with the help of a peach and the distracting task of shining up the broadstick. As the terrain for Hole N$^{o.}$ 1 was about worn out, Sam grabbed his pail of a dozen gutty balls, his golf bag, and a scythe, then set out to a space along the western property line. The scythe was purchased from a tool man that was passing through. The salesman didn't earn Murchison's business, but he did Sam's. Twenty yards south of the first green, Sam looked at the land before him, took a deep breath, and started cutting. The tee box for Hole N$^{o.}$ 2 was made ten yards long and five yards wide before Sam tired out on the first go. The loose ends were gathered and after a short rest, he placed a golf ball in the back-middle section of the fresh cut grass. This was a once-in-a-blue-moon time that Sam Stallings would hit a golf ball in overalls. With the broadstick in hand, he eyed as long of a distance as he figured he could hit a shot. The body and mind stood ready as he walked up to the ball, maintaining his far-off gaze. The greatest distance possible was something Sam hardly ever yearned for, however, this time the ball was positioned further up than normal in his stance so as to achieve just that. Into the back swing, his worn-out-from-using-a-scythe arms summoned all might and let it all go at a shot that flew straight as an arrow, up and across the golfing grounds. Near its landing, there was a slight curve left but, for now, it was lost in the tall grass.

Eleven gutty balls were pulled from pockets and dumped hard to resist, even after it was said that just one good one would be hit to decide the distance needed for a proper fairway cut. Ten yards were stepped off and the scythe went flying and swiping to save the lost golf balls. The strip started at three swoop-lengths across and grew to twelve as it neared even with the oak. The right side was running tight along the thicket, meaning a long spot where trouble could brew if a shot sailed away. The wire was moved and the animals corralled to the southeast quadrant. Not long after, they were all put up for sale with an advertisement at the mercantile and then sold to a passerby within a half hour. Taking down the grass was under control, and selling the animals made for three less things to fool with. There was a breather under the oak tree consisting of water and another peach, then Sam went back to swiping grass and looking for golf balls.

During another break, a rag from the back pocket was used to wipe the grass clippings from his sweaty forehead. The sun was quickly setting, leaving Sam working in a darker shade than the rest of the place off to the east. Cool shade was enjoyed for a moment and then the attitude became that daylight was burning. He was about to get back to the last rows of swiping for the day, when the corner of his eye caught a stunned glimpse of a figure standing atop Dead Horse Hill. Not Murchison, this person was short.

Sam stood motionless, mirroring the unknown subject until he couldn't stand still any longer. Ending the ongoing stalemate across the acreage, he turned back to the new tee box and gathered his tools. Even though movement might have been the sign that the unwelcome visitor needed to encroach, Sam walked on anyway. Retiring himself from the work day and walking to camp, the intersection of the road and the ridge sat hidden by the oak tree until he arrived to the trunk and peered underneath the thick web of branches. Worn out from all the work and in no mood for nobody, luckily the figure was gone as it should have been. And, though plum tired, Sam wasn't going sit and mull over who was putting their nose in his business either. He pulled two golf balls from the box and went on to knock shots down to the first hole, over and over to the time of the moonlight finally slipping behind a wad of clouds and the darker morning not allowing sufficient visibility. The walks between each two shots were quiet, other than an occasional cricket sounding off, and eerie. Sam felt like eyes were watching. The hope was that the loud cracks of the broadstick were warning off whomever might have been lurking. Also, even as tired as he was from all the work, he slept with one eye open that night.

Before sunrise the next day, the task was back to cutting grass on N$^{o.}$ 2. The dozen golf balls were soon found scattered a good stint past the oak tree, where the left side edge of the new fairway started widening away from the thicket. The cut went on for too many scythe swings and two hundred more yards. A good thirty-yard stretch of grass was left tall and beyond that, the spot where the second green would be constructed. After a day filled with all that swinging of the scythe, there was just too much grass to haul off to the heaping pile in the southwest corner. The hauling would have to wait for tomorrow. Sam was even more tired and beat at the end of that day, but played five times through on Hole N°. 1 in the evening. The next morning, soreness demanded the day off.

Sam fashioned a hammock using a piece of canvas that was tied between a post and the lowest branch of the oak tree, and it was all together suiting him fine on that lazy day. He positioned the lounging spot so as to have a bird's eye view of Dead Horse Hill and anyone showing themselves. He sat up and kicked his leg over one side while chewing the last bite of a ham sandwich, then swallowed when there was that man standing atop the ridge. The sun was shining bright, revealing a short pair of overalls and a round head. Sam was in the darkness of the oak and waited to react on any encroachment. The man stood looking about the forty acres like he had a certain interest in it, something for sure. Sam watched him bend and peer down under the oak, then the man took a long look at the home site and the materials over there. The very moment Sam pulled his eyes away to pick up a glass of water, the man made a move and was headed down the hill. Sam pulled his other leg over, rockingly, and felt back into canvas for the broadstick. He hopped down to stand still until he could tell if it was a passerby, or if the man had some kind of business he was trying to get into.

About even with the oak tree, the man stepped off Main Street and began trancheing a line toward the camp. Sam stepped out from the darkness of the oak, broadstick in hand, to meet the young overalled man at half way. He was in deed short but not that short. Much stouter than Sam, carried a much bigger smile too. Right off, about the only thing in common was the buzzed haircuts. There were no immediate words, except for a "Hidey" from the stranger as the two drew near. The golf stick switched from the right hand to the left and then there was a formal greeting.

Duley Short was his name, owner of Lot 4, the seventeen-year-old boy of the hardware man in Greenville. Sam, at first, kept pretty quiet and did not divulge much of anything. He listened as usual, let the visitor spill his deal, and slowly found a comfortable way into the exchange. Duley most definitely carried the conversation. Kept asking questions, really. It didn't take a New York minute for the topic of the conversation to turn to golf. Duley asked so many questions about the game and the grounds that Sam took a bit of a liking to it and, little by little, gained enthusiasm in the back and forth. Still, at the same time, he was making efforts to dismiss himself with work to be done. Duley asked why no golf on that day. Sam couldn't resist saying that he was about to get started with the afternoon round, as soon as the green was swept.

Well, Duley wanted to stay and watch. Sam went on to display some of his best efforts, and Duley just wouldn't leave. Sam, finally, gave him a shot. None were pretty, and Sam was generous enough to toss down more golf balls as he said, "Try another." On that day, Duley became the first person ever allowed the honor of swinging the broadstick. Sam didn't much like handing it over but chalked it up to charity's sake. Duley was awful and had completely whiffed at the ball on his first swing. On his next attempt, the ball was killed by the knee-high grass just feet away. Another burned left toward the oak, the next try was a gash into the black earth, and finally a decent strike but into the thicket. There were several more whiffs, a couple of gashes, two more thickets, and one that came back toward the entranceway. Sam kept feeding him pointers and, after all, there was tremendous improvement. After one into the slough, Sam called it quits on the new player's lessons. Nonetheless, Duley caught the fever and clearly did not want to leave, citing more sunshine remaining. Sam put forth an invitation for Sunday, two days from then, and began politely ushering Duley toward Main Street. Serious thinking was ready to commence regarding tomorrow's job at the N°· 2 green.

Leading the chatty visitor out off the grounds, Sam was privy to be the first in town to hear the news about the lumber yard and hardware store. Duley told that his father had elected to sell the gin, forgoing another family-owned location. His old man was leery of a construction boom in the area and had received a generous and enticing offer from the more prominent J.K. Elliott Hardware and Lumber Company. Elliott owned three stores already, the flagship one in Dallas. Sam had stopped in for supplies on his trip. Also, a Denton County location and another in McKinney. Duley was not wanting to stay around Greenville any longer, in his father's store. He'd been working there since he was six or under. So, he chose to keep his lot and claimed to be in the market for a job. Duley Short dang sure wasn't going to work for J. K. Elliott, nor Murchison. Murchison had a reputation around the area for working his employees too hard. Sam understood the gist of this, though kept it to himself. Sam assumed Murchison was aware of the gin sale and kept his mouth shut about it as well. Murchison was pleasantly surprised and motivated at the fact of J.K. Elliott coming to town, when he finally learned of the news a week or so later. Lastly, Sam let Duley know that from then on, he was shagging his own golf balls. Duley left, and Sam hunted into the night, finding all except the one in the slough.

In the days after meeting Duley, Sam was back to hard work with the scythe. At the end of the second fairway, he walked over the thirty yards of tall grass and started shaping the green. For whatever reason, he was feeling creative at that time and wound up carving out a bean-shape with the radicle part on the tee side. The grass was taken down as low as he could muster, about a half-inch and slightly shorter than the fairway. The last trimming of the day happened when he went over and cut down the grass in the twenty by twenty square patch. A foot-wide border between the green and the thicket was left a half inch taller. The shreds were moved to the hay pile and the square green at N$^{o.}$ 1 was now comparable to N° 2. The red flag at N$^{o.}$ 1 was ripped in two, tied to another identical branch, and posted leaning out of a new glass jar. The grounds were ready for real golf, putting included, rather than just target practice. Before lunch time on Saturday, golf on two holes had begun and didn't stop until under a Sunday morning moon. Any sort of nourishment was forgotten throughout that whole entire day, aside from swigs of water between the working and the golfing.

On Sunday, Duley showed up early and golf commenced directly thereafter. Sam continued affording Duley the luxury of using the broadstick but it was first made clear that if he planned on doing more playing, a golf stick of his own was required. The play that day turned into more lessons and despite, at the end of twenty holes, Duley had more than twice the score Sam did. Out of that, the newcomer was more than twice as good as he was when he first walked over the hill and into the game. The off-subject chit chat throughout the day was favorable to both and comedic at times. Deals were even made between the two new pals. Sam promised to help with golf and necessary equipment, as Duley was desperately wanting to craft a new stick for himself. Sam was ready for Duley to have his own, as well. Duley offered his construction knowledge and skills to help Sam build a house, and a better lean-to. Over a peach under the oak tree, the two discussed grounds and game. Sam promised that new golf sticks would be a priority tomorrow, it was on his mind anyway.

While looking around the place at all the work that was piling up on the to-do-list, Sam had a heck of an idea. Duley was offered a job, and accepted right away. Sam still had some money held back, needed the help to make the place a humdinger, and smiled big when he shook the hand of his new groundskeeper. After a short time of the monotonous battle with the grass, the land owner had grown sick of it and the chore took up too much golfing time. That didn't mean he completely left the grounds alone, there was just help with the hard work. One thing that was made clear to Duley, work was priority over golf for him. It was the other way around with Sam.

Monday morning, as rearing to go to work as the two were, it was decided that gathering appropriate and sturdy enough materials for new golf sticks was going to be a challenge and take big-time luck. The boys sat under the oak tree and it wasn't more than a minute before they were planning out a house and, an hour later, hammering and nailing. And, not just any house. With Duley's smarts and help from Murchison's memory, over the next weeks, a near exact replica of Judge Jackson Merit's dream home was constructed at Sam's chosen site.

The job required a few trips to the hardware store in Greenville. Sam never went. Golf never took place before work in the morning and always after with what light was left. The home ended up grand and beautiful, resembling something you might picture when reading a novel set on a small and lush southern plantation. Whitewashed inside and out, except for the flooring, left natural, and the doors, painted black. The only difference between what was now there and Judge Merit's vision, was that the big front porch was moved to the back porch and vice versa. This for the lone reason of having more space to sit out in the late evenings and enjoy looking out over the grounds. Once the house was finished, a wooden split-rail fence was erected around the perimeter with a single opening left at the jaunt of an entranceway Sam had created with the wagon.

Sam couldn't get the smile to leave his face. He was happy as a lark with the new place. Not to mention that it was a house fit for a judge. And, a retired one at that. Once the details were completed and the place was furnished, with help from Murchison and the stash of items collecting dust in the barn, Sam was feeling at home like never before. The three-bedroom place had one for sleeping although he never slept there, always on the back porch. One room had a cot for any potential guests, whoever that might be. Another room, upstairs, would soon be set up as a golf stick workshop. The full kitchen was never used and the parlor seldomly. A new outhouse, over by the rebuilt shed, replaced digging a hole in the thicket.

Duley solicited the help of his two older brothers and they all began work on a small cabin-style homestead at Lot 4. Bright and early each morning, Sam lent a helping hand for the week. There early, only after spending an hour playing golf under the first light of each morning. The house at 04 Main Street went up like clockwork, which left for a little recreational time. Though sharing the broadstick among four players was not favored, the brothers received a hefty dose of golf each evening. It didn't quite seem to catch on with them like it did the youngest. Afterall, the two older brothers were married, had kids, and each running their own hardware store. Duley sure was busting the mold in that family and his new occupation was seen as foolish in the eyes of the four parental figures he had. If his papa had anything to do with it, Duley would be making lumber deliveries come next week. The thing was, Sam had played things just right. Papa couldn't compete with the wage Duley was pulling in at the golfing grounds. The two brothers might have had a small taste that made for a little understanding, when they each hit a single decent shot and a fun time slid on in. The older one asked, "You get paid to do this and cut grass?" "Better than Paw pays?" followed the middle brother.

While things were finishing up at Lot 4, Sam spent the weekend arranging belongings inside his house and knocking out some much-needed work around the grounds. Early that Sunday evening, he started playing as many holes as he could get in before dark. Six holes in, he realized the quiet stillness lurking across the grounds and the sense of lonesome that was apparent on that day. Sure, he enjoyed playing alone but there was something to be said for having an opponent around to beat up on. Sam felt like he would be a selfish mongrel if he kept such a pleasing thing all to himself. Others needed to see it, play it, experience it. Nobody besides him and Duley would ever have at it, unless told about the place. He stopped his round on the fourth time through Hole N° 2. Holes were dug and two posts were planted on either side of the opening in the fence. By candlelight, Sam whitewashed a board that was left over from Judge Merit's lumber package and carefully stenciled out two lines of letters. Midnight slipped by as he filled in between the lines with the last of the black paint, and the sign was left to dry.

Duley was roused from a sound sleep in his new residence before the sun came up, and the two pals were right at it carrying the sign from the back porch. The white placard with black letters was nailed to the two posts out front, thus marking the opening of The Judge Merit Golfing Club. Serious golfers only. A dollar to become a member, which would be turned over to a town fund. Cost of a nickel a hole, to be used for upkeep and maintenance as well as to help cover Duley's newly negotiated salary.

Sam and Duley, over anything else, put themselves to nothing but golfing business. When the topic of finding hickory wood for golf sticks emerged, Duley had an extraordinary remembrance. Way up northeast into the thicket was a hickory hollow, full of the trees. The problem was the rumor of an old man, a stubborn and possessive hermit, that owned most of the land and did not like anyone coming into his neck of the woods. The story was that years ago, a group of young teenage boys had ventured into the hollow while playing war games. All of the sudden, the boys found themselves in the middle of what seemed like a real battle. Musket shots were fired and they were run off right directly by the crazy old man hollering from the depths and threatening their lives. Duley hadn't heard of anyone else in all of the county schools that had been brave enough to venture into the hollow.

Sam didn't think twice and stood on his feet to head out. Toes were pointed out the door when Duley expressed his hesitation about going, so he gladly stayed with assignments to tend to around the grounds. The broadstick was picked up and tucked through the belt loop, Sam wanted to make sure Duley was working and not playing. The hired hand had certainly caught golf fever. Sam grabbed a peach and walked the remains of Main Street until he disappeared along with the trail into the denseness of Brown Cat Thicket.

Duley worked, stayed worried, and made regular glances into the thicket every hour. As Sam did not return by night fall, the groundskeeper fell asleep on the back porch after imagining endless golf shots going across the pristine grounds. Each swing that went through his mind sent a golf ball over the slough. However, the young rookie had yet to gain the ability to knock the snot out of the ball and keep it straight. Sam was a no show the next day. Duley continued cutting grass and patiently waiting to play some golf. He was now staring into the thicket every fifteen minutes, wondering if all was well with Sam. After dinner at home, Duley returned to lie in wait at the golfing club. Finally, as the darkness was slipping in, distant cracks of snapping branches could be heard echoing through the trees.

The man from Hickory Hollow was named Hopper Hackman, a wretched and scruffy, grimy and grubby, old man that lived in a mucky shack in the depths of the backwoods. Hopper was a self-described hermit and a self-prescribed moonshine drinker, as he put it. Sam ended up making a new pal and went out to the bottoms on exactly the right day. The old, perhaps unstable, man was out doing something around his vast stretch of property and got himself stuck in a deep mudhole. When the old man heard the branches cracking and echoing into the depths of the hollow, he called out. Sam was able to locate the cries for help and, using the broadstick, plucked the hollering man from his predicament.

All the hickory in the hollow was bestowed and Sam left for home with a head-splitting hangover, while carrying all of the wood that would fit in his arms. Hopper let it be known that there was more where that came from and Sam gave news of the bar and golf grounds, with an open invitation to each. The old recluse looked at Sam like they were both crazy and quickly rattled off the true story of why he didn't get out much. "I'm damn eighty-six years old!" he said. The man claimed to have not been out of the hollow in ten years, but promised pondering a visit to each establishment.

Sam explained to Duley that the 'hardest-to-find-and-get-ahold-of' part of a golf stick was still not in hand. Duley racked his brain and made an imploring and unfruitful trip to his father's hardware store. His papa wouldn't have anything to do with it, not even in asking a favor of the local blacksmiths. It ended up that both iron workers were too busy to mess with anything less profitable than railroad work, anyway. With that, and other failed attempts, the broadstick was shared for too many more days and lots more rounds. Meanwhile, an assortment of hickory shafts were whittled down and fine-tuned by candlelight on the back porch.

At the end of the month Sam brought Murchison two dollars to initiate the town fund. One from Duley and one from himself. They would certainly not be paying by the per-hole fee as they would both go broke right quick. Murchison, surprised, moved, and very grateful of the thoughtfulness, notified Sam that the old blacksmith Finus Ryan had arrived to town and was due back tomorrow with the last of his equipment and tools of the trade. A small lot on the west side of the gin had been purchased and a small shack constructed for the purpose of pounding and shaping iron. Sam ran back to the grounds, and double-timed it, after collecting Duley and the newly crafted hickory shafts. The boys realized they had time and played a ball each to the gin, then played back home when Sam recalled that Finus was not due back until tomorrow.

Sketches were drawn up on paper and the next day was spent loitering around the new workshop, hitting golf balls up Katy Trail, and waiting on the blacksmith to arrive. Finus, a washed-up looking fellow that appeared much older than he was, showed around lunchtime and had already been informed by Murchison about the likely potential for a golfing club job. After helping unpack a heavy load from the wagon, Sam and Duley sat down with the tradesman inside the small darkened shack and put their heads together. Duley dozed off to sleep late that evening, likely because he was full of all the listening and learning that went on and on. Sam stayed tuned in with anxiousness, even as the discussion turned long and the night grew to morning. He and Finus, who showed to be ardent about the project himself, burned the midnight oil and cooked up a plan. The shop was going to be up and firing in the next days, and the products would be delivered to the grounds once finished. The newest resident would be in touch if there were any problems or questions.

The golf holes were being trimmed quite regularly and made for a mountain of hay in the far back-left corner. To add to it, Earl Hardin, the windmill man was there with his crew to work. He didn't say much other that weather talk, or seem to give a flip about golf, but water was running two days later. As soon as the sucker rod was pumping, pails were carried down and poured on the critical greens and tees. The place was looking fresh and magnificent, though definitely still becoming. Steady emissions of the fractured grass loomed in the air while the grounds were providing the best golf Sam had ever played. The satisfying lies left the scythe worn out and the tool was starting to barely cut it. Over three or four visits to the blacksmith's shop, Finus, beginning to think the boys were asinine, had run the blade over a whetstone until there was not much of anything left. Sam and Duley were staying quite worn out themselves, each taking a somewhat lop-sided fair share of swings. Referring to two different types of swings that were going on- the dullness came with one and skills were sharpened with the other.

Maintaining the grass had become quite redundant, thankfully Duley made things easy upon returning from one of his trips to Greenville. The visits to lend a hand during the busy mornings at the hardware store usually took place on Saturdays. Sam permitted the time off because it provided a morning for solemn and soul-filled golf, during which the mental part of the game was so eloquently refined. Duley's horse was always tired when they arrived home in the early afternoon. The rider was hurrying to get to work on the grounds, so plenty of golf could be played in the evening. This Saturday was different. Duley snuck off with a wagon and was late in his return. Not that it mattered. The boss man at the golfing grounds never stayed on a timely schedule to begin with. The Saturday before, Duley was running late and Sam had asked why he was back so early. Duley was tardy because he had been repairing and fine tuning a grass mower that was abandoned at the store in non-working condition. He paid off his father for the 'junker' the moment he walked in the door. A Hills "Archimedean" brand, push style, and very welcome by the groundskeeper and the golfer. The gift was certainly a big surprise to Sam and time after time reimbursement was refused. Duley was as tickled about the new toy as anyone. He enjoyed mowing the grass nearly as much as he did playing golf on it, only for a short time though.

Turns, still not fair ones but just turns, were taken between mowing and playing Hole N$^{o.}$ 1 and Hole N$^{o.}$ 2 with the broadstick. Finally, Finus showed up a week later with a box full of gems. The blacksmith was paid in full and then some, including a promise of free golf for life, membership included, if he ever wanted. The golf part of the payment was directly refused in lieu of a bad back and worn-out, callused hands.

In the new upstairs equipment and repair room, Sam and Duley went to work over the next days piecing together golf clubs. All sticks were made under the watchful eye of Sam, who bolstered the selection in his own bag to include a hickory-headed driver with iron facing, an angled-face chipper for short shots and hitting out of trouble if there was any, and a finely-tuned putter. Over the next nights, more than a dozen sets of four sticks were manufactured for potential sale to any new members. Duley worked on a set for himself, almost identical to Sam's. There was the one big difference, the broadstick. Duley put together an imposter and, despite being shot down by the real deal so many times, always felt it was as good. That's how Sam put it, telling the apprentice that one golfing stick was as good as any other and it was the player that needed to come around. That next week was Duley's birthday and Sam gifted him a new leather golf bag, complete with yardsticks and a brand-new Folgers can. Even had his name burned into the leather.

Duley had worked over a couple of days trimming the surplus of grass down to two inches all across the whole place, including a new fairway that was cut at N$^{o.}$ 1. Sam didn't use it, he was straight to the green off the tee. Others might not want to have so much of a risk with the slough and the thicket guarding like all the king's men. Sam had been working on getting a better watering system started. He wanted fuller and greener grass, the best folks had ever stepped on. Duley suggested fertilizing the place, which was refused by Sam because of his new habit of finding a blade of grass to chew on while a puzzling shot was assessed. "Any man in his right mind wouldn't chew on fertilizer." Sam said. And, that stopped the discussion. The chewing of the grass had become a necessity. He had run out of tobacco and didn't much care or feel the need to go for more. That routine was fine being out the door because it wasn't doing the golf game any good, he didn't need to seem older, and, in the last days, the nervous tensions had suddenly disappeared like in an Ellis Fair magic trick. Life was good and easy at The Judge Merit Golfing Club.

The two tees and the fairways were always mowed down to a half inch, and manicured to perfection. The green was cut down even lower. Sam noticed that the lawn mower wheels were doing a great job at laying down the short grass of the putting surface, thus providing a smoother roll. Duley went that day to the hardware store for more supplies. A dozen old lawn mower wheels on an axel with push handle rising from either end was used every day to smooth the greens, after they had been swept with a broom. This became routine, every morning and every evening. Hose arrived via special order from the hardware store and a spare water barrel was affixed to a small cart. A good hickory handle and solid wheels made for easy pulling, though Sam insisted the water wagon stay on the walkways. Because of this insistence, more hose had to be ordered. A thorough watering always followed each golfing session. In the battle with the Texas sun, a good watering was needed even on the few days that saw a late summer storm pass through.

The moment complete sets of golf sticks were ready, the boys had hit the grounds for ten holes. Half of which were in the dark. Then, somewhere around sixty holes were played the next day. They lost track when the run reached into its extended nighttime hours. While the grounds were in fine shape, the two were taking advantage. When there was need for a mowing, golf would stop and they would mow. Mowing and golfing is about all that took place. They would stop to eat when they were hungry and bathe in the river when they were stinky, but not much else.

An early and brisk fall was settling in and Murchison's curiosity brought him out to check-in, as he had not seen a sign of either of the boys in some time. He hadn't seen the sign hanging either, or the house, or any of the improvements for that matter. He was enamored at Sam's memorial acts and tributes but even more so, becoming filled with sadness and joy at the sight of them. The aging man was taken back as he looked about the breathtaking golf landscape and gave a big ol' laugh when he heard a crack and saw one fly through the air from the first tee. A golfing club wasn't one of the businesses Murchison had hoped for, but he was smiling while taking it in and onboard with it being a part of town.

Sam laughed and smiled big, too. He was surprised by the visit and proud in seeing Murchison so elated. The golfer pointed around showcasing the ins and outs of the holes, which included a decent briefing on the rules of the game. Murchison was inspired, tuned in, and following along each move of Sam's finger. He remarked what he could on the game, or a shot, and filled Sam's cup with compliments. No additional lots had been sold and no one new had come to town. No Arwin Rank and no cafe. No J.K. Elliott Hardware and Lumber Company. However, there was good news, railroad work was starting back up at the first of next month. Murchison also notified the boys of another auction that would be upcoming, this time with promising advertising. After no discussion, no vote, and a no-questions-asked decision, paperwork would be filed for an official town name, Merit. Perhaps, like what was thought at the golfing club, a name would help the draw.

Duley went off to work around the N$^{o.}$ 2 green, leaving Sam and Murchison at the first tee box. Sam didn't say much, just hit golf balls. Murchison watched and did not disturb, standing in silence as he looked around and admired the place. After filling himself with the grandeur of the golfing holes, there were often looks to the oak tree or into the thicket. Between shots, Murchison let Sam know that he would be sending a letter to Mrs. Mary Merit to apprise her of the blessing that had come to town in the name of The Judge Merit Golfing Club. She would be overjoyed at the news, and he was needing to check in on her anyway. Murchison was told he had an honorary lifetime membership, to which he giggled and said he would take it. "You don't have to play to stay a member, do you?" he asked. Murchison headed home because he hadn't armed himself with a bottle of Overholt, then returned twenty minutes later for a proper toast to the golfing club and the spectacle of Sam hitting golf balls across the bruised sky, through the falling Texas sun, and into the moonlit Merit night.

CHAPTER 6

Little to no activity continued passing through the intersection that Fall. All the while, grass around town was up to tall weeds and had begun losing its luster. The turf at the golfing grounds was the opposite, seeing plenty of rounds and still showing at a prime color of green. The rough areas snuggling the trimmed fairways were allowed to grow up to four inches, held an even darker green color, and sat more similar to town. They hadn't seen a lick of action, now that Duley's game was coming around. About the only regular noise in Merit came from Finus pounding iron or loud cracks of the golf strikes echoing out all day long. Aside from the occasional passerby on Katy Trail, the customer base of Murchison's General Mercantile was limited to the four town residents. The bar had three regular customers. Finus didn't drink. Call it two and a half, Sam couldn't be counted as a whole. He was there only one time that month, to celebrate Duley's first hole-in-one. Duley was known to frequent the drinking establishment for one or two after leaving work, or play, on most days that end in 'Y'. Drinking was another family tradition.

The Judge Merit Golfing Club had its two resident regulars and the blacksmith shop one. Sam kept Finus super tied up with golf club work, anticipating the railroad jobs would soon consume the blacksmith's work hours. In turn, as the days were shorter and the nights turned chilly, the boys kept themselves busy after-hours making golf sticks. At times, the repetitive and tedious work seemed useless and they'd go back to golfing until after dark or until their noses and earlobes couldn't stand the cold any longer. The various clubs piled up at the top of the staircase and thoughts simmered that no one would ever use, much less purchase, the equipment. Still, vision and hopes remained and work ramped up during that early winter. By December, you could say the boys were running a golfing stick factory. Hands and brains worked with wood, wire, leather, thread, iron, and intuition. All of the new golfing equipment underwent plenty of examination and experimentation once completed. Each golf stick received a round of shots under its belt, courtesy of Sam. If he liked one in particular, it would be kept upstairs. All others were bundled in an appropriate grouping and lined up along the back porch, a selection of brand-new bags included.

On the day crews showed to begin work continuing the dead-end rail line, the foreman roamed down to the mercantile and tried to hire Sam and Duley as they stood with Murchison watching down Katy Trail. The offer was refused and, once all the noise started, the boys headed back to the golfing club. Finus quickly had a full schedule and with no more golf sticks to piece together, Sam and Duley found themselves doing other handy work. They hashed out an idea for a much-needed accessory in the golfing holes, and wooden blocks were whittled out to fit down in the bottom. Glass jars were pulled out and the holes were made larger, supposedly the official size for the game. Once the holes were plugged with the new contraption, the flags stood perfectly erect out of a hollowed-out cavity in the middle of each wooden piece. Putting became a little easier and you could hear a bit of a rattle each time the ball fell to its goal. All of the work took place during the night time, because if the sun was out Sam was playing. Although the weather was colder and the winds more brisk than desired, nothing much else could occupy the boy. The young man's game had become tuned in and he was hitting the ball the best he ever had, saying that teaching Duley how to play was helping to improve his own game. There was no letting up on the number of golf strokes that were taking place. Cups were rattling constantly.

The railroad crews kept the bar busy while in town, then they all moved along like a tumbleweed in an open field. Finus moved along with the work and wasn't seen again until summer. Murchison was happy with the quality of work that ran through town and was motivated to add to. As the crews finished up, he hired The Bateson Brothers to construct a small train depot, on the north side and near the former 'End of Line' sign. Boardwalk extending to the northeast corner of the intersection included. The new additions were according to the railroad commission's plan and extended the length of the passing track. The Bateson Brothers made quick work over a two-week time period, so the project caught Sam off guard when he stumbled into town. The trip made for food, and food only. Sam had become a boy living in a golf bubble. As he looked over the new construction in stunned disbelief at the sudden transformation, the first freight train roared through without a stop and left a wall of dust falling down on the white collared shirt.

The depot would see zero stops during the last of that year. Only freight was passing through and there was nothing being imported to, nor exported from,

Merit. Once in a while, an engineer would stop in the middle of the intersection and run to the bar for a quick drink. Murchison invited the golf boys down and provided feasts for the holidays, and free drinks to celebrate the new year. Those were pretty much Sam's trips to town, other than the occasional grocery run. More often than not, Duley was making the runs as part of his job when work, other than general maintenance, around the grounds began to slow. Sam was quickly becoming a type of Hopper Hackman himself. On New Year's Day, the first passenger train roared through without a stop and many more like it would follow in the days ahead.

The second Monday after passenger rail service began, Sam stepped out from one of the rare shopping trips at the mercantile and looked east down the rail line. He suddenly paused his steps at the edge of the porch when he noticed an army of men, clad in white, marching in chivalrous form down the southside of Katy Trail. Warden Berle Loudy, a tall and burly man dressed in all black including a cowboy hat, rode on horseback down the middle of the ruts and yards out in front of the convoy. All around, a half-dozen mounted guards dressed in black pants and sky-blue collared shirts flanked the rows of convicts. When Sam noticed the iron jailing around each ankle, chains in between, and caught the whole picture, he about turned back inside. Then, after more moments of staring down the trail he heard the chains dragging along, and went back in the store and pretended like he forgot something.

Warden Loudy was greeted at the intersection by Murchison, who was briefed about the train having broken down a mile outside of town while carrying the load of prisoners on a transfer to the penitentiary down in Huntsville. The engineer expected a day for repairs and the convoy was seeking any kind of accommodations while waiting. Work to keep the prisoners occupied would be best, if there was any. Murchison didn't much want the convicts right there in town as it might drive off any potential residents, which it wasn't likely for any to show if the prior days, weeks, months, and now years were any indication. In the back of his mind, he was figuring that Sam just as much would like to have the help at the grounds, because that's who he looked to first. Young Sam did not know what to make of it when Murchison's hard stare bore through the glass windows of the mercantile and a long index finger called for his presence in the middle of the intersection.

Duley stood in the middle of the first fairway, bug eyed and looking snake bit, when Sam came over Dead Horse Hill leading the band of convicts. Shocked at the sight, he nearly took off into the thicket to hide. Waiting instead, he wondered what-in-the-world, as the men marched down Main Street and turned left into the golfing club. They all gathered under the oak tree and after Duley crept up and had a close look at the mean-faced bunch of men, he all of the sudden remembered that he was supposed to be in Greenville to help his father that day. Sam called him out on the fib and Duley was sent to Greenville anyway, after being told that he better hustle it back right away with every shovel, hoe, and rake that was in stock. Showing up still bewildered, he was back in two hours flat with an exhausted horse and all of the tools that could be carried. The whole plan for the grounds was organized well before and standing ready for implementation, Sam had just fine tuned it on the walk up. The next years of progress were going to take place right then. While waiting for Duley's return, everything was laid out to the guards in very specific detail. The prisoners, stretched out in a line on their hands and knees, had been crawling the entire place from south to north, and back, scouring for anything that stuck out as not belonging. This first order came from Warden Loudy and was likely given simply to kill time.

All of the rakes and shovels went to work. A perimeter group was assigned to make their way around the grounds clearing any and all brush for five feet on either side of the split-rail fence. This made the place look much nicer and more defined, though also helped rid the borders of many potential hiding spots an errant golf ball might seek out. A small group was sent to the $N^{o\cdot}$ 2 Hole to dig out a pit, along the frontside of the green. The second shot was already a tough one and an obstacle such as a sand bunker would make it even tougher, similar to the slough at $N^{o\cdot}$ 1. The extra dirt was leveled out across the green and graded down, thus raising the entire putting surface and surrounding area by two feet. This meant giving up the hole, likely until spring when the grass grew back, but it would be worth it.

The three oldest and least-capable-of-grunt-work prisoners grabbed rakes to dethatch the dead grass in the fairways, plus six feet into the swath of taller grass surrounding each. The largest group, ten prisoners most of whom were the big and gnarly looking ones, were assigned to dig out the slough. Sam wanted it longer, wider, and deeper. Earth was pulled, and pulled, and pulled from the muddy slough, then moved and layered across nearly all playing surfaces. Now, sat a plenty steep grade between the No. 1 fairway and the mudhole. If your tee shot was just short of the slough, it was likely going to roll on in. Duley and his mule went to work pulling a flat drag around the place so as to compact and smooth the new dirt surfaces. A small group of prisoners followed Sam and were met by wagonloads of dirt in the southern part of the property. A new, raised tee box was going in, Hole $N^{o\cdot}$ 3.

The mower was pulled out from the shed and, whichever prisoner it was that had the honor of pushing it along the third fairway, sure had a smile on his face while doing so. This seemed to tick off the ones that were digging, but they kept their heads down and stayed working after a click of Warden Loudy's shotgun. The N°· 3 fairway was formed long and wide, made to bend just a tad around the oak tree before it stopped ten yards shy of the prospected location for the new green. While the mowing was taking place, Sam began work on the putting surface with a convict named Kelly Ray Carroll, a man heading to Huntsville with a death sentence for a double murder. As the two worked side by side, Sam offered as much freedom as he could by answering questions and telling the rules and strategy of the game. Also, a good golf story or two. Guard J.T. Wilbanks commented that the condemned man had never behaved better. The new pear-shaped and sloping green was created on the north side of the oak tree, hidden from the tee box, and made to fall west to the new portion of the slough. As a shot was landing, it was going to be one way or another at the sharp crest that crowned the middle. The slough was continuing to grow wider, deeper, and more treacherous by the minute for any approaching shot at both the N°· 1 and N°· 3 greens.

The Judge Merit Golfing Club looked like the prison fields throughout that day and into the evening. A partially filled slough existed no more, it was pretty much a dirt hole. The channel in front of the N°· 1 green was wider and connected to a decent-sized pond that cradled the west side of the new putting surface. Load after load of the dirt was moved to here or there, all to Sam's liking. Once all was kosher with the landscaping of the grounds, the long day was called and Sam put on a short golfing exhibition for the inmates until the sun went down.

The guards went through the night sleeping in shifts, while the prisoners crashed heavily all shackled together around the oak tree.

While barely sleeping a wink, Sam's brain was thinking until morning and at first light he was up with Duley constructing a walking bridge over the narrow part of the water way. Warden Loudy rode ahead to the broken-down train and returned shortly thereafter with notice of another twenty-four hours of time needed for repairs. Murchison strolled out for an early morning visit, toting breakfast of ham and fresh biscuits for everyone, and learned of the extended stay. Right away, he put a crew together working the plow up and down the last part of Main Street. Before noon, the road on the northside of the ridge was better than on the southside and the ruts running over Dead Horse Hill were carved out into a manageable incline and decline. The entrance way into the grounds was made to match the street and came to a 'T' just off the front steps of Sam's house. The new bridge was also in place, ready and waiting for some iron railing work by Finus.

Bits and pieces of dead grass, all the way down to the roots of any showing weeds, dirt clods, rocks and pebbles, and any other debris of any kind were picked and plucked from the grounds until late afternoon. New and improved tee boxes and greens at N° 1 and N° 2 were raked, packed, and smoothed to the likes of absolutely level. The N° 3 green was quite different with the slight ridge separating front from back and the vicious slope down to the hugging slough. Grass would need to get busy around a good portion of the playing areas, meaning good golf would have to wait. Sam was fine with the short wait, spring would arrive soon enough and there was plenty of land to play on elsewhere. Besides, the place was shaping up like a dream.

After a lukewarm beer for each prisoner, the group fell right to sleep in their spot chain-ganged around the oak tree. When word of the train being ready came in the early hours, Sam handed over a two-hundred-dollar donation to the Warden along with four sets of new golf sticks and twice as many golf balls. The donation was to be used for more balls and upkeep and maintenance of a golf hole in one of the prison yards. Warden Loudy hesitantly accepted, though made a promise and said the promise would be kept.

Sam and Duley about didn't know what to do with themselves, not able to play golf on the holes for weeks. During that time of the year, the grass was just not growing in around the bare spots that were created in the recent renovation. Mainly, the tees and greens. After morning waterings, time biding rounds were played up and down Main Street and over to the gin. On one occasion, they played for miles and miles down through the southern prairie using a far-off tree as each hole. The boys arrived back in town a day later and Murchison was set up and ready to go for tomorrow's auction, with more than a dozen wagons lining Katy Trail. The auction had been advertised in a dozen papers, including ones in Dallas, Ft. Worth, and Texarkana. Also noted by Sam, was the front door to the other corner building standing open and a large wood-burning stove sitting on the porch.

The rest of that evening and the auction were skipped by the golf boys in favor of going ahead and playing the holes, despite the grass still lacking in spots. These were the first rounds of three holes and Sam said that he couldn't, shouldn't, and wouldn't wait any longer. For another two days, they shot rounds until they couldn't go any longer. Finally, they gave the grounds a break and the greens were meticulously raked, rolled, and watered. Then, the same prescription was given to the tees and fairways. Duley worked on building another water wagon, while Sam did the watering, because it was going to be needed. One water wagon simply did not keep pace and would no longer be sufficient, especially when spring and summer were in full effect. After a good week of going full tilt at the golfing club, Duley finally caught some time off to run home. He also caught wind of the recent sprawl when he went over the hill. Sam would not be privy to the surprise until the morning.

Over the next months, Merit was buzzing like no other town in the region. Murchison sold all lots on Main Street, except the ones across the street from the original buildings. More lots were marked off headed west from the intersection, down both sides of Katy Trail, and sold for the highest dollar value. After they sold, more lots were marked in the south and they were quickly sold before the next weekend's auction. By March, it would come that upwards of twenty-thousand acres of the settlement were sold off and the town held a population of just over one-hundred. Murchison was a busy man, but a happy man. Any hint of depression in his body had apparently left, because it was rare to see him without a smile in those days. Staying busy kept his mind off certain things and that's the way he preferred it. It's the way he was raised and the way he went through years at the service of Judge Merit. Murchison's time was so thin that in the weeks after the auctions he hired Ross and Otis as full-time employees at the mercantile and the bar, respectively. Convincing those two young men to move to Merit took Murchison offering up a place to stay for Ross, the small building next to the bar, and a round of golf twice a week for Otis. Otis would sleep in the bar until small quarters could be built out back and, one day, Ross caught wind of the golf deal and wanted his own share of rounds each week. Murchison paid the membership and per hole fees directly to the town fund. The cost of a new set of golf sticks with bag, four dollars, was deducted from each of their pay checks over the next six months. One dollar per stick, and a free bag with purchase of a set.

As the lots were sold, homes were built and businesses began popping up. The cafe was the first new establishment to open doors. Arwin Rank and his young wife, Jill made their living quarters upstairs and served up just about anything you could imagine, including frog legs, downstairs. Sam and Duley never had intentions of being everyday customers at the cafe, but the food was so good that's exactly what happened. Sam always for breakfast. Duley always for lunch. And, more often than not, both for supper unless there was work or golf that had carried over. The same kind of thing transpired with Arwin Rank, he didn't intend to be an everyday customer at the golf course but that is what happened. The golfing was so good he couldn't resist it. Arwin was a chubby fellow with cheeks that looked like they were constantly full of food. His neck didn't exist and his shoulders were broad as a hog, though he spoke in a higher-pitched voice which lessened his brute. His eyes were near permanently squinted and his smile would only leave for a moment before returning, no matter the predicament he was in. Which, Arwin seemed to be an ace at finding his way into predicaments. As the cafe was up and running, he was sold on a set of golf sticks and a club membership. The restauranteur was out to play a round of holes early every morning as he learned the game. When eight o'clock rolled around, he would head into work at the cafe. Come to find out, he was not leading on as to directly what he was up to each morning.

J.K. Elliott opened up his hardware store at the gin and business was booming from the start. Twenty-three homes went up on Main Street, as well as six buildings across from and identical to the existing ones that Sullivan had built. The porches connected to the boardwalk from the train depot and, when more commercial buildings were built along Katy Trail, the whole downtown area of the small and forming community was connected with wood walkways to keep your boots out of the black mud and dirt. In crossing the intersection, you could do so on red bricks that were installed across each road. All of the commercial buildings were constructed in the same style at Murchison's insistence, exactly how Judge Merit would've had it. A colleague of the Bateson Brothers completed all of the matching construction. A number of homes went up off in the countryside, some inside the settlement land and some not. A new road, 1st Street, was cut and smoothed one block west of Main Street, running not quite to the start of the incline to the ridge. More lots were marked, sold, and more homes were built.

A few weeks stretch of cold and late winter weather didn't seem to deter any activity, not in town and not at the golfing club. Other than the onset, Sam and Duley were pretty much unaware of the sudden growth in Merit. More so, they just didn't pay much attention to it all. Their heads were still stuck down in their own golfing world. After studying any book on gardening or agriculture he could get his hands on, Duley was still trying to work the grass to perfect. The cold nights were spent learning and the days were spent aerating, watering, not watering, mowing grass and letting grass grow. Pulling weeds and taking extra care of the bad spots were the focus most of the time, and wits ends were reached with both. J.K., himself, recommended a fertilizer which was reluctantly tried and tested in assorted trouble areas. It seemed to do some good, so the mix was sprinkled about the rest of the grounds. Sam left the grass chewing behind and started chewing on half a toothpick, available at Murchison's store. Timing seemed right when, days later, days of rain came pouring down. Dried out, things were looking up with the grass despite even colder weather blowing in.

The sun had continued doing its work. The place was rougher than what was desired, but not too bad for the tail end of winter. Things were shaping up. The waterhole would have been out of the category of an eyesore if it had more water.

A stockyard and stables were put up and opened for business on the other side of Finus, followed by Wilkerson's Home Furnishings around the corner from Murchison. Fulton & Son's Funeral Home, The Fine-Cut Barber Shop, Dell's Creamery, Patton's Pharmacy, Harwood's Sausage & Meat Market, Salisbury Wagon & Wheel, the businesses, jobs, and people descended into Merit before spring. So did electricity, by way of the poles coming down the tracks and up the streets. For the meantime, the power stopped at Dead Horse Hill due to the incline. The First Methodist Episcopal Church of Merit was built and established at the end of February, east of the train depot. The following week construction started in an adjacent lot on the First Baptist Church. Murchison allowed J.R. and Lily Beth Kearney to open the largest building, one of a different style. Next door to the mercantile and extending south on Main Street for a jaunt, the two-story Merit Inn consisted of ten rooms and had the nicest parlor in five counties. The place was complete with fancy furniture and chandeliers, a piano, as well as its own small bar. The Bateson Brother's workers were still putting finishing touches on the building when three newcomers took up short-term residence in the place. No golfers. However, they were all drinkers and the only regulars at the hotel bar. Any others and the most prominent socialites in Merit were at Murchison's bar, the bar that still didn't have a name.

Sam struck a deal with a young Lowell Fields, the barber. Nine holes free in exchange for each burr haircut. Sam tossed in the membership fee and offered a loaner set of golf sticks. In about the same amount of time that it takes a man to grow the need for a haircut, Lowell caught the golfing fever and was by far surpassing the free nine-hole offering. He purchased sticks and played every weekday morning before he flipped on the red, white, and blue pole. His game wasn't much to talk about, but it was clear he enjoyed the time on the grounds.

Since the actual date was not known, Murchison settled on the sixth of March as Sam's birthday. That year, he was presented with new flags for the golf holes. The red rags were taken down and new pennants were hung on each of the three flagsticks with pieces of wire. These were nice, handmade, cream colored with blue trim and blue numbers. Not everyone in town received gifts from Murchison on their birthday, perhaps that was one of the perks that went along with the first resident merit badge. Duley painted six small blocks of wood to match, and to mark the space on the tee box from which a golfer must hit behind. The game was growing more precise and sophisticated at The Judge Merit Golfing Club.

The town bustled on into spring, so much so that the Bateson's opened a new office and another stretch of twenty-four homes were built on 2nd Street, west of and parallel to 1st. People from all walks of life settled into Merit. The population, by Murchison's count, had reached near two-hundred. Even with all of the new residents rolling in, there was no jump in golf memberships. Sam kidded that it was because the grass at the golfing club was struggling to stay green. He only said it a time or so, but Duley worked harder because of it. Of course, the two golf-struck lads had been playing daily round after round throughout the cold winter months. They played in freezing temperatures one day and seventy-degree sunshine the next. In snow for about two days and ice for half of one. Sam called it quits on the icy day after an embarrassing score appeared for nine holes. That evening he played three rounds without ice, both the score and the temperature came in at a chilling and dazzling 15.

Arwin had continued to come play his round of holes every day, until Jill found out that he was not working over at the blacksmith shop on preparing a new grill but going up over the hill for a game. He might have started stretching his usual two holes to three or four once extra help was hired in the kitchen, however, he got caught. The next morning at breakfast, Sam was accused of driving Arwin's taking-up of the game and somehow, he explained his way out of it. As a matter of fact, he convinced Jill to try the game as well. After lunch on the next Monday, the Rank's showed up together at the golfing club. Jill paid her dues and the Rank's went to putting in their best efforts. Arwin gave quite a few snarls to Sam over the next weeks.

The economy in Merit was neither languishing nor thriving, perhaps just surviving. Murchison was doing well and putting most all the cash right back into Merit. Most businesses were banking on the prospect of the railroad, which was beginning to pick up. More passenger trains than ever were moving about the country and finally connections were made, putting Merit along a decently trafficked run of track. With the railroad loop complete, the town was the last stop before a split for the eastbound trains thus making it a common transfer station. If anything, there was either whiskey or ice cream sold to those waiting for their next leg. As the town materialized, train engineers took notice and the creamery quickly became the most popular reason for making an unscheduled stop. The mercantile, bar, and cafe received a fair share of passerby business but nothing to get excited about. Word about the delicious ice cream at Dell's Creamery had spread all over and it was indeed the biggest draw, especially as a warm spring settled in.

The most dramatic change that occurred in early spring was the entire slough filling up to the brim by the grace of more than a week's worth of rain. That, and Duley ventured back into the thicket to find a beaver dam clogging the crick that fed onto the property. After something close to a tussle, the dam was destroyed and the rushing water pretty much flooded the northwest corner of the grounds. For a week it was impossible to get to the first green and a walk all the way around the oak tree was required to get to the second tee, as the bridge was useless. The hole and flagstick at N$^{\text{o.}}$ 3 had to be placed on the upper half of the green, while the lower half was swallowed up by the bustling edges of the slough. In a few days' time, waters finally subsided and it was back to normal golfing.

Right quickly, bright sun took over a better part of the days and all began to blossom around the golfing grounds. A row of young crepe myrtle trees came out of nowhere along the northern fence line, and Sam's peach seed that he had planted almost a year ago had become a fantastic juvenile specimen in its spot over by the shed. No peaches yet, maybe next year. Trips to the mercantile for his favorite snack continued now that they were in season. A pair of willow trees sprouted up just off the left side of the back porch and another on the right side. The beginnings of magnolia trees were showing along the right side of the first fairway and line of pine trees had shown in the earliest jump all along the second. They were all just a foot or two tall, maybe the peach and the willows were three, and all under Duley's green thumb. Too many bluebonnets to count were covering a wide, but tolerable, portion of the rough areas and were left to bask in all of their purple glory. Not one was allowed to stay in a fairway. After grabbing a few flats full of flowers from the nursery section of the hardware store, his father's in Greenville, Duley dug out flower beds all around the house and planted a wide variety of colorful flowers mostly zinnias and hollyhocks. Sam saw the gardening as taking away from golfing and golf work but went with it anyway. He did insist that honeysuckle was planted on either side of the gate because of the divine smell that would linger, this known from his catching it along the trails every now and again. Despite all the color, Sam was most impressed that all of the grass had turned to the most prominent shade of green that had been seen yet. After another day of rain to brighten everything, it was all business as fair weather play finally commenced and a player went out there enthralled with the game and his surroundings.

Spring in full bloom, Duley had been staying busy working more on the grounds and golfing less. Indeed, not so for Sam. In fact, things had turned the other way. After so many times of playing the holes in different orders, there became the desire to mix things up. Sam used any chance he had to take a new shot of some sorts, the only thing certain being that it involved hitting golf balls at something. The shed, the fence posts, the oak tree, the sign out front, from here, there, and everywhere. A fathom worth of small, identical divots were littered all over and about the golfing grounds. Sam would drop balls and hit them at whatever hole while chatting with Duley, wherever he was working. Hitting golf balls, and talking about hitting golf balls in between hitting golf balls. Sam finally realized this hammered on Duley's nerves. Sam was laying down work for the groundskeeper right in front of what was already under repair. Duley might have felt that Sam could at least do it out of sight. Duley's watchful eye for bare spots was keeping his golfing at bay more and more each day. Day and night, hour after hour, minute by minute, Sam had a golf ball flying, bouncing, or rolling in some direction around the golfing grounds. There were no blisters popping up, his hands and fingers had become hard callused and unrelenting to the over and over again rubbing of sweat-soaked leather.

Nature, beauty, wildlife, and Sam's game were all flourishing. Duley was always busy keeping the grass down somewhere and Sam just took to playing around him, all day, every day. Not only were birds, butterflies, rabbits, and rodents moving about in the ideal weather, people were too. Sam wanted to take the time to encourage others to come out and play the game, which meant giving up his lean to hermitism and perhaps going ahead and reaching himself out there more. Not too much. There wasn't any kind of big sway in his keeping to himself, he was just allowing folks to be around more often and longer before he excused himself back to the grounds. Those occasions were mostly at the cafe or mercantile. Murchison did all the advertising Sam needed, and even began using the golfing club as a selling point for potential land buyers.

Jim Ainsworth was the first one to town that already owned golf sticks. He was a retired lawyer that gave into his wife's pleas to move to Merit, after hearing her main selling point of the golfing club. He became a Saturday regular and certainly wasn't there for any kind of social aspect, which made for an ideal member in Sam's eyes. Ainsworth would play his holes and be gone. Sam's favorite pastime other than playing, was to spend time talking about the game and discussing all of the different rounds played. Conversations with Jim would occur at the café and, as said, never at the grounds. One Saturday, Sam and Jim played a round together. Sam was in the hole with two shots on N$^{o.}$ 1, three shots on N$^{o.}$ 2, and two shots on N$^{o.}$ 3. Jim walked off that day, saying that Sam was in a league of his own and didn't need to be ruining a man's weekend. Jim laughed after the comment and so did Sam, but they never played together again.

D.L. Jenkins, a gardener with a vegetable stand in town, came out to secure a membership and purchased a set of golf sticks. He played that day, but never again. Duley suspected that he was up to something, as every Saturday afternoon D.L. would leave the stand with his golf bag and head toward Greenville. There were no golf holes in Greenville.

There was also South Main Mal, Malvin Matthews. A young, tall drink of water that wore his pants too short, yet always had new shoes. His pants weren't really too short, his suspenders were too snug. He might have been trying to show off his new shoes. That's the kind of guy he was. He and his wife moved down from the north and purchased Lot 3. In the first days after settling in, the Matthews kept to themselves until Duley intervened with golf talk in Mal's ear. His wife was a hefty woman that rarely ventured out of the house, though she would get out on the front porch to crack a whip if necessary. If not at work running the front desk at the new inn, Malvin was home as required. Once in a while, if he had an ounce of a chance, he would venture out of the house. Venturing out meant corralling the children in the front yard. If any one individual was lingering outside any of the businesses, Malvin was hanging at the southwest corner of his lot chatting up the patrons, or whomever. Once catching wind of the game, he saved back money and secretly purchased a bag of sticks on the condition that he could keep the set out in the shed at the golfing club. On his off days, he would wait for the kids to take to themselves blowing on dandelions and sucking on weeds, then he'd sneak off. The reason they called him South Main Mal was that no matter if he was walking north, he was looking south, always keeping an eye out for his old lady coming to snatch him up.

At first, the plan worked for the sly, chatty, and lanky man. He could get a round in and get back home without the wife noticing. Mal was quickly caught with a hankering for the game and turned into a half-way decent player. His problem was, before and after each shot, he was trying to peer up over Dead Horse Hill and down Main Street for fear of being pulled back home by his ear. All boiled to a head on the day his second-in-command boss, Mr. Kearney, stopped by the Matthew's home for a favor. They said that you have never seen something so big move so fast, as Mrs. Matthews waddled her way up the hill and to the top of the ridge. Mal saw his old lady the instant she was there with one of his south on Main looks and dropped everything. From then on, his right ear was stretched out and much bigger than his left. Days later, he showed up at the grounds wanting his golf sticks and said he was ready to play. Mal had threatened to leave his wife over the matter, so she conceded to one round a week. As Mal would get to the second, third, and fourth rounds he would chuckle and tell that she had no idea what a round was, then he would turn and aim his eyes south down Main Street.

It didn't take long for the minister at the new First Methodist Episcopal Church, Reverend Hayden Oliphint, to catch wind of the game. He purchased a membership and golf sticks, and provided a blessing over the grounds. There must have also been a prayer over his game. After a week he sure could hit the ball right where he wanted nearly every time. Rev., as he came to be called, started off neck and neck with Duley in the game and played his way to even give Sam a run for his money in the months ahead. On one occasion, closing out the sixth round of the day, Sam holed out a bunker shot on Hole N$^{o.}$ 2 to make-up a stroke. Then, a prayer was answered when he sank one, from the fairway on N$^{o.}$ 3, for the win on the eighteenth hole. Sam upped the intensity of his practice rounds after that, though gave every effort he could to get Reverend Oliphint out to play more. The reverend was simply dang good competition. One wouldn't think it, but the only time Rev. was regularly able to make it out was on Sunday afternoons. Pastor Oliphint would tease that he would come out on Monday mornings, too, if Sam would ever come to church on Sundays. Rev. knew exactly what Sam was doing on Sunday mornings, so he didn't give too much of a hard time.

After that near loss to Reverend Oliphint and learning that Sunday was the minister's only available day for golf, Sam implemented a new policy at The Judge Merit Golfing Club. Sundays were by invitation only. Serious golf would be taking place and there was no time to deal with customers. Arwin had inched his way back to playing more, once the cafe started breaking even and more help was hired. He was about the fourth best in town and his game was coming around, so he received an invitation. By all means, Duley was welcome. His game was storming along. The Monday before, he shot his best score so far of a 75 for six rounds. Work was generally minimal on Sundays, anyway. Reverend Oliphint and Sam completed the foursome of men that would play eighteen holes every Sunday beginning at two o 'clock sharp.

Sam was always the winner, but the other three kept on trying. Even as such, it was decided that no more invitations would be sent out, no matter who wanted to come play along with. The weekly meeting of the four men would become a rich tradition and it came to be well-known that the grounds were altogether closed on Sundays because of. Not that anyone was knocking down the gate to get in there, Sam mostly wanted his new friends to have their own special time for playing the game. And, the competition was a change of pace from round after round, and shot after shot, of solo golfing. Word of the private round eventually got out and made some golfers out of the new regulars a bit jealous. Certainly, Lowell Fields and Ainsworth. Neither showed at the grounds for a month, and the talk was bare from those two in the days and weeks after. Sam even got a bad burr hair-cut out of the deal.

Four Methodist Episcopal Members joined when word got out that Rev. Oliphint was a member. Likewise, several Baptists in town went ahead and joined up while still waiting for their church to be completed. When Sam was asked by any church member, why he didn't attend church services, the same answer was always given. "I get my sermons on Sunday afternoons." Stories on golf and stories from the Bible were always shared, and the two were often made relative to one another. Rev. Oliphint and Sam enjoyed time spent walking between holes on Sunday afternoons and evenings, as much as they did playing the game with each other.

As spring was fleeing and the heat rolling in, businesses began to do well in part because there was an expansion in the railroad schedule and more trains were stopping on the way through. Incoming deliveries to the mercantile had also expanded and Ross was finding it challenging to keep the shelves stocked. Around meal times, the cafe was nearly always full of people eating and gossiping. Barstools at Murchison's place were pretty much always taken and there wasn't ever more than a vacancy or so at the inn either, especially on weekends. Dell's Creamery most often had a line out front waiting, often all the way around the corner on Saturdays. Same at the barber shop.

Other than flashes in the pan, The Judge Merit Golfing Club was not often drawing any new customers. Sam didn't give one droplet of care about this. His focus was on his own game and nothing else. Anymore, he really didn't give too much worry about the grounds unless he wanted something special done. Duley had it all under control and looking as fine and dandy as ever. The grounds of The Judge Merit Golfing Club had become his baby, the game was Sam's child.

Five, six, or seven little old ladies had all moved to town and congregated like flies in deciding that Merit didn't have enough accouterments. They formed a committee to promote their agendas and, as a business owner, Sam was asked to be a part. He was reluctant but went to the first meeting at Murchison's urging. About ten minutes in, there was an interruption. Howard Dobbs was his name and he wanted to share a refreshing drink of Coca-Cola with the group. Howard was in town pitching the product and brought a glass to each committee member sitting around the meeting table in the back. Sam, having just finished twenty holes of golf and sitting cotton-mouth thirsty, turned up the bottom. The ladies in the meeting went to carrying on about what all the town needed, and Sam wasn't sitting keen on getting himself too involved. No doubt he hoped for Murchison's success, but sat on the fence as to whether he desired more customers at the grounds. If you went so far as to call Sam stubborn, it would only be in that he didn't want others in the way of his own golf. The Judge Merit Golfing Club was not a business, it was golfing ground. The talk in the meeting all sounded like more people coming, most likely not golfers. Also, most of the ideas being tossed out were ridiculous. Murchison even gave some eye rolls in regard to certain topics the ladies brought up. If the most of the committee's aspirations were to come true, the town would turn into a metropolis before the start of summer. The Coca-Cola had Sam worked up and near as anxious and jittery as he had ever been. Sitting still in the meeting was not easy to begin with and the soda made it even worse. The same sort of thing was happening with the others on the committee. The talk accelerated fast, was abundant, and at times grew even more nonsensical. After ten more minutes, Sam politely excused himself to a dire emergency at the golf grounds and stood to make his way out. When asked by the nosy lady how on the green earth he knew what was happening at the golfing club, Sam responded that his groundskeeper had stepped to the front window with a dire wave, then ran off. "It must be something awful." he said, bolting out of the store. Outside Sam accepted seconds from Howard Dobbs and proceeded to run up Main Street to play twelve times around, thirty-six holes, at record pace.

The committee, which Sam abandoned altogether and nicknamed, continued on and was always trying to get him to do this or that. Help out with this, donate to that, pay to advertise the golfing club in the weekly newsletter, come to this meeting, visit this town with us. The begging, inviting, and soliciting was constant. Murchison left the group as well, being that prerogatives were mostly aimed in an unwanted direction. "Those ladies just want to get together so they can be in everyone's business, then talk about it." Murchison exclaimed. Sam always did what he could to keep the grounds of the town as cleaned up as his own, and continued his loyalty to helping Murchison out anytime he needed it. The easements were pristine and the field next to the churches was kept well-groomed for picnics, play, and other community activities. About every other week, or as needed, Duley would drag a blade down Main and get it back to smooth. This was all enough to keep Sam's conscious clean about being a good citizen and, maybe, golfing too much. He wasn't comfortable with it, but Sam extended himself plenty as far as socializing with the townsfolk. Worrying about who all was around became something Sam didn't much fall to anymore. However, with more and more moving in and all the out-of-towners venturing off the train, the old habits began to come to and he was fighting with his intentions of showing himself out in public more for the sake of promoting golf business. Lately, Duley had been the only one dealing with the occasional customers and visitors that were showing up.

The committee was quick to organize all types of events, one in particular, the booking of a traveling circus. When the train rolled into town, Sam and Duley headed to the tracks to catch the parade of pageantry. The show took place in the field beside the churches and when finished, Sam thought he had seen it all. His first live view of any such function involved lions, tigers, bears, elephants, contortionist, two sets of identical twins, a bearded lady, all sorts of balancing acts, a strongman, and a not so impressive magic show. But it was magic nonetheless and memories of Mr. Fair returned. Sam and Duley stayed out of the general audience, preferring to hover around the back entrance to the tent. No kidding, at one point that old bear got a little rough and out of control, knocking the tamer to the ground. Sam, standing right there with broadstick in hand, gave one crack to the furry skull with the iron end and the grizzly shaped up and settled into his manners. Sam and Duley took part in drinks at the bar as they were heading home from the circus grounds, and ended up fraternizing with a group of the performers. That was an entertaining hour. Waiting for Duley to finish up a drink, Sam stepped into the middle of Main Street, dropped a golf ball, and let one fly into the night sky with all he had. The ball was centered down the middle of the road and quickly vanished into the far-off darkness. When Duley stepped out, Sam was laughing like crazy as he had just turned down an offer from the ringmaster to hop on the train and join the circus.

More trains rolled thorough Merit as summer was nearing, and there came to be some interesting visitors to the town that was seeing the growth spurt settle. A rookie writer from the *Dallas Times Herald*, Skip Sherrod, traveled out to produce a newspaper article about the sweet treats that were available at Dell's Creamery. Unfortunately for Skip, he arrived to town late on a Saturday after the shop had closed and Dell's, like The Judge Merit Golfing Club, was also closed on Sunday's. Skip decided to take in the bar for a drink before turning around to go back home without a story. It so happens that Duley was sitting at the bar and struck up a conversation with the newspaperman. "The best business in town is not the creamery." Duley said. Sherrod moved a barstool closer and sat on the edge as Duley went on about the game and the golfing grounds. After that one drink, they were headed up Main Street.

The next Sunday morning, a full-page article came out on the back page of the *Times Herald.* 'Golfing is King Over Ice Cream in One Small Texas Town' the title read in bold letters. The article told about different parts of Sam's journey to Merit and about his affection for the game, including the story of the establishment of the golfing club. Sherrod described the rules of the game, as told by Sam, and gave a substantial amount of insight to the reader regarding the beauty and grace of the grounds. Sam was labeled as an up and comer and one to keep an eye out for, if golf ever took off as a legitimate game around Texas. A trip for golfing was recommended for any and all golfers, and a trip for 'what they say is good' ice cream for those that weren't. The article closed out by declaring that the author had come into town to write a story on Dell's Creamery, but the ice cream shop was closed so he could not speak to its taste. 'The boys at Judge Merit Golfing Club said it was delicious, though one could tell they didn't give much of a hoot about ice cream.' Sherrod wrote.

With a healthy distribution, the article went out far and wide beyond Dallas and Merit. A baker's dozen of new members joined over the next month, all out-of-towners, and although most told Duley that it was the best golf course they had ever seen, only a few ever returned to play again. The reserve of golf clubs sold out right quick, so Duley went on a trip to see Hopper in Hickory Hollow and, thankfully, Finus showed in town at the right time. Duley and Sam both went to producing more golf sticks but couldn't keep up so a back order was initiated and the task left to the apprentice. Sam was way more interested in using the clubs than he was in making them. Ice cream sales went up that month as well and, in appreciation, Mr. Dell granted Sam free ice cream for life. Sam always got vanilla then added his own peaches. Once Mr. Dell caught wind of it and had a taste, that flavor was made available as a featured selection in the shop.

After the release of the article, townsfolk seemed to take more to the game of golf being around. Sam was always being instantly recognized any time he carried the broadstick, and he was known to the majority of everyone living in Merit. He was a little more lenient about who was able to come play, it was getting to the point that the business was needed. As such, many tried their hand at the game. Men, women, and children, though with only a few did the love for playing the game latch on and sink in. If people weren't playing golf, they sure were talking about it. There was a fever about and it seemed everyone was hootin' and hollerin' that they lived in Sam Stalling's hometown, home of The Judge Merit Golfing Club. Some locals sent donations because they thought it was a garden club, supposedly from all of the chatter about the beauty of the place. Many of the people in the surrounding counties that had some sort of business they were conducting in Merit would wander out to the attraction and then want to wander around like it was an arboretum or something. All of the chatter about golf and the grounds that was going on in the cafe, the creamery, the inn, or the bar was often overheard by someone off the train or stopping on the trail, and they would want to go have a look see. Both Sam and Duley could typically tell what a person was coming for as soon as the visitor walked atop Dead Horse Hill.

The buzz started toward a big climax when a lavishly outfitted N°. 1 train rolled into town on a fine Sunday afternoon. First off the steaming locomotive was a gang of six men clad in black suits, all carrying pistols inside their jackets. They were putting eyes on everything and fanned out like a starburst the moment their boots hit the ground. One man stood at the train door and two headed straight for the cafe. There were not many residents out and about, but those that were had their every move under watch.

Not a soul else had budged from the rear passenger car of the shorter than normal train. The duo that entered the cafe returned minutes later and boarded the train. At one o 'clock sharp, the two men in black were followed off the next to last car by the President of the United States of America, Benjamin Harrison, and a small entourage of assistants, advisors, and associates. The President ate frog legs at the cafe and while visiting with locals, naturally, The Judge Merit Golfing Club found its way into the conversation. Arwin said it was Murchison that brought it up, however, Murchison never fessed up to it. Whatever it was that whomever said, made President Harrison decide that he needed to head up to see for himself. Murchison led the way. Duley tried to charge the group a dollar each for the newly implemented visitation fee, until he was waved off by Murchison. Sam didn't much like the visitation fee, but Duley promised it would cut down on the riffraff garden admirers. Duley straightened right up when he learned the identity of the esteemed man and then went to fetch Sam, who was putting behind the oak tree over at N°. 2.

Sam shrugged off the visitors, even when told of the stature of the visit. He told Duley that no one interrupts a golf game, then went on to tee off at N°. 3. In the middle of Murchison explaining the rules and the grounds, President Harrison turned south to watch Sam drive a golf ball that was headed directly at the politician. Three of the men in black suits stepped forward and raised their elbows, shielding The President from the oncoming object. Murchison cooled their jets after the ball fell to a near perfect lie in the middle of the fairway, a hundred or more yards from the conglomeration. Sam made the walk up the short grass with a couple dozen eyeballs staring at his every move. He continued on with the next shot, a lengthy broadstick swat that lipped in and out of the hole. The effort drew applause from Murchison, then the rest of the small audience followed suit. Sam tapped in for a 3 and walked over to a handshake from President Harrison, a pat on the back from Murchison, nods and fake smiles from the entourage.

"I've never seen the game but you sure seem to have a knack for it, young man." The President said.

"Well, thank you, Mr. President. It's quite a game." Sam replied.

"That's quite an oak tree, reminds me of one on our property in my boyhood days." President Harrison told, "The Jackson Oak we called it. Looked just like yours there."

"Isn't that something." Sam said thinking of Judge Jackson Merit. "That's the name of this one."

"I'll be." said The President.

"Perhaps you would like to take a turn at the game." Sam offered.

"Oh no!" said The President, with a belly laugh, "I am liable to embarrass a whole reputation. I don't believe the American people would take too kindly to their president playing a game. I suppose I am expected to be working."

"Well, I suppose everyone needs a little time off. To me, golf seems like the perfect game for a president. I understand you are a busy man with a lot on his mind, and I couldn't think of a better way to relax. My vote is that we play a couple of holes." Sam said with a wink and a smile.

"I think you should, Mr. President." Murchison added.

President Harrison leaned over to a young man with a notebook and whispered in his ear. The smart and important looking cohorts and assistants joined in on the whispering and then The President turned back to Sam and said," Alrighty, let's give it a shot here."

"Sounds like a plan." Sam said

"Yes, indeed." Murchison seconded with a single smack of his hands.

Duley smiled, and then got a look from Sam that told him to go fetch one of the extra bags of golf sticks from the back porch.

"Go ahead and throw me a lesson or two." President Harrison said to Sam as they walked shoulder to shoulder to the first tee.

All others, except the black suits forming a perimeter around the grounds, were excused over Dead Horse Hill. Murchison insisted on watching from atop the ridge, and was not told to budge. He even made the walk home for some Overholt and returned just as the pairing was teeing off at N°· 1. Duley was allowed to stay. He carried the President's bag and also served as an advisor, just like the other business-looking folks that were in tow. In lieu of The President being at the club, Rev. Oliphint and Arwin were turned away at the ridge shortly before two o'clock.

Three holes were played that Sunday afternoon between Sam Stallings and President Benjamin Harrison. The President never would have known it but Sam slacked on purpose, and won by only one stroke. There was no scorecard kept because of orders stating that there should be no record, whatsoever, of The President's partaking in the game. There are no records prior to that first golf round by a president and it would be many years before any commander-in-chief let on that they were a participant of the game. No news articles about the round ever appeared in any of the local papers, but rumors were flying that storied Sam and the golf grounds even more. With the hearsay, there were a lot more visitors and no new members. It was like a lot of people thought they were going to meet The President out there at the golfing club.

Recently retired, Doctor Newman Smith sat down in town on a misty late-spring afternoon. A sweeping Saturday downpour lingered to rain itself out over Merit, instigating unwilling downtime at the golfing club and a trip to Murchison's Mercantile for Sam. That morning's golf was stopped short when the cats & dogs came barging in and, for the meantime, a wet golf ball lay abandoned in the middle of the N$^{o.}$ 2 fairway. Gray clouds had been rolling in from the west since Sam's opening shot and they eventually collided with the clear sky above to make it split down the middle, the west a dismal gray and the east a wispy blue. Loud thunder and a bolt of bright lightning cracked overhead, turning the walk up to the lie into a run for cover beneath the Jackson Oak. Sam was on a hot roll in his first sixteen holes and, by golly, going to wait out the electrical storm under nature's umbrella so he could finish the routine six rounds. Once leaning on the massive trunk, he started in like he always did with thinking about the next move to best improve the grounds. A look over the slough made for a wish that it would fill back up, summer was beating down and a swell swimming hole was getting to be a necessity. There would be nothing better than finishing a hot day of golf and then taking a cool dip in the fresh water hole. Twin and triplet strikes overhead signaled the bottom falling out, thus sending the dampened golfer on a soaking scamper to the house.

The back porch served as a reminder to Sam that he was needing to pick up a pair of rocking chairs that were purchased last week from the mercantile. Neither of the two boys at the golfing club were growing lazy, nor even close to retiring. Sam and Duley just needed a place to sit during their late-night discussions about the grounds and golf. Duley would soon be returning from his weekly trip to Greenville and, by reason of Mother Nature, the day was not showing as being good for anything else other than sitting and talking about what they would rather be doing. In the pouring rain, a drenched Sam figured what the heck- grabbing the chairs now, during this delay, will keep from cutting into golf time at a later date.

After changing clothes and after noon, Sam hung his raincoat on the ear of a rocking chair and then had a seat for a second trial during an amusing conversation with Murchison. The two tickled men were laughing off a Judge Merit riddle about dogs and trees, and bark, when an older and very pale gentleman with round-rimmed glasses, wet and wiry gray hair, long black coat, brown vest, and a western-style bow tie stepped onto the porch of the mercantile. He was a scientist, not a doctor. His name was Doctor, and it turns out that he would end up taking a much different type of interest in the game of golf.

Murchison made the introduction, after he had guessed correctly on the identity of the new stranger. "You must be Doc Smith." he said, thinking back to recent mail correspondence.

"Indeed. Not to be particular, but no Doc. I've been called Doctor my whole life. I'm not a Doctor, just named that way. And, I'd hypothesize that you are Murchison." Doctor Newman Smith responded in an intellectually sounding, calm, and silvery voice.

"Yes, sir." Murchison replied. "Glad you could make it. Welcome to Merit."

"Thank you, kind sir. The last part of the voyage was quite muddy due to all of the precipitation, though nothing that would stop a wagon wheel from rolling. Nonetheless, I am here." He removed his raincoat. Murchison had his mouth open and was deciding what to make of the new fellow. Sam had his mouth closed but was probably doing the same. "Is this your boy? Hello, young man." Doctor asked.

"Afternoon, sir." Sam said, as he stood from his new chair.

"Doctor Smith, Sam Stallings," Murchison said in a proud tone. "Owner of The Judge Merit Golfing Club, Merit's finest and most enjoyable business. Next to the ice cream parlor, that is." he added, followed by a click of his cheek and a thumb poke into Sam's rib cage.

"Well, I saw the ice cream parlor around the corner. And, Samuel's place is next door." Doctor said, rattling Sam's hand and holding on past a generally customary time. He looked Sam in the eye. They were nearly face to face, which could be attributed to the elder gentleman's lean in. "Now, what kind of a club is it?" he asked.

"No, sir." Sam said, smiling, leaning back, and cocking his head to the side so he could better see the man's eyes. "My place is north of town, over the ridge. I do believe it was a quip that my place was second best to that tasty ice cream over at Dell's."

"Oh, I see." Doctor said, followed with two brief and minutely audible laughs as he turned away. "You are on the other side of town." he continued, and ended with one more guff that turned to a short and frail cough. Doctor moved his glasses to his forehead, let loose of Sam's hand, and turned to fully face the rocking chair before having a seat in the third of many more handmade pieces of furniture that were still on the market.

"Do you need a rocking chair for the porch at your new number twenty-four, Doctor Smith?" asked Murchison.

"I may be retiring from my career, but I do not plan on sitting in a rocking chair per say. In this universe, there are endless opportunities for experimentation and new discoveries that have yet to be realized. Knowledge only leads to more knowledge and science only leads to more science. I may have quit my job, but my work will never end. Young man over there, Samuel, intelligence gained is wasted if one does not reach to expand it." Doctor was rocking back and forth, looking and speaking to the awning above. "Besides, I've realized that there is no need for a rocking chair on the porch at my new number on Second Street in Merit, Texas. If I feel the need to rest in a state of periodic motion, the Boston style rockers at Murchison's Mercantile sit reposefully sufficient."

All three had an out loud laugh, Doctor first and his was only a ha.

"Speaking of number twenty-four, Doctor." Murchison said, as he sat forward on the edge of his chair. "I'm sure you are ready to go have a look-see. Let me run next door to grab your deed, then we'll head up."

"Already had a peek on the way in. Yes, I am worn from the travels, the deed would be nice. I could get started unloading for the night." Doctor replied.

"Sit tight and I will return in a moment. Sam can answer just about any questions you have regarding town." Murchison said in an increasingly louder voice, as he stepped off into the heavy sprinkle and began his way to cross Katy Trail.

"Do you require any help with getting things moved in?" Sam asked across a vacant chair.

"Well, son, I expect the storm will pass in the next hour and twenty minutes. I shouldn't have too hard of a time once the weather is not hassling the task. Don't you have a business to run, Samuel?"

Sam went on to explain the gist of golf and The Judge Merit Golfing Club, including the stories about Judge Merit and the dedication of the grounds. The deed arrived and an hour and twenty minutes later, after the storm passed, Sam was busy helping unload the new resident's wagon until close to sundown. Moving was prolonged by the interesting cache of supplies the scientist insisted on showing off. After a few general science lessons and the last box, Sam grabbed two rocking chairs and made it home with barely enough light to pick up his earlier round that was left soaked in the N°. 2 fairway. He finished sixteen, seventeen, and eighteen to total a fine score of 62 that day. There was another change of clothes, a late supper with Duley at the cafe, then a small gathering to get to.

Late that night, under the stars of Merit, an 1880 brass Lornhofer-Marks refracting celestial telescope was set up in the middle of the Main Street and Katy Trail intersection. Sam, Murchison, Duley, Lowell Fields, Arwin along with Jill and her mother, Mr. Dell, J.R. and Lily Beth Kearney, several hotel guests, South Main Mal, and a handful of other residents all enjoyed Doctor's astronomy lesson and an up-close show above. As turns were being taken to see the last constellation of the evening, Ursa Major, Doctor stepped away and got into Sam's ear about golf balls.

"I've been thinking about this game you were speaking of, Samuel."

"Yes, sir."

"Golf, you said."

"Yes, sir."

"And, you told that one of the objects of this game was to strike a ball down the range."

"Yes, sir."

"And, do you have one of these balls on hand?"

Sam snatched a gutty ball out of his back pocket and handed it over. Doctor lowered his eyeglasses from atop the wiry hair and put them right back up. He reached into his vest pocket, pinched out a monocle, and squinted it into his eye socket. The ball was held above his head and away from his body, then Doctor turned his back to the bright moon.

"Well, what the hell is it made of?" he said.

"Some kind of rubber, not really sure. I've used all kinds of golf balls. Rocks, carved pieces of wood, stuffed leather ones. These fly further than anything else." replied Sam.

"Yes! Young man, that is exactly the subject of which I was going to provide you a little schooling." Doctor exclaimed. The man spun and pulled the golf ball down, dropped the monocle into his waiting hand, and laughed one huff. "Just give the dial around the eyepiece a little turn in either direction to focus, Mrs. Kearney." he instructed toward the skyward telescope.

By now, Mrs. Kearney was the only person not listening in for what Doctor was going to say next. Sam was particularly tuned in. Doctor slid the monocle and golf ball, together, into his vest pocket. Then, the scientist went to grab the long and narrow cherrywood case sitting across the arms of a nearby rocking chair that Murchison had pulled over. "Hold this, please." he said, turning to Sam and placing the case in the young man's hands. "Do you keep one of these for your stick? I am assuming that is your golf stick that you use to hit the ball, lying over against the porch at Mr. Murchison's place." Doctor inquired, as he unbuckled three brass latches and opened the lid of the box.

"Yes, sir, sure enough is." answered Sam.

"And, what's material is it made from?"

"Iron, the part that makes contact with the ball. Hickory wood for the stick, sir."

"Uh huh. Hold that right there." he instructed. "Mr. Kearney, did you have enough of a look there?" Doctor asked, as he stepped over to the telescope and pulled a lens cap from the same pocket as that golf ball. "Gentlemen and ladies, the experience has been a pleasure this evening. I hope it has been fascinating for you to discover new stars over your old home. It has been fascinating to rediscover the old stars over my new home. I believe I will retire there now."

A short and singular round of applause came as Doctor pulled a handkerchief from his back pocket and plucked the device from its tripod. Most of the small crowd went to heading home while looking up and recalling the brightest stars. Mal hustled back home and went in the door quietly. Lowell stopped the forgotten barber pole and went to his place on 1st Street. Jill and her mother went through the cafe and upstairs. Arwin went inside the bar for 'one'. Mr. Kearney turned on the vacancy sign at the inn, the switch had been flipped earlier at Doctor's request. Murchison put the rocking chair back in front of the mercantile and waited to be the last to leave the scene like he always did. Duley walked over to grab the broadstick. Sam stood by holding the opened cherrywood case while the lenses of the telescope were wiped clean.

"So, do you have a case for the stick?" Doctor asked, again.

"No, sir. A bag. There's more than one stick." Sam replied.

"I see. Now, let me tell you what you need to do in order to achieve a maximum distance with your ball."

Sam immediately thought to the golf ball put away in the man's vest pocket, there was no way it was going to get away. Right then, he laid one eye on the tucked-away ball as Doctor leaned over and carefully placed the telescope in its case. The lid was closed, Sam ears were wide open, latches were flipped down, and then the owner took the case in hand.

Doctor continued, "You need to freeze those golf balls."

Sam said nothing and was waiting on an explanation.

"Freeze 'em and they'll fly further. When an object is cold, the object is more dense. That is because the molecules are closer together. It's more rock solid. That way, when you smack it, the distance will be much greater." explained the scientist.

"Yes, sir."

Sam was thinking freezing golf balls would be more trouble than what it was worth. And, the rock-solid part wasn't making too much sense either. He could hit the wooden balls further than the chipped rocks he'd used, leather ones further than that. Murchison spoke up, opening the door to the new freezer in the mercantile and offering a bowl of water to put the golf balls in before they were shut away below 32 degrees. Sam said he would get with Murchison next week and went back to pondering Doctor's suggestion.

With the telescope case tucked under his arm, Doctor was having a word with Murchison about something to do with the electricity in town. Duley was asking if Sam wanted to stop in the bar before going home, and handing over the broadstick. Doctor finished up what he was saying to Murchison with a handshake, and eyed the golfing stick as he began to step away in heading home.

155

Sam was just about to speak up about the item needed for his game back to the golfing grounds.

"Good night, young men. I'll hang on to this ball, Samuel. See what I can do to make it fly further." Doctor said, turning away to walk on.

"Yes, sir." Sam said, in utter disappointment. He felt like someone had taken his puppy and was planning on giving back a big, grown dog.

Sam went on home for the night and Duley stopped in the bar for just 'one'. Murchison too, except he had a flask of Overholt with him all evening long. Doctor would go on to all sorts of golf evaluations, experiments, tests, and suggestions. Not all would prove to be helpful, like freezing golf balls.

Sam did have his curiosity plucked by Doctor's first recommendation. Monday morning, he showed at the mercantile with four gutty balls in his back pocket. Three were put in a bowl of water and stuck into the freezer on the bottom shelf. The fourth was played back home to the front sign post of the golfing club in a record number of 4 strokes with the broadstick.

Tuesday morning, Ross helped chip the ice off and a frozen golf ball was dropped on the dirt road in front of the store. The first shot zoomed left like a scared cat and wound up around the corner in Mr. and Mrs. Miller's front yard. The second took off in a line drive and caught the right side of the road before hitting a rock and bouncing into the vacant property next to Duley. The third shot careened back across to the left side and stuck in the ditch between The Mosely's house and Mr. Goldwire's wagon. The hack out was a looper that never went anywhere but across the street. Number five went down the road a jaunt, and managed to stay. Six put him back on the left side, all the way over beside Herkimer Horowitz's house at 23 Main. Seven barely peeled over Dead Horse Hill and took fifteen minutes to find in the thicket across the way. Eight snapped thorough branches and made it back out to the road. Nine got the ball even with the Jackson Oak and shot number 10 was a lucky one that wasn't meant to hit the sign post, but did. After all of that, Sam wasn't up to playing with those two other frozen balls. He figured they probably weren't even frozen anymore. Anyway, he went to the $N^{o.}$ 1 tee and let all three fly. All ended up in the slough, and that would be the last time Sam Stallings ever froze golf balls.

Most of the scientific endeavors ended up being harebrained ideas that helped as much as a stick in the eye, though Doctor did have a piece or two of advice that served well here or there. Out of the freezing thing, came the heating thing. Those gutty balls would tend to get misshapen after so many beatings. Heating them up and rolling them in between the hands helped to round them back out. A coat of grease on the bottom of the golfing shoes helps to keep mud off the bottom. Though, unless it was a rainy like the day that golf and science met, it was hard to find mud at The Judge Merit Golfing Club. The grounds were back to a prime color green and full of diligently manicured grass. It was tough to find a bare spot anywhere. Doctor's weekly weather reports were helpful at times. The predictions, along with most all of the other suggested experiments, prevailed like a coin flip and were now being delivered to Duley at the cafe. Duley would later pass the information on to Sam at the golfing club. After so many weather reports, Sam would tell Duley that they were golfing all the time and if they wanted to know what the weather was going to be like for golf, all they had to do was look around.

That Tuesday, Sam had just finished an evening eighteen and was sitting on the back porch eating a peach for supper when Doctor showed with a gutty ball in hand. Now, Sam didn't know what the scientist was up to when he took the thing. And, he sure didn't know what to expect when it was returned. One certain thing is that he never thought, due to Doctor Newman Smith, the lost golf ball total would grow on up to four. The man had only been in town four days. Doctor had taken that ball and drilled about a half dozen small holes all the way through it. Sam later commented that the ball looked exactly like Doctor's brain. The scientist said that the ball needed lift to fly further. All of the holes exposed more surface area and created space for air to take control of the ball, lifting, and keeping it in flight longer. Dark was settling and Doctor headed back to town for a star-gazing date with Jill Rank's mother. Sam placed the manipulated golf ball on the first tee, right away. He saw it shoot up and go right, corkscrew left and down, then back up and right. The ball has never been found. However, on a hot day that summer, Sam swam to the bottom of the slough and scavenged those other three.

Summer started off with great golf and there was a lot of it. The grass was really greening up and the weather had been pleasant, not too hot yet. Sam took to getting in three rounds per day, with a swim between each. Usually he would play eighteen in the morning, eighteen after lunch, and eighteen late in the evening. Duley was managing to get nine in on his lunch break and most often joined Sam for the late rounds. In contrast, it seemed that the enthusiasm and excitement had worn off with many of the other current golfing club members. Lowell was there pretty regularly, and it had become a shot in the dark on Ainsworth making his Saturday round. Ross and Otis were there a lot, and always begging Duley for a job. They knew not to bother Sam while he was playing, which made them good candidates. Growth in town had leveled off even more and Murchison was searching harder than ever for any way possible to create another draw, even going so far as attending a couple of meetings to try and straighten out the prerogatives of the committee.

Murchison showed with sad news on the first day of June. He wrote a letter to Mary Merit some time ago, and had not received a reply until the day before. The letter showed joy in the news about the property and sorrow that Judge Merit would not get to enjoy the times. Mrs. Merit agreed that the Judge would be tickled at the sight of the golfing grounds and commented that he sure did love the game. This was a big surprise to the former right-hand man. The Judge was a regular old President around Murchison when it came to his golf game. Mary Merit promised a trip to see the town and the golfing club in July and could not wait to do so. Sadly, on that day, correspondence was received from J.W. Cole, the longtime lawyer of the Merit's. Mrs. Mary Merit had passed away shortly after mailing her letter.

Before leaving the grounds, Murchison shared stories about the couple and reminisced the memories. Telling Sam, Mrs. Merit would have been in heaven when greeted by the honeysuckle, her favorite. Sam sat somber on the back porch as thunderstorms rolled in and out, dropping a welcome shower. Another big batch of rain clouds came in from the west keeping any golf from happening before darkness fell. The next day was the first in a stretch of slow and hot ones around Merit. Murchison temporarily closed the bar to everyone, except himself, and a trend began to emerge around the settling town. By late June, business owners had vacancies, and surpluses, and were peering out their windows and doors looking for customers. There were no new residents that month, in fact a number of 'For Sale' signs went up along Main, First, and Second.

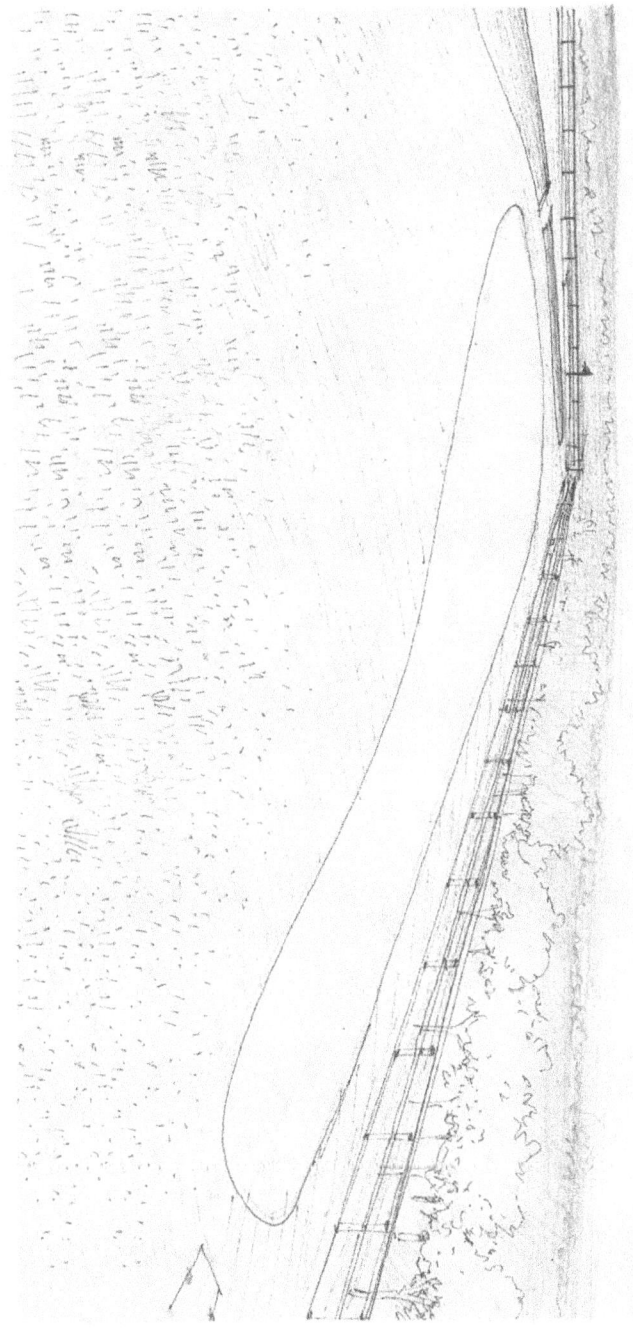

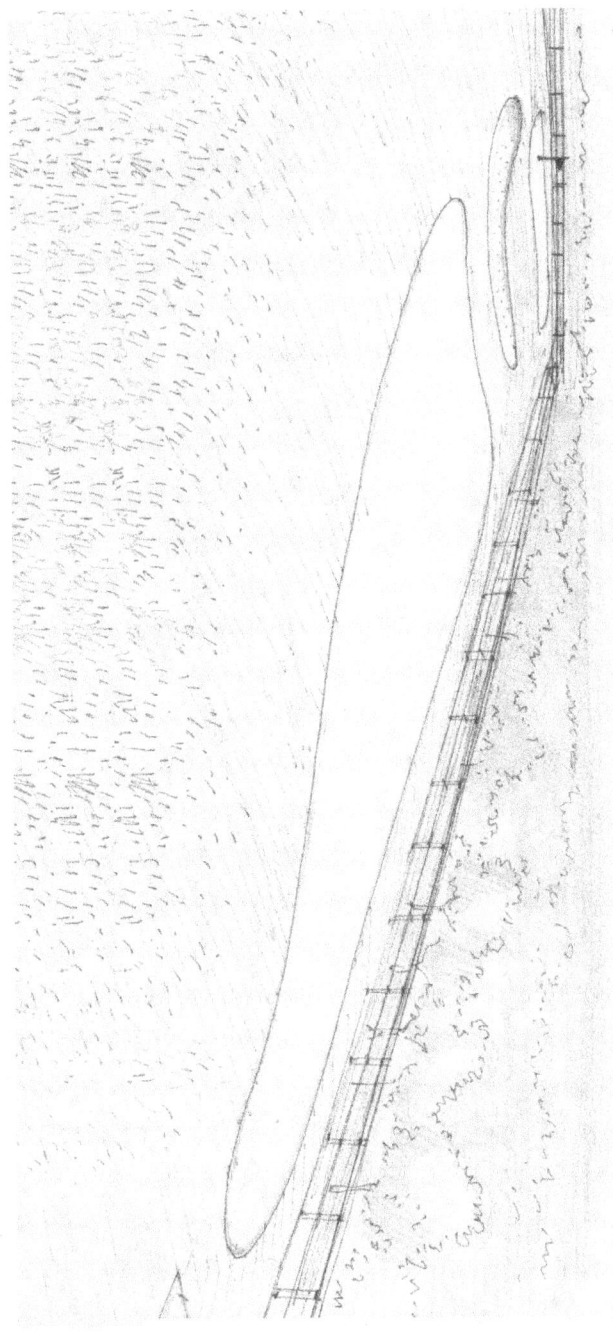

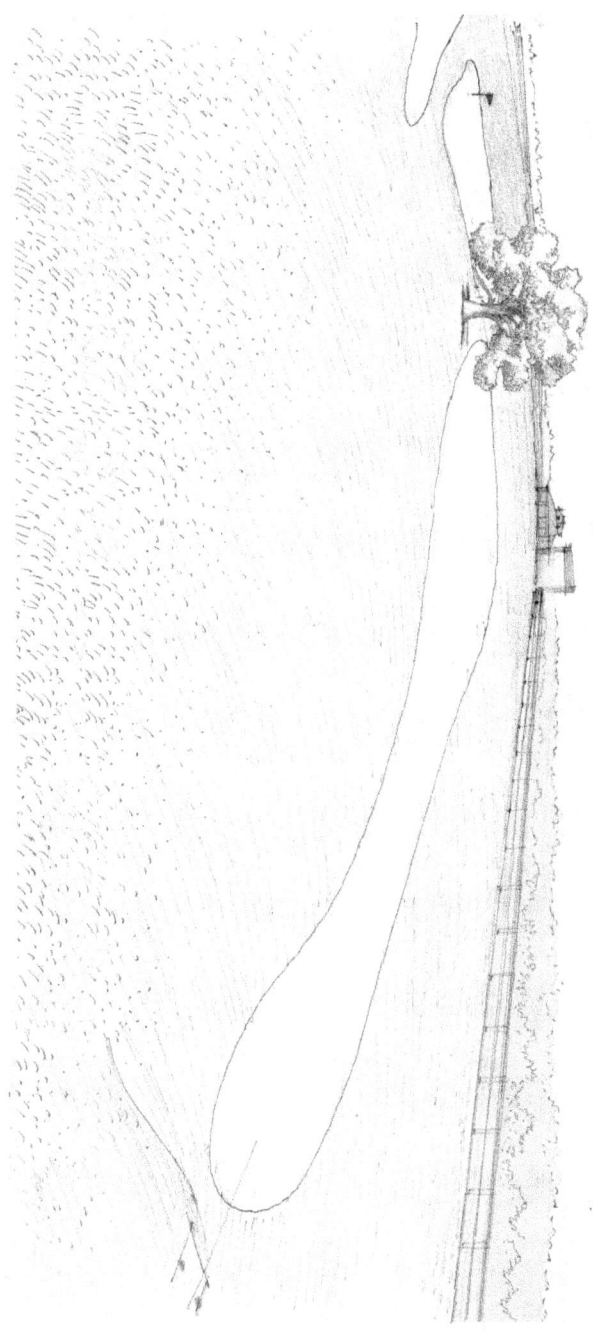

CHAPTER 7

On a mid-Sunday morning that was gleaning assuredly ideal weather, a peanut-colored cloud of dust put forth from the busy black dirt lingered above the two rows of whitewashed buildings and subtly faded into the solid blue sky above. The cloud would become an even more prominent nuisance after church dismissal. It was the first weekend in July and Doctor Newman Smith was cooking up a spectacular display of fireworks for that evening's celebration, all orchestrated by 'The Busy Committee'. As far as that group, Murchison was up to the level of not tolerating much besides straight-forward business. The extra-curricular this and that had him fit to be tied. The need for more growth and the fact of it being a holiday, had helped to lean the pressed man toward more cooperation on this go 'round. In the middle of the otherwise he was keeping up with, even subjecting himself to sitting through meetings and planning sessions with the group of little old ladies. Earlier, he stepped out on his front porch very pleased to see that so many had shown up and were out and about. People dotted Merit everywhere. Loitering, browsing, shopping, buying, soliciting, prodding, galivanting, gossiping, and, in general, stirring dust. The day many had waited for found Murchison with a smile and going around, shaking hands, like he was running for mayor or something.

The splendid evening, announced to all surrounding counties, was to include an array of games, prizes, entertainment, activities, and festivities that would culminate with the grand finale firing off into the dark sky from atop Dead Horse Hill. Things were looking toward a grand time, as clamoring men, women, and families from near and far had been rolling in with excited anticipation of the upcoming affairs. Leading up to, Sam was quite oblivious of it all and any other on-goings that were taking place outside the boundary of the golfing grounds. His mind was about as preoccupied as ever. Running, was a bad streak of the golf ball not falling in the hole as good as need be and, for the last week, he had vehemently been out to stop it.

Out-of-towners began filtering in on Thursday and although you could see sky for miles in all directions, prime spots near the epicenter of the party were long gone. There was no vacancy at the inn, nor at the stables and stockyard, and an abundance of wagons and carriages were scattered about Main Street and down both directions of Katy Trail. Horses and mules were tied up at any and every spot that would accommodate a clove hitch and a bellyache helping of people gathered thick as thieves on the boardwalks and along the right of ways. The line at Dell's Creamery already went on and on as others shuffled into the cafe for a late breakfast. The stock on the knick-knack shelves at the mercantile was slimming fast and Kearney's parlor at the inn was standing room only, accompanied by the piano jingling and jangling on. There were thirty or forty camps posted in the southern prairie, the last open space left available, and more wagons were rolling in every minute it seemed like. Merit was a full cup that day.

There had been some golf business to wash up with the wave of visitors. Two foursomes of first timers came out to play Friday, one in the early morning and one in the early evening. Duley handled everything, greeting, instructing, and cashing out the new members. Sam kept his distance, two holes behind, and playing an extra golf ball because those ahead were advancing along so slowly. One of the first-timers apparently thought he could do the same and took out a second ball. The man got one extra shot in, before Duley hollered and waved it off with not much of an explanation. One ball played per man was the rule. Of course, there was the one young man that was an exception to that rule. Sam's first golf ball scored an 18 for six holes. The second ball completed the two rounds in 19. During evening time play, both balls rolled in at 17 for six.

A pair of gentlemen, golf sticks in hand, had showed up earlier that morning but Duley, hand trimming grass around the N$^{o.}$ 3 green, cut them off at the front gate with notification of the advertised 'Closed on Sunday' policy. Duley probably looked like a lying fool when he rattled it off because right then and there, dead in front of the beleaguered men, a loud crack and a golf ball flew from the N$^{o.}$ 1 tee. Sam finished two loops with a total score of 21, then prepared to head into town. Once he caught sight of all the traffic, there was hesitation at the top of the hill. Kicking a little dirt, Sam turned around and walked over to the fence so as to be within earshot of Duley.

"It's the Fourth of July!" Duley hollered, "Independence Day!"

Sam headed back south, retracing his steps down Main Street. The trip to town was reluctantly necessary as the standard minimal food supply at home was down to nothing but peaches and wild dewberries that were sprouting up at the edge of the thicket. That reason behind the number one errand which was fetching some glue from the mercantile. Earlier, while striking the second shot on the second time through Hole N°· 2, the wire and twine that served as the ferrule of the broadstick busted and a crippling jiggle came to the connection. Sam had left more than a little to be desired with his drive, so applied more muster to the next one. Whatever went awry with the choice golf stick on the next shot caused the ball to career down much shy of the normal landing spot on the green. He finished the fifth hole of the round in five strokes and gave about the same number of sideways shakes with his head when finally pulling the ball from the cup. The treasured club was down, out, and in need of repair before the traditional Sunday afternoon round against the boys.

Broadstick sidelined, the chipper was used as the replacement for the second shot on the third hole and left the third stroke to be taken from the short fairway grass on the left side and just past the trunk of the Jackson Oak. The chipper was used again for the third stroke, a thirty-or-so yard pitch to the crowned and sloping green. A tough ball to get stopped and a bad roll past the hole left a ten-foot putt from the edge, one that broke toward the slough. He made it, barely, to reluctantly come home in 4 rather than the desired 3. Each shot of the unsatisfactory round played through the aggravated head as he walked up to the house, frustratingly and not so gently left the golf bag on the back porch, then headed south to the ridge.

Below the cloud, there were more folks in and about town than had previously been seen in any of the big city stops. In this case, it was a different story of simply mixing in, which was near impossible around Merit though not so much desired anymore. Although, that day was different with all the strangers flocking. Main Street was thin and anything more than nods and howdys were thankfully avoided on the walk in. If Sam hadn't kept a steady and purposeful clip like he did, conversation would have been inevitable before he got to the cafe, which was half full with regulars and hummed loudly from the chatter of the many others.

Mayor Benny Abernathy, in from Silo City, stood from his table and, as the fedora was removed, extended his hand to be the first to greet Sam with a handshake. The scruffy-bearded and freckly mayor then introduced his wife, who smiled big and gave an elbow nudge to the short and round politician's rib cage prompting the introduction of her younger sister, perched next in line. His wife, Bernice or Denise, was a well-off, well taken care of, well made-up, well-endowed, and all over glamorously-presented woman in her Sunday best. Mr. and Mrs. Abernathy went together like an old sock and a new shoe. Her much younger sister, Denise or Bernice, made Mrs. Abernathy seem like she might have fallen from the ugly tree and was about as beautiful of a woman as there was in town. Sam politely shook hands with the mayor, gave a gentlemanly nod to the women, and stepped on around to give a hurried-looking eyeball order to Mac back in the kitchen. Both women gave a uphauled huff to the mayor when Sam walked away without choosing to galivant. The huffs were shunned and the pudgy politician turned back to watch Sam's next moves, like every other person in the room from the surrounding counties.

The two women would have been more flabbergasted if they saw the smile and wink that Sam next sent across the room to Daisy Williamson, the lovely, striking, blond, and beautiful daughter of Mayor and Mrs. Dash Williamson of Denton County. Dash represented the party opposite Mayor Abernathy, whichever one was which, and had been out for golfing twice. One of those times, a hot summer day, Daisy came along and carried cold drinks for her father and his associates during their rounds. Sam played closely along behind and shot a 28 for three, three-hole loops, his worst score ever. That's as far as the pass would go, a smile and a wink. Sam was too shy and would have never gone up to say a word to hardly anyone, especially not that pretty young lady and especially not on that day. There were more important things to be taken care of.

Earl Hardin, his wife, and their two kids were at the next table. Earl was one of Sam's favorites in town, always good for a grass or garden tip, and had still only been out to the golf grounds for the purpose of building the windmill over a week's time. Earl worked building windmills and fixing wagons, mainly, but could also repair just about anything else and very well knew the ins and outs of farming. The kids were not yet school age and, after the initial greeting of the couple, received the first attention from Sam, a loud buzz with his lips coinciding with a ticklish poke to the belly of each child. The playful act drew hysterical giggles from the kiddos and also relaxed Sam tenfold in the packed room. Mrs. Hardin, a teacher at the small, two-room, new school that had not yet held class due to it being summer, quietly asked if a nature tour of the grounds was possible. Sam gave consent and suggested it take place at any time of her choosing.

Sam slid over to say hello at the scooted-together tables holding a group of local, older gentleman gathered for their traditional pow-wow over coffee before church services. Some of the crew he knew, some he didn't. Some he had seen before, some not. Most were farmers or ranchers and rarely ventured off their land except for church, coffee, feed, or fertilizer. Ainsworth, the Saturday regular at the golfing grounds, was the open door for Sam to step over, occupy a little time, and feel less bothered while waiting for his food. Merle Stills, the accountant in the area, had brought his son-in-law out for a single loop during the golfing frenzy that fizzed a month earlier. Arlis Gilwhip, the local chicken supplier that had moved over from Blue Ridge, joined the golfing club in early spring, came out for three or four days in a row, and hadn't been seen since. The other men at the tables had never been out to play and probably never would. Just the same as with Jim, Merle, and Arlis, Sam shared a handshake with each man at the tables. Even though introduced by Jim to all, he wasn't offered the other names. By the looks, most of the men likely thought the game was foolish and the grounds were a bad use of good farmland.

Next, Sam was motioned over by Inez Garlan to a table full of gossip and the First Baptist Church ladies. Inez explained to the table that she had been over the hill to see Sam's lovely garden, the ball he hit with a long hammer went on forever, she thought the mallet or the ball one was going to come flying at her, she couldn't believe it, had never seen anything like it, and the tulips were beautiful. She also announced that her brother's wife's cousin was also named Stallings and there could perhaps be a relation down the line. There were no tulips at the golfing grounds.

As he moved on through the cafe, Sam tried the best he could to keep his eyes and his distance from those that were known to tie a fellow up with small talk. A number of other hideys, how are you doings, and handshakes later, he finally made it to Murchison. Both men always up to their ears in their own respective businesses, it had been more than a couple of weeks since the two had seen each other. Murchison said he would fetch the glue. The store was sold out, but a jar was thought to be stashed away under the counter. Sam requested to go along, and that they leave as soon as his breakfast order was ready. Doctor Smith suddenly interrupted the conversation for something deemed immediately important and Sam gave a roll of the index finger to Mac, then right back got a signal to come to the kitchen window. Ham and biscuit in hand, Sam made eye contact with Murchison and subtly motioned that he was going out the back door and over to the mercantile.

The horn on the N°· 56 engine blew one time, dull and proud, as the passenger train approached from the west. All of the regular engineers knew to blow only once if they were coming through town after eleven o'clock on a Sunday morning. At that moment, Sam stepped out on the south boardwalk and tucked a small bottle of glue into his back pocket. The visit to the mercantile was successful though extended. Ross put on hold a long line of customers and took the time to rummage around trying to find the glue, to no avail. Murchison finally showed and then, finally, found the glue. During the wait time, Sam looked to browse about for a sack full of food to purchase, however, the shelves were near empty. With all the visitors in town, stock was bound to be running low everywhere. There might have been some jerky in the golf bag that would serve for supper, and it would do on a Sunday.

The line went down and the store cleared out, then a bulk of chit chat ensued after Murchison called off church for himself because he wasn't going to make it in time. Sam walked out of the place feeling like he had lost a chunk of the day and was wanting to hurry it back home. The broadstick needed fixing and fine tuning before two o'clock and that was going to take time, it was in a bind. As he was ready to hustle home, there was no way he was going to make it across the tracks before the long stretch of cars crept through the intersection on its way to a stop at the station.

Sam sat on the front steps and gazed over the crowds while waiting for the dust from the passing locomotive to settle closer back to the haze that it was. The first families and groups to step off the train rushed into the churches, tardy, and that was way more than routine disembarking. Merit was lucky to see more than one or two off the № 56, a leg on a coast to coast haul that ran on to St. Louis. Nine out of ten times, the feet that did hit the platform from 56 only stuck around until the train to Tyler came in.

Next off the train was a long exodus of well-to-do looking men and women. Gentlemen in new suits put on their new hats and popped open new umbrellas for the numerous ladies who were all dressed in new, colorful, and elegantly patterned dresses. Three personal butlers wearing black suits were hustling about to retrieve small pieces of luggage for the women, as the group congregated on the planks of the platform in front of the ticket office. The stream of about thirty or so began flowing up the boardwalk along Katy Trail and, like Sam, everyone else that was still out on the streets had their eyes locked on the new arrivals.

Realizing that any more of a delay would place him in the crosshairs of the crowd, Sam crossed on over the tracks and began to head up Main. A look back east as the corner of the building was beginning to cover up the train depot revealed another man, and company, exiting the train. A man if you could call him that, more like a behemoth, was surrounded with an entourage that was stuck to him like honey and heralding the larger-than-life figure as he stopped and gandered over his new whereabouts. Hovering over the scene were gentlemen with tripods and cameras, as well as several others carrying notebooks. They were clearly newspapermen.

The big fella certainly stuck out more than anybody. Sam did a double take and slowed his walk to get a better and longer look before the white washed corner of Fulton's blocked his view of the giant. The man was a clear foot taller than any other person around and when turned sideways, stood thicker than a normal sized man. There was a gut, but toned muscles overshadowed it and most prominent were the Herculean arms that hung out of a tight, white, collared, cotton shirt and away from the hulking body. His back and shoulders were that of a bear and made small a set of struggling suspenders holding high a large pair of brown short-pants. The baggy knickers, cuffed with a button right below the knee, were met with high patterned socks that looked like they belonged to one of the women in the preceding group off the train. The lower half of the big body narrowed. The knees wanted to knock but didn't and the calf muscles were lacking for a man that size. Feet were small too, matching the legs but not the height nor torso, and were fitted with a shined-up pair of brown leather dress shoes.

When stepping off the train, the giant man crowded the exit and the big jowls heaved up a wad of spit and let it go right there on the side of the ticket office. Sam stopped in his tracks and when peering back around the corner after witnessing the disrespectful act, he found a strong glare coming right from the culprit's eyes. Sam did not budge his bead first and made it through the stare down with the solace that a disappearing act was another step north.

A reflection glistened from above the head of a partially grayed-up, old, colored man with a back that curled like a bad golf shot, and that was the last sight before the long glimpse east was blocked. Sam stopped in his tracks and peered back around the corner. Still, he was not alone in this act as everyone else around had also moved their stare from the flamboyant procession of the rich and fancy over to the giant of a man. Mumbles about the huge-sized figure turned to astonished and outspoken words, then children became tickled as they called out in amazement. Despite the distance, some of the younger ones seemed frightened at the man's presence. Sam wasn't particularly captivated with the big fellow and zoned in on the shiny reflection that had caught his eye. A turn of the crooked back revealed a fistful of golf sticks hoisted over the shoulder of the aged, colored man standing clad in white. Sam saw exactly what he thought and then had a hard swallow as he ducked around the corner and began his steady clip back up Main Street.

Teenage boys came flying off of a back car, cornered the posse, and immediately sought autographs, which were conceded by the smiling and grinning, chummy looking, big guy. Then, adults, including some locals with no idea who they were talking to, stepped up to the commotion and asked for a signing or a handshake. Even if you didn't know who the large man was, it was clear that he was a draw of some sort. The activity on the platform was swelling by the minute as more and more passengers unloaded from the train and the touted entourage began walking the boardwalk to town.

The suddenly nervous and hurried young man was almost to lot one and picking up pace when he heard the call come from Murchison, "Sammy!"

A turn back caught the dreaded wave over. Not that he minded helping or stopping to visit, but there was a storm brewing and it was coming down the boardwalk. Sam changed directions, then quickly walked over so as to send a message that he was being slowed down from a crucial beat. The message was never received or ignored, one of the two.

"Yes, sir?" Sam said.

"I'll never get you to stop it, will I?" Murchison shot back, double-barreled with the piercing glare.

"If you haven't by now, then it's not likely." Sam replied.

"Just like a stubborn old mule." Murchison poked, then smiles and draws of laughter were shared. "Come in here a minute." the bar owner suggested.

"Sure thing." Sam replied, after a look back at the throng coming head on.

First thing once inside the hushed and dark room, Sam's attention was caught by the portrait of Judge Merit on the wall. Months had passed since he last visited the establishment and though the familiar portrait flashed to mind near daily, tip-top shape always came when seeing the storied painting in person. The picture served as strong motivation after the fits of the morning round and the peal of the broadstick. Sam was needing something, and right then.

"Did you see the size of that man?" Murchison asked as he stepped behind the bar.

"Big ol' fella." Sam spoke below a whisper.

"I wonder who in the world he is. I guess they are all over him because of his size, like he's a circus character." A blank silence occurred because of no reply. "Perhaps he's famous. We've seen 'em before, haven't we?" Murchison said as he set out two glasses.

"Sure have." Sam replied softly as he ceased his stare into the painted eyes.

"Run grab a case of Overholt from the barn, please." Murchison ordered to the bartender, Otis, who was wiping off tables. "Church is not yet out, but it won't hurt a flea. Drink?" Murchison asked Sam.

"No sir. Sunday round against the boys at two."

"There you go again with your stubbornness." Murchison remarked with a quick laugh. "How are the grounds looking these days?" he inquired, and began to pour.

"Holding up to the heat, so far." Sam answered.

Murchison tossed the empty bottle into a trash bin and then reached under the bar and pulled out a golf stick, then laid it across the bar in front of Sam.

Sam didn't know what to say, so said nothing. He was about to ask if a drunk golfer had left it. His eyes opened wider than normal and then he looked to Murchison for an explanation.

"You know what that is?" Murchison asked.

"I do believe it's a golfing stick, a middle iron." Sam declared.

"Have a look there." Murchison insisted, with a finger pointed at the handle end.

Sam pulled the golf stick from the bar and swiftly stepped back to assume his routine stance. It was very similar to the broadstick, even a bit sturdier. The head was lighter but seemed stouter and also appeared to have met many less golf balls than his well-seasoned own. The head was given a few back and forth waggles and then Sam raised his hands for a squinted look at the letters J.M. scrawled on the nub of the grip. He instinctively flipped the hickory shaft of the golf club to his collarbone, coming to rest like he had completed a fine shot. His lower jaw made a slow and slight drop. "Jackson Merit." Sam said.

Murchison nodded with a sincere and proud smile. "Found it yesterday while making space in the barn. It was in one of those crates back there. I wanted to bring it to you right away, but I was tied up and forgot all about it. Too much going on."

"You reckon Judge was a golfer?"

"Judge *was* a golfer. Found a record of his score in the same crate. Have a look." Murchison asserted. He then pulled from the cash drawer a small and worn card marked with faded lead handwriting.

Sam laid the golf stick back on the bar and took the card. With a thumb hiding the final result, he began going over the round ever so closely. On the twenty-ninth of May, 1875, six holes were played by J. Merit, Big Jim, A. A. Pearce, and Lokey. At this moment Sam would recall to himself, years ago, Jack Malley mentioning a great local golfer by the name of August Pearce, probably the first known man to play golf around the Dallas area. Mr. Malley told that Pearce was the kind of man that knew all of the important people in town, the high-up ones that were running things. This because of his athletic prowess in the game of golf and an apparent eye for winners in horse races. There was something else that he excelled at, too. Some other game he played in college, another game with some kind of a ball.

All men scored a four on each of the first two holes, except Pearce who posted threes. On the third hole, Big Jim and Lokey put up a six and a seven, respectively, while Judge and Pearce both came in with fives. Judge Merit had the hot hand on the fourth, recording a two. A. A. Pearce maintained a one stroke lead with a three and Big Jim and Lokey put up fours. Hole five saw Judge with the hot hand, again, as he was in on three strokes and Pearce and Big Jim were down for fours. Lokey notched one further back with a five.

Sam had all of the numbers stuck in his head when he looked up from the card and then summarized the round, so far, to Murchison.

"One hole to play and Judge is knotted up for the lead." Sam declared, as he looked at Murchison with big eyes and a rich smile. A smile that had grown while adding up each count, each shot, each stroke gained and lost that carried the fate of the final scribed totals for the players. Murchison grinned and nodded for Sam to go on. "Looks like he was at the very least a darn decent player. A. A. Pearce, too. You know him?"

"Never heard of him, nor Lokey." Murchison answered. "Big Jim was the Attorney General of the state, then Governor."

Sam popped out his lower lip so as to say, 'Isn't that something.', then put his eyes back on the next to last column of numbers, the last still hidden under a thumb. Lokey's eight stuck out first, followed by Big Jim's seven. A. A. Pearce scored a five and Judge cashed in with a four. Sam ran back through the row labeled J. Merit followed by the one labeled A. A. Pearce. He quickly tallied the math in his head, then removed his thumb from the circled totals. Lokey thirty-two. Big Jim twenty-nine. A. A. Pearce twenty-three. Judge Merit twenty-two.

"Judge took the round!" Sam exclaimed with raised eyebrows, as he held the card away from his eyes and had another run through of the top line.

"Sure enough. Never would have guessed that he was even familiar with the game, much less played it. Although, doesn't surprise me that if he was playing the game, he was the winner. Always was." Murchison claimed.

Sam turned the scorecard over to find an inscription that was confirmed as Judge Merit's handwriting.

Play commenced early on a fine Saturday with the short grass of the pasture carrying a fair amount of morning dew. We all had a crack out of Big Jim suggesting for the next game, we bring along an old pair of boots with nails drove through the soles for a better hold on the earth while taking our golf swings. August A. Pearce sure does know the game well and if not for lucky rolls on my behalf, and a couple of bad bounces on his bill, my pocketbook would be two-hundred dollars lighter than it is today. Jack County, Texas, 1875

"Sounds just like my friend." Murchison said, as he and Sam laughed and relished a moment in memory of Judge Merit.

As the moment went on, Sam spoke up. "That is something else, Judge Merit played a little golf. Puts a smile to my face, thinking about those darn golf holes out there on his place. I've doubted it, but I reckon he would get a kick out of it. Maybe appreciate the place."

"Me too, Sam. Puts a smile to my face, too. And, you are dang right, he would love it. He'd probably be an everyday customer." Murchison said with a wink. "More than anything, he would be proud that you've done good with it, Sam. It's a fine place."

Sam gave a solemn smile and, as he looked up from the wood floor, Murchison pointed a finger and said, "That's yours. I'm not sure if it is up to your liking for use, but take it with you."

"Now, are you sure you don't want to hang on to it?" Sam asked.

"You are the one that does the golfing, and you know good and well that I'm not going to be using it." Murchison said.

"Figured it might have a sentimental hold and you might want it as a sort of keepsake."

"I think it tickles me even more for it to be in your hands, Sam. Take that card with you, as well. Put it up out there where it belongs."

The card was slid into the front pocket of the white-collared shirt and then Sam graciously grabbed hold of his new golf stick. He went right to studying with a fine eye, so as to immediately decipher all he could. The solid and sturdy tool was crafted by someone that well knew what they were doing and it was most likely that the thing originated from far off across the pond. Used, but not too much. After all, and to Murchison's confirmation, Judge Merit was a busy man.

Murchison was pouring up another drink. Otis was stocking the liquor and Sam had moved to eyeballing the grip. The front door of the place sprung open and a loud and rowdy voice tolled into the bar. "Where in the hell does a fella get a drink in this dust bowl?" said the giant man who filled up the doorway and hence ducked to get in. His tone was bass over the many others that were jawing up a storm behind him and, when he stepped through the doorway, it was like he never stopped coming.

"You can put your money down." Murchison quickly rang back.

Change was pulled from the big front pocket of the big brown knickers and sent tumbling off the bar and crashing to the floor. "Get on two whiskeys then, you old codger." he said with a smart-ass pause between the order and the insult. Murchison raised his eyes and chin, as did Sam. Most of the followers seemed to know the attitude as the norm and didn't flinch at the surly display.

The big guy had already placed eyes directly on Sam and was in the middle of a short path across the room to the stammered young fellow. The rest of the mob, no locals, filed in like they owned the place and began hollering for drinks on the double. Murchison held Otis at bay on serving anything and watched, ready to deliver something else over the bar depending on what ol' jumbo was up to. Sam found his eyes and chin raised high, as he cocked his head back to look the towering man in the eyes.

"Are you even old enough to be in here?" belted out the big, loud, and deep voice.

"I'm in here, aren't I?" Sam replied in his young and sharp sounding way.

"That's questionable. A man's liable to miss you, unless he's looking hard enough."

Sam was heated up from the disrespectful talk to Murchison and was about to heat things up more by firing back with a line about the bully finding him just fine, and doing so right quickly. Don't think for a minute that he didn't consider and rehearse through his mind for a long hard moment about exactly what would happen if it came to be that he needed to crack this big ol' boy a hard knot on his noggin with Judge Merit's old golfing stick. Like a gavel coming down for a hard sentence. Sam neither replied nor budged and, for the moment, was dismissed from the confrontation while the big bully looked around the room and then gave an angry and scowling nod to Murchison so as to say give me my drinks. Most everyone else in bar had already caught wind from Otis that there would be no drinks until noon.

"I've got more than a dozen brands of whiskey." Murchison countered to the scowl.

"Overholt!" the deep voice called as everyone watched and listened over the domineering conversation.

"Nope." replied Murchison.

Standing at the corner of the bar, Sam snickered but on the inside only. The beast was still right there before him.

"Whatever's in your hand and hurry the hell up." the deep voice growled.

The big man's attention then turned back to Sam and the grump took a head to toe look of the cool young man casually leaning against the bar, feet crossed, right elbow posted, and the recently acquired prestigious golf club clutched at his left hip.

"Munroe!" The brute voice of the big guy called over his shoulder and through the bar.

The noise in the room cascaded down to murmurs and a slow alley parted amongst the crowd. The bent over colored man, still with golf sticks posted up on his shoulder, seven of them, hobbled through and came to stand right off Sam's left shoulder.

"This young lad here is holding on to a golf club, here at the bar. Must be looking for an ass-whooping." A big laugh, a raspy old laugh, oohs and ahs from the bar patrons, and a slight bend at the waist later, the big right hand was reaching for the sacred golf stick in Sam's left hand. Budging nothing more than a finger, Sam swung the wood and iron like a pendulum until it was out of the extensive reach. Then, the eyes of the two men met hard like cold rocks.

The horde inched in closer and Sam was in the last place that he wanted to be, the spotlight. And, right up in the middle of a brightening one. The door had yet to close from the parade that had yet to cease from entering the bar. Locals were also making their way in now, and the ladies and gents in the room that were in the know of a rivalry brewing were talking it up in the background like they were discussing the gospel from the Sunday sermon.

The big man pulled away and, while fiercely staring down Sam, spoke to Munroe saying, "I didn't see it at first, thought it was a cane. Thought the scrawny rat was a cripple, not a golfer." There was a deep snark of a laugh and then whooping and hollering from not everyone, but nearly.

"You sure we have all the clubs, Munroe? This kid swipe one off the train?" asked the big man.

"Yessir. All seven here. Yessir." Munroe responded in his gruff voice, as he looked his boss in the eye.

185

"Make it eight." The Whammer muttered, then cackled with laughter. "From the looks of it, a decent iron if it is in the right hands." The giant laughed on as he looked back at the club in Sam's hand and contemplated his next move. Silence had come to the room. Sam, knowing he probably couldn't take the big fella in a fist fight, was ready to take out the back door, golf stick in hand, at the drop of a hat. Though, there was no way he would leave the fedora behind either. The large right hand reached, again. "You better hand it over or you're liable to thump a knot on your head." The deep voice groaned and a majority in his gaggle erupted with another chorus of amusement.

"Hey now!" Murchison yelled out from behind the bar, "Just who in the hell do you think you are?"

A newspaper columnist, Marty Satterfield of *The Houston Post,* chimed in above the chatter to Murchison and soon everyone was tuned in. "Old timer, you don't know who stands in your bar? The greatest golf ball striker in the country. Never been beat." he said. "Best one we will see in our lifetime, isn't that right gentlemen?" the man continued, speaking over his shoulder. Oh yeahs and uh huhs came forth from a lot of suits. "Meet The Whammer, sir." Satterfield said in a voice that resonated like it could have just as well come from over a speaker.

Sam immediately recalled Jack Malley's mention of The Whammer and how he made it sound like the man was the Zeus of the game already. A man in the process of becoming a new type of player that would unleash power and strength on the finesse-style of play, thus reducing any kind of short game to child's play. The Whammer was such a large baby that it was a news story all over the United Kingdom. He was born on golfing grounds and by the time he was a teenager had supposedly defeated hundreds of men across the countryside of England, out-driving and out-playing all challengers. The family migrated and the boat missed the United States, ending up in Mexico. Early on, in his stint south of the border, the young man played the beaches and makeshift holes off the gulf. After leaving out on his own, the young golfer spent time playing and traveling through the deserts and mountains of western Mexico. He found his way on over to the hills of California where his latched-on convoy of buddies, mediocre golfers, fans, and rumor driving news reporters assembled. That's how, when, and where he really began to drum up the notorious reputation with his displays of might and domination over any and all that dared to take up the game in his presence.

California, and the fruit bearing economy of the gold rush, allowed for access to some of the best equipment, materials, weather, and locales for golf. The locale, and all with it, also allowed for the rumor and hype to proliferate. The Whammer made quite a name and quite a lot of money playing the game by the time he was twenty-five. His name hadn't reached the east coast, yet, but it was said that he was well-known all over the west. The purpose of the trip to Texas was a sportsman's exposition in Houston, the big guy was the headliner and the California caravan was now on its way to Chicago and picking up weight along the way.

"I don't give a damn who he thinks he is." Murchison said, as he slammed his fist down on the bar. "He's not going to come into this bar, or this town, trying to throw his big weight around like he's doing."

"Listen here old man." The Whammer said as he turned his attention away from Sam and directed it in full force toward Murchison.

"You listen here." Murchison interrupted. "You might do elsewhere what you are doing here and get away with it. But you got another think coming around here."

The Whammer reached out to snatch the bottle of Overholt that was sitting out and there was no telling what he would have done with it if Murchison hadn't beat him to it.

"And, if you don't watch it, you'll get your ass beat with a golfing stick while you're here." Murchison declared as he stepped away and pointed the bottle at the big chest.

Sam shivered as the place fell silent.

"Wait!" Satterfield said, as he put a brave arm in front of The Whammer's chest. "Are you saying there are golf holes around here?"

"Sure enough, and a mighty fine set at that." Murchison responded.

The Whammer was already back on Sam. "You play golf in this dirt hole?" the deep voice asked.

Sam stood stone cold silent and still, composed on the outside but not within.

Murchison was looking ten times as mean as the day Sam rolled into town. "You are doggone right!" he said, as his fist pounded on the bar another time. "And, if the grounds don't eat your golf ball alive then my boy Sam will." he declared as he pointed to Sam and continued to stare down The Whammer.

"Sam boy." The Whammer said as he moved his look back to the youngster, who was still looking cool as a cucumber. In the meantime, more interested and attracted parties had stepped into the bar and the rumble was escalating. Half of the room was already going back and forth, egging on a game between the two, and the tension was about to put flight syndrome into Sam. "Sam boy doesn't stand a chance, folks." The Whammer announced to his entourage, and everyone else.

"Two-hundred dollars says otherwise." Murchison blurted out, silencing everyone. Again, Sam about shivered and a nerve almost gave away the impenetrable and unbothered swagger in his pose.

"Game on!" The Whammer said.

Glee and jubilation filled the bar and drowned any momentary discussion of the proposition. Satterfield was trying to say something.

Sam kept his frozen pose, and butterflies swarmed with the ham and biscuit.

"Hold on, now. Hold on." Satterfield said, "How many holes are there?"

The chatter went silent.

"Three holes." Murchison said in a hot grit.

The bar was now past standing room only and the flurry in the room had risen to its busiest and loudest yet. Wagering on the contest started up immediately. If there was a tally of the books, it would have shown things to be quite one-sided. The dozen or so from Merit that were in the establishment put their money on Sam, while everyone else that filled the place up was betting on The Whammer to win.

"Three holes." Satterfield shouted over the buzz as he held three fingers high in the air, then raised his other hand so as to quiet the room. The bar fell back to silent and The Whammer finally stopped staring down Sam. "Here's what we've got." Satterfield continued, "Three holes. Standard golf rules. Man with the lowest number of total strokes after three holes wins."

"What kind of holes are we talking about?" The Whammer seemed to require.

"Golf holes! Did you want a gopher hole?" shouted a local voice that sounded like it was Hopper Hackman, who was quickly becoming known as the town drunk ever since Sam's revealing of the bar. Duley had agreed to keep the type and source of the wooden shaft's out of Murchison's ears.

"The best golf holes you ever stepped foot on." Murchison hollered.

"We'll see about that." The Whammer replied. Munroe mumbled something in accompaniment.

"To make things more interesting, I'll toss in another hundred." said one of the reporters that most certainly had to have come along from the west coast.

"I'll throw in another hundred." added Skip Sherrod from the *Dallas Times Herald*, there to cover the holiday celebration, not Sam nor The Whammer.

"Make it three from me." Murchison said, "A five-hundred-dollar prize will make a better story in the newspaper for you boys."

"Five-hundred dollars to the winner!" Satterfield announced over the room.

A collective gasp came about and then the tumble of chatter and predictions accelerated. Stakes on wagers were rising, too, and a variety of side bets were in the process of debate.

"Won't be much of a contest. What we will see is a remarkable display of The Whammer's fine skills. It'll certainly make for a great article. 'Whammer Takes Down Hot Shot Kid in Texas'" said one of the west coast reporters that was following along with the traveling entourage.

"Whammer is gonna kick the horse shit out of that scrawny kid." yelled out one young man that was obviously all-the-sudden a golf want-to-be and completely taken to a gullible look by the presence of the notorious west coast big boy.

Right behind Sam, one of the rich ladies could be heard giving her opinion. "The gentleman will be finished up and that poor boy is going to still be trying to figure out what to do with himself." Followed by an unimaginably high-pitched and screeching laugh.

"I will put up for wager, one hundred dollars guaranteeing The Whammer knocks each and all tee box shots the furthest." said one of the highfalutin men from the train. Another slick gentleman with a lady around his arm raised the bet a hundred and accepted it with a handshake. "The kid will get him on a short hole." was the reply that came while placing the bet.

Standing at the bar, a man named Milam from over by Greenville leaned to one reporter and said, "The wind is supposedly picking up out of the north here after noon time and going to play right into the big fella's hand on hole two, probably three as well. This kid don't have a chance in hell on his own grounds, if that guy can really get a hold of the ball." Milam had been out to hack a round of golf once or twice and in each instance did more talking than golfing. The reporter went on to ask numerous questions about the lay of the land and each hole. All of the answers would later be deemed fairly inaccurate or exaggerated, including the wind bit.

"The Whammer is going to beat this child like cornbread batter!" said a man clearly off the $N^{o.}$ 56.

"Five dollars says the fat man don't win." offered up Hopper Hackman, indeed the man that had smarted off earlier. He was ripe-smelling of alcohol, already, and quick in doling out insults to all the strangers that were showing their loyalty to the rival. Two men in coats tried to escort the drunk man out, but they were starting to have hell with it and Otis stepped over to put a stop to the squabble. Murchison's order.

191

All of the official conversation between Murchison, Satterfield, and Sherrod was interrupted when Neely Jamail, a cattle baron known as the richest man in the area, called out that he was doubling the prize money.

"One thousand dollars to the winner!" Satterfield declared.

After another gasp from the still developing crowd, the stir began swirling and people outside the establishment were now trying to jam themselves in. There was a quick nonchalant smile shared between Sam and Murchison. Sam's was a reluctant response of a half-smile.

Skip Sherrod whistled loudly. Noise went down a couple of notches but talk and jabber ensued. "Now, to ensure that all is fair, we are going to need a man to oversee the competition and make sure all rules are followed. A judge of the competition." he said.

"Where is Reverend Jessup?" called out a voice from down at the front door end of the bar.

"Still in church." replied a lady sitting at a nearby table.

"He's the one." Murchison insisted.

"He's the most trusted man in three counties. Knows golf, too." said another man in the back vicinity.

The ones speaking were identified as being from Leonard, a stop on Reverend Lassiter Jessup's charge. Although the veteran preacher never ministered in Merit, near every other town in the area was or had been on his circuit. Reverend Jessup was likely the most trusted man in five counties and was in town at the request of Rev. Oliphint to deliver a prayer before that evening's festivities. Partisan denominations had 'The Busy Committee' on the verge of a quarrel over who would give the blessing, Rev. Oliphint or Reverend

Barnabas James of the First Baptist Church. Truth be told, Revered Jessup knew the game via his visits with Rev. Oliphint.

"Sherrod and I, the gentleman behind the bar, we will speak to the reverend once services have been dismissed." said Satterfield.

"Now, gentleman, I hate to put a damper on things but the train will be pulling out at sharply one o'clock." said a butler that was accompanying one of the well-to-do couples.

"Train's broke down." said Bose Gentry, a notorious gambling man from Bonham that was the second biggest guy in the room and stood surrounded with a lowdown looking posse of cowboys. He put his hand on his pistol for reinforcement, then his well-practiced eyes aimed right at the engineer of the N$^{o.}$ 56, Sim Goodman, demanding a delay. "Right, Sim Goodman." The cowboy and the engineer had never met, and the guess was not hard as to how Bose likely knew Sim's name.

All suddenly reverted back to still and quiet. Sim Goodman looked around and had a bunch of fierce eyes drowning any bravery, or will to adhere to the schedule. "That's right. There's an issue with the Johnson bar." he announced, "Not sure how long it might take. Fireman is flipping over the switch and sending any through-trains around on the passing track. We're going to be stalled out for the time being."

"Ok, sounds like we are a go." Satterfield called out.

All-the-while, Sam was standing quietly amongst the hype but had coyly slipped around the corner of the bar to create space between he and The Whammer.

"Looks like your boy here is trying to skin out." The Whammer said to Murchison, then turned to Sam. "This kid couldn't hit the broad side of a barn. You in or not? Munroe and I will take these people's money on to Chicago."

Satterfield quieted the room with a hush that was echoed and encouraged along by others. The Whammer even slowly looked up from whispering more smack talk into Munroe's ear. Sam pulled the fedora down on his forehead and took the half-step around to the front side of the bar. He glared hard eyes right at The Whammer, causing the rising chatter in the room to come back to silent.

Fierceness came to muster at an ounce of thought rising from a few short years ago and the fabled rounds that had put Sam on the run. On this day, The Whammer was presenting himself just as mean and dirty as the rough boys down in Georgia. Same type of hooligans though the situation was much different in hometown surroundings, on his own turf. Murchison was the only one that knew the story of what happened down in the Peach State and he certainly wouldn't put up with those antics here. A Colt Single Action revolver would have The Whammer and his clan hemmed up and pinned to the city limits sign if there was any retaliation like there was in the deep south.

Tension was thick and mounting by the moment. All eyes were on Sam, and all ears were waiting.

"Half a mile up Main." Sam said sternly. He slammed the iron head of the golf stick into the wood floor like how a judge calls a recess, then turned to march himself out the back door.

The colloquy inside the place heated up like train brakes and the room was scattering and situating in all different directions. Murchison left his post and quickly stepped to catch Sam before he made it too far.

"Sam!" Murchison called out.

"You are crazier than a pet coon." Sam said as he turned back. Murchison winked and they both smiled.

"You'll take it. I know you will. Keep your head on top of it and do your thing." Murchison urged and encouraged.

"Here's the deal. You have got to go back in there and buy me a little time." Sam said, as he grasped his back pocket to ensure the glue was still there and then went north behind the row of houses lining the east side of Main.

Murchison returned to the bar and chimed a spoon five or six times on his whiskey glass, the only one that had so far been poured in the bar that day. "Here now, here now." The glass was chimed and chimed, again, and all patrons slowly fell silent. "Here now, listen up. Churches dismiss in one half hour and folks will need time for lunch. The competition will start at one o'clock on the dot."

"One o'clock tee time." Satterfield called out to all.

Some folks began begging to order drinks, others waited, and others scattered about town. The line at the cafe was back to extending out the door as did the one at the mercantile. Howard Dobbs, the Coca-Cola man, arrived right on time and opened up his wagon for ice cold soda pop. Hamburgers and hotdogs were quickly cooked up and served by the husbands of 'The Busy Committee', which eased the wait at the cafe before church let out. Carnies started with their ballyhoos and pitching of Ring Toss, Bottle Knock, Shoot Em Up, Buzz Wire, Fool the Guesser, and other games that were set up under tents on the lawn beside the churches. One smart young man fetched his father's putter and a glass jar from home, then dug a hole in the ground and quickly had the longest line in town of adults and children alike at a penny per putt. When the doors to the Methodist Episcopal Church swung open, the first service to dismiss, word of the showdown spread like wildfire on a scorching hot day.

195

At Murchison's request, and for a free bottle of whiskey per man, Bose Gentry and his gang were riding to the top of Dead Horse Hill and saw to it that no one crossed over until a quarter shy of 1 o'clock. Otis was boxed in and business was pressing. Murchison summoned the help of Jesse James behind the bar, not the famous gunslinger. J.J. was Otis' father's bar back and happened to be in town taking in the festivities. As said, he was not the gunslinger, though he could serve drinks as fast as one might imagine the outlaw drawing and shooting. And, the second round always came before the first one was finished. Glasses were full, and all in the packed bar were satisfied in no time at all.

Reverend Lassiter Jessup stepped onto the front steps of the church, clad heel to toe in black, and was startled when cornered by Satterfield, Sherrod, and Murchison. At first, he thought they were there with a generous offering for the collection plate. Prize money was handed to the reverend and the four men went behind closed doors in Murchison's place to lay out duties and ground rules.

Aside from the general golf rules, which were pretty cut and dried, it was established that tee markers and holes would be placed in new locations prior to the start. Murchison assured that Sam changed them regularly and would have no problem with it. In the case of a tie, an extra hole would be played, staying with the same sequential order and starting over with N$^{o.}$ 1, until a winner was decided. Winner takes all. Reverend Jessup would make judgements on any disagreements or controversies, ensure that both players were playing the game in a fair and honest manner, keep the official record of the score, and have the final say on all matters. Murchison would bring Otis and Ross for crowd control and have in reserve, the help of Bose and his boys if needed. All four men would walk, and inspect, the grounds beforehand while placing tee markers and switching around the holes. The men shook hands and stepped outside to head up Main Street where at the north end, a deep collection of people had gathered before the line of horses that were perched atop the ridge. The church bells never rang.

Sam reached home and found Duley having just cleaned up, from mowing the greens, and standing dressed in his favorite Sunday golf attire. "Everything in shape? All set to go?" Sam asked as he ducked inside the tool shed to grab spools of twine and wire, then headed toward the porch. Duley walked near tucked in his back pocket.

"Sure enough. Everything except for putting the flags out. She's looking good as ever, going to play a real nice round for us this afternoon." Duley replied.

"Let's hope so, but it's going to be a different kind of Sunday round today. Don't worry about the flags. I'm sure when they get out here, they are going to want to move 'em."

"What are you talking about, Sambo?" Duley asked.

"You have a clean pair of coveralls?" Sam quickly replied.

"Sure enough. My tans just came back from the laundry."

"Go put them on. I need you to carry my bag today."

"Carry your bag? What the hell is going on, Sambo?"

"You will find out here shortly. What did you pick up my sticks for?" Sam asked as they arrived at the back porch and an upright, organized golf bag.

"Why, they were scattered all over the place. I figured it was a bad shot until I saw the broadstick. It's in there with the others. What the hell happened?" Duley asked.

"We'll talk about that around the corner."

"What in darn heck, Sambo?"

197

"Turn your ear to Dead Horse and listen there."

Both gazed away, then at each other as they shared the silence and listened for the distant blaring.

"Uh-huh." Duley said with his mouth open and while still trying to listen.

Sam got busy scoping out each stick in his bag. "It's all coming this way and going to be here in a hurry." he said. The battered broadstick was pulled out and placed with iron standing on the wooden porch and leather laying over a bent leg. "We're going to have the golf of a lifetime here directly and it's going to be tougher than nails. Go change. When you get back, tell Murchison to keep everybody off the short grass. Then, come on in the clubhouse." Sam said as he snatched the Judge Merit Special from its lean on a post and slid the new golf stick down into the foremost part of the bag. Duley took out from the porch with a baffled look that Sam never saw and headed to fight through Bose and the burgeoning wall of people, over and back. Sam grabbed the broadstick from its lean and looked at it with surgeon eyes, then slid through the back door and drew the shades in the windows.

CHAPTER 8

Main Street, Katy Trail, and the southern prairie had all been left in the dust and sat occupied only with a plentiful number of empty camps, parked wagons, grazing horses, and a 'broken down' train. All businesses had 'Closed' signs hanging in the windows and the barber pole was making only occasional and partial rotations from the cheap breezes of wind. Otis ran off the stragglers from the bar and, shortly thereafter, everyone had cleared from the boardwalks and intersection. The fireman was not tending to any train repairs, he and Sim Goodman were walking up Main Street. A group of carnies, after sipping around on bottles over at their convoy of wagons, brought up the tail end of the last to head north.

The gathering of waiting ladies, gentlemen, and children of all ages spilled over the edges of the road and extended from the tip-top of the hill down to Lots 14 and 16. Bosc and crew continued to hold the flood at bay while Murchison, Satterfield, Sherrod, and Reverend Jessup walked past the long line of baby crepe myrtles and to the front drive of Twenty-Five Main Street. Ross and Otis tailed closely behind, both in white mercantile employee vests. The walk was mostly silent until, once over the ridge, Satterfield commented while the group marveled at the lush grounds and the accompanying fruits of nature. The five men stayed just off the steps, admiring the quiet and still landscape, while Murchison went to the back door to give it a knock.

"Change 'em!" Duley called out as he peeled back a shade and peeked outside through the window.

Ross and Otis, following in Murchison's tracks, made a quick stop at the shed for tools. From their time lingering around the grounds, the two had a decent idea about changing the holes out. Both had come to hanging out at the grounds before and after their shifts, with Sam mandating that they loiter only on the back porch. They worked so much that they never had time to get more than a hole in, so they hadn't been playing a whole lot with the new three hole minimum. Shooting the bull with Duley on the back porch and at the bar, Ross and Otis had picked up plenty of knowledge on the work that was taking place.

The group of six set out to make a walk-through of the golfing holes, and inspection began at the first tee with the men gathering in a huddle for discussion. Murchison was the one overruled, three to one, in the decision-making process. Ross pulled the two blue, wooden markers from the edge of the short grass and moved them back eight feet to the elected spot. The game would begin with the first hole stretched to make the shot over the slough as long as possible, from the very back part of the tee box.

The group had a pleasant walk down the fairway, although each man chose a different path. The smell of fresh-cut grass and a charming day were soaked in more than anything was inspected. Along the way, Murchison picked a blade of grass and inserted it between his teeth. A sure sign that he had a dose of nervousness in his mind. They all lined up to walk the bridge over the full-to-the-brim slough and to the square-shaped first green. Ross cautioned that they should all keep their footprints on the playing surface as few and faint as possible. On the fringe of the green, there was another huddle for brief discussion. Then, using a handy tool Duley had made up, Otis cut a new hole in the right front corner. A yard away from either edge. Ross removed the wooden plug from the old hole and placed it in the new one, then smoothed the edges with gentle fingers. Otis filled in the old hole with the cylinder of earth that came from the new one and then, leveled it out with several taps of the boot. Reverend Jessup watched closely and when all was deemed ready for play, he posted the flagstick.

As the men walked on, Satterfield called out. "One stroke lost if a ball goes into the water and cannot be played."

"Sure thing." replied Reverend Jessup. "Same rule applies for Brown Cat Thicket."

"If one goes in there, one is added to get them out, and three will be the next one." Sherrod stated.

"That's right." Satterfield confirmed.

The men were at the N°. 2 tee box and decided on the middle section of that space as the spot for relocating the two blue markers to each east and west edge. Then, they walked on down and without much discussion, the routine was followed, and a new hole was placed in the dead center of the bean-shaped N°. 2 green.

"All set here." Otis said, as he raised from a knee.

Ross checked over the work, adding a couple of taps with his sole. All men agreed and, after another look around, Reverend Jessup posted the second flagstick with an affirmative nod to Murchison. "All set." he said.

Work moved to N°· 3 and with no vote, only a brief discussion while they were on their way, markers were placed at the very back quadrant of the rectangle. This was further back than ever before. On the way to the third green, there were compliments galore. Sherrod and Satterfield talked of the beauty of the place, and went back and forth with some specifics on the challenging nature of the layout. Sherrod said it was a world class set of holes, the best he had ever laid eyes on. "Every golfer should come here to play." he said. Reverend Jessup commented on the sheer beauty, as well as the inspiring and creative work of the oak tree.

Murchison was proud walking the last stretch and as his feet moved through the fine green grass of the fairway, he had the notion that day was the best Merit had ever seen. His chin was proudly raised, though he was preoccupied for the moment and nervously wordless. Chewing on a blade of grass, he took a moment to wish for the judge's presence and shed a tear while considering the thought of his dear friend missing out on something that he would have truly enjoyed. As they approached the third green and Murchison walked elbow to elbow with the other dark suited men, he looked back and listened to the anxious noise coming over Dead Horse Hill. Then, said a silent prayer for a young man's triumph.

It was decided that the hole on N°. 3 would be placed at the back, left part of the green. All the way down the slope and a near impossible reach from any spot on the fairway. The changing out of the hole routine, vote included, went off without a hitch and the final flagstick was posted. As the grounds had been deemed ready for play, The Whammer, closely followed by Munroe, could be seen making his way through the front gate of the golfing club. Murchison whistled up to Bose and gave a wave, signaling to open the passage.

The Whammer and Munroe walked up on the official talk of the four men, now gathered at the N°. 1 Tee Box. After looking down the chute, over the water, and at the No. 1 flag, the tallest and biggest eyes appeared dazed and caught up in the equation of how to maneuver through the lush grounds. The big guy was gazing around in his own world and failed to respond to questions from Satterfield. He looked befuddled and with clouded aim. The bully had momentarily lost the edge in his attitude and obviously any other conscious sense.

"Whammer!" Munroe vaulted the big guy back into reality, "I do belief dis da goodest lookin' golf grounds we's eva been at. Ain't it?"

"Hell no." replied The Whammer. "What in tarnation are you talking about, Munroe? This dump? I've seen better grounds at the bottom of my coffee cup. Look at the pig sty down here. What is that?" he said as he nodded toward the slough.

Satterfield, Sherrod, and Murchison all gave a quick roll of the eyes and had even more quickly dismissed the comments. Murchison nodded at Reverend Jessup, a nod that rolled toward The Whammer. The preacher man stepped forward with the grace of a lion tamer.

"Yes, sir. Reverend Lassiter Jessup of Leonard Methodist Episcopal Church." The minister introduced himself, then shook hands with The Whammer. If you ever saw Reverend Jessup holding The Bible you would know that he had very large hands, though it didn't look like it during that handshake.

"The hometown boy is the one needing the prayer, mister minister." The Whammer said. Munroe cackled and the big boss echoed that.

"Blessed be us all." replied Reverend Jessup. "Sir, per the club rules, a fee of a dollar per man required for play. You and your bag man." he stated.

"Awe hell!" said The Whammer. "Put your pocket change in the man's collection plate, Munroe." The Whammer turned to Munroe and watched him count out four bits. "Eight, Munroe." he demanded. "You think I'm carrying any change in my pocket. I'm about to play a dang round of golf."

Munroe handed over eight shiny quarters, of which were passed to Murchison. Murchison looked the preacher in the eye and nodded, as the member fees were handed over. "Per hole." Murchison whispered.

"Also, Sunday rate is a dollar per hole. You can pay for the set three. Any extras, there won't be a charge." Reverend Jessup informed The Whammer, and stepped away like he knew the man and his side kick were going to need a moment to sort things out.

"You heard the man, Munroe." said The Whammer.

Munroe put both his hands in his front pockets and began digging around.

"Don't tell me you ain't got no cash Munroe. What, did you burn all of that Houston money on wine?" The Whammer was gritting his teeth and growled the words. "Yardley!" he called out. A man that was wearing a fine suit and had been inconspicuously hovering in the background took several quick steps while reaching inside his coat. The man pulled a pocketbook and handed over three crisp dollar bills. "Are we all set with the B.S.? The Whammer asked Reverend Jessup.

"Bible study was at ten o'clock this morning, young man." Reverend Jessup replied.

Murchison accepted the rest of the money and left to get with Ross and Otis, then the three rushed over to stop the invasion at the entrance gate.

"Grab that bag, Munroe." The Whammer said, "Let's go down here and putt a few."

"I suppose that would be fine." said Sherrod.

"It sure is." The Whammer called out as he walked off the first tee, then started down the slight slope of the fairway. Munroe hung in his hip pocket.

"The other player will be entitled to do the same." Reverend Jessup called out with a smirk. The Whammer never looked back.

Sherrod and Satterfield both gave an assuring nod and a smile, after they peeked over to make sure The Whammer was not looking.

"Stand firm. We are behind you Reverend." offered Sherrod, moments later once the men felt comfortable in speaking and not being heard.

Murchison stood tall in front of the bustling convention that was resonantly blanketing Main Street and still filtering over the hill. He raised both hands in the air so as to seem even taller and to gain control of the noise spilling out from the increasing press of people. This act did not accomplish much beyond an immediate eyeshot, so the tall man stood up on the fence rail and climbed another one higher, grabbing the tall sign post for balance. He paused, taking in the moment as he looked over the parade that was coming in. A proud smile was showing, one that came with a feeling like no other that had surfaced in years. Once again, there were immediate thoughts to Judge Merit and what he would think of it all. Golfing was probably the one thing that the pair had never, not once, discussed. An internal laugh bellowed as he considered the game of golf driving it all, and what the thoughts would be on that considering the Judge's newly revealed playing talents.

Murchison put the wonders and memories aside and turned back to his serious-business face as the last groups, followed a clip back by the carnies, were closing in on the mass. He put his right hand up in the air, left one still grasping the post, and said, "Welcome, folks. It is great to have everyone gathered here today. It's a fine day and it's going to be one hell of a competition. First off, a grand fourth of July to all!" he exclaimed. There were hollers and hoorays and, after a moment, Murchison waved his hand higher to gain back the attention. "Listen, here. These are the spectator rules." Calls for quiet could be heard going out to the back of the pack. "Number one, stay off the tees, fairways, and greens. In other words, the short grass. Stay off the short grass." he said in a stern tone. "As we move about the course from hole to hole, it may be necessary to cross over a fairway. If so, this will be done in a designated area so as to not trample all over the good grass that is primarily used for playing. Ross and Otis, here, will direct you to those pathways. Bose Gentry is here, if extra guidance is needed. The rule that comes before the first rule is that you must keep complete quiet while a player is evaluating and playing a golf shot. Bose will address, accordingly, any non-abiders."

Once again, chatter started amongst the crowd and Murchison regained control with a wave and a raise of the voice. More calls for quiet went out.

"Listen up, listen up." Murchison said, "Give the golfers, and the golf balls, plenty of space. Even when they are in the tall grass. We don't want anyone hurt. Also, please, maintain respectful behavior at all times. With that, welcome to The Judge Merit Golfing Club!"

Murchison raised an open hand to the sign above which incited an explosion of fanfare as people of all makes, models, sizes, and ages began to pour through the front gate on a day that had the freshly groomed grounds looking as fine as ever and that refreshing smell of fresh-cut grass abounding in the air. If you have ever seen water run down a hill, that is what it was like. Against the flow, The Whammer and Munroe were making their way back up the N°. 1 fairway and were immediately surrounded by a rowdy troop of admirers as they reached the left side rough.

Reverend Jessup, Satterfield, and Sherrod had moved to the back porch and were discussing any matters that could potentially come up, when Duley stepped out from the house with Sam's golf bag slung over his shoulder.

After a nod to the gentlemen, Duley stood quite shocked when he noticed the magnitude of the onslaught of people. Ones in the know of the game went quickly to secure a spot either around the first green or first tee box. Along the right side of Hole N$^{o.}$ 1, there was quickly a deep stretch of a crowd that filled the entire space between the fairway and the fence. Dewberries were getting squished. It was the same thing on the opposite side of the fairway, except thirty or forty deep with the gallery thinning out, for the meantime, as it reached the green. No dewberries had grown in on the left side. Those wanting to avoid the bustle, and many of the older and elderly, situated themselves as an amoeba under and around the Jackson Oak. The small willow trees out back were the popular location for those that were still wagering, and between there and the first tee it was packed thick with people. In the shade on the north side of the house, the carnies found themselves a place to pass around their bottles. Murchison arrived to the back steps and ordered Otis and Ross to clear a pathway for the players to make their way to N$^{o.}$ 1.

The Whammer bumped his belly into the tight wad of fans and made his way to the first tee, then began taking practice swings that were mired over by everyone surrounding. A sizzling whoosh came from each draw and the same, though heavily multiplied, with each thrust. He stood with a closed stance and knees moved a notch from together as he rared back to cock the hammer. There was an odd twist of the hips and large torso, then all hell came to be as a sleek and big-headed iron club was driven way around, past his middle, then onward like a powerful machine, through, and over his right shoulder. He was a southpaw and the powerful upper-body was, no doubt, doing the work. The man would step back and spit on the tee box every three or four swings. Then, after grinds into the well-manicured and freshly trimmed grass with his shiny brown shoes, he would have another go with another series of big whoofs. Munroe stood patiently, off to the side, scoping out the grass, shining the putter, and eyeing the distance of $N^{o.}$ 1. Reverend Jessup, Satterfield, and Sherrod made their way down the pathway and readied themselves behind the tee box, well away from The Whammer.

Waiting at the back steps, Murchison put his arms wide to secure some room from the traffic. Folks were scattered in clusters everywhere, giving the poor grass a beating like none other. Though, thankfully, most of the trampling was taking place in areas not so desired by a golf shot. The breezes gently swayed the thin branches high in the oak tree and the flag down at $N^{o.}$ 1 hung undisturbed under the undeterred sun that was showering its bright light and sweltering heat over all. Rich folk's colored patterns could be spotted in clusters throughout the jagged assemblage, mostly on the front rows and in the prime spots. Umbrellas dotted the drove and the more populous dark clothed portion of the turnout filled in around. Littered about were men in suits standing together, but away, as they smoked their cigarettes, cigars, and pipes, in the spare spaces. In the vacant areas behind the strategically gathered crowds, were children laughing and playing about. Chase looked to be the favorite pastime amongst the young ones. Older kids pretended to hit golf balls with their make-believe golfing sticks, then rejoiced as winning long shots trundled into the far-off hole. All the people everywhere made the grounds seem like the most festive place on earth. Quite contrary to the way it was preferred for golfing.

Quiet stillness absorbed for a brief moment and eyes were closed while the necessary parts of focus were summoned to. The knob to the back door turned and Sam stepped into the chaotic spectacle flooding his normally quiet paradise. There was a small burst of cheer with the appearance at the steps. A little hollering and a round of claps were followed by a bit more. Murmurs came to and then sounds lessened to the dissonant hum of continued ambling and jockeying for spots. An enamored Sam, fedora tucked tight, head down, and both hands in the back pockets of his Sunday best navy-blue pants, took two steps and was directly greeted with a firm and welcome handshake by Murchison. The right hand reached out and the left hand stayed in its pocket with thumb and fingers fidgeting the best ball he had in stock. One that had been sized up, identified as a gem, broken in, wrapped in a rag, and saved back in his top dresser drawer.

"Good to go?" Murchison asked.

Sam gave an affirming nod while eyeing a way to start off the walk to the N°· 1 tee box.

"Give those newspaper boys a hell of a story."

Sam received a pat on the back and stepped in behind Murchison, who hollered ahead with arms waving to, "Clear the way!" Sammy, Sambo, Sammer. Boy, kid, kiddo. Encouragement came from many locals that Sam had no idea even knew his name, maybe they didn't. Not that he was hearing a peep. The endearing fare was there but tuned out as he turned right to take the familiar, though dramatically different and now significantly narrowed pathway. Duley followed and then got caught up, having to patiently wait for the pathway to widen in accommodation of the J.A. Folgers coffee can trailing off his left side.

Sam's head was down but raised up when he knew it was Hopper Hackman calling out in the rugged old voice, "Swat with that hickory stick all you got, my boy." In the immediate congregation, the golfer found and sent an assuring nod to the old eyes. Sam turned back to find Duley and, during the quick glance back, did not. He kept on walking. Duley was back there and coming. Forward, The Whammer's golf club appeared in a blur then disappeared in an even more blurry state from high above the heads of the surrounding bodies. Appeared, then disappeared. Appearing, then disappearing. Again, reappearing as Sam made the steps down a partially cleared channel of rising clammer.

At the first tee box, Sherrod and Satterfield were ushering back the anxious incher-uppers in the herd when Sam arrived to the meanest of looks. The Whammer stopped his swinging and started a stare that seemed like he had a bone to pick. The two men stepped together like at the start of a prize fight and Reverend Jessup stepped between. Duley and Munroe each hung at their respective player's back. Murchison, Satterfield, and Sherrod gathered around. Ross and Otis took over crowd control and near silence had fallen when Reverend Jessup pulled an 1875 Liberty Head twenty-dollar gold coin from his front pocket.

"Gentleman, three holes. Winner takes all, one-thousand dollars. We will play one extra hole, as necessary for a tie break." Reverend Jessup said, as he looked back and forth between the two contestants. "Now, I think the three of us have a clear understanding of the rules of the game. Are there any clarifications that need to be made?"

"No, sir, Reverend." Sam replied.

"Let's get on with this show." responded The Whammer.

"You, sir, are from out of town and will make the call on the coin flip. Winner of the flip chooses to go first or second. Heads or tails. Call it in the air." Reverend Jessup directed toward The Whammer, as he flipped the coin in the palm of his hand showing either side. After both sides were shown to Sam, the coin was tossed above all of the heads and in midflight, "Tails!" called out The Whammer. The coin came falling to a tumble and took a short spin in the green grass. When examined closely by Reverend Jessup, "Heads it is." was shouted for all to hear. There was only a small amount of cheering and more sulking from those that were near. Murchison grinned. Reverend Jessup pointed to Sam.

"Second." Sam chose, then stepped to the back of the tee box, turned, and leaned into Duley.

It had become clear that The Whammer was going to hit first and excitement built rapidly across the golfing grounds.

"Hand me the new stick." Sam said.

"Not the broadstick?" Duley asked, puzzled as he handed over the new one and received no reply.

Sam rubbed the head of the JM Special like he was summoning up magical powers from within, and tried to relax as he stood by. The Whammer was eyeing down the pin and going back and forth with Munroe about a best strategy for the shot. Ross and Otis had the crowd in check and silenced, with help from Satterfield pitching in to get things where he wanted it. Reverend Jessup stepped up onto the tee, away from the Whammer. He raised his right hand and in a loud preacher voice spoke out, "Ladies and Gentleman, up first, all the way from the west coast, the hills of California, undefeated in golf play, the great Whammer!" There was loud cheer that rousted from further and further away and, in the end,

211

from a distance far beyond the reach of Reverend Jessup's introduction. The minister stepped back and took position near Sam. The Whammer, raring to go, grabbed a small can of sand from Munroe and kicked his back leg out as he bent to pour a half-inch hill between the tee markers. Fans looking to be amazed inched closer. All eyes were watching from everywhere, seeking a gigantic blast. Sam was thinking about nothing other than how the new golf stick was going to handle getting a ball over the water.

"What the hell is he doing with that sand?" Duley leaned over and whispered in Sam's ear.

"Watch here. It's part of the game, Duley." Sam whispered back, "We're going to need some, too, if we're going to make the slough."

Duley was looking perplexed and like he was fixing to run for sand. "I got it." Sam said, as he looked Duley's eyes to the pocket on the golf bag and then back to the action at the tee.

A shiny new gutty ball with a black insignia was handed to The Whammer, who placed it atop the sand tee. Munroe backed away. Another discharge of whooshes came from a final set of warmup swings. Again, everyone was impressed but this time no one reacted. There was a long stare at the N$^{o.}$ 1 flag, then The Whammer assumed his position off the golf ball. The iron was lined up, hips wiggled, there was a draw, and then fury was released. Screams, yells, and cheers went out but faded right away. Mouths were open and eyes were watching. The ball shot up like it was headed to the moon and before it started downward travel, Sam knew it was to the green and would be lucky to stop there. One could hear sighs and yells from across the water when the shot hit dead center of the green. Up by the tee, it was hard to make out what had happened. The ball was out of sight. Ahead, faint hearsay was starting and rumors flew up the golf hole as quick as the ball flew down. It was either in the hole or in Brown Cat Thicket, according to the chatter. Most, including The Whammer and Munroe, were leaning toward the thicket.

Sam stepped forward into the spotlight beneath the sky of blue and pulled his best ball from his back pocket. Duley followed and the two walked as far away from earshot as they could, while still staying on the tee box. Shoulder to shoulder and both staring at a tranquil flag, right front, Sam cleared his throat and lightly whispered, "What do you think about any gusts down there?"

"If you get over there to the right, liable to be something out of the hollow to blow it back short. There were light gusts churning out of there an hour ago." Duley whispered back.

Sam looked to the sun with a squint and back to the surface of the green. "Grass rolling good?" he spoke quietly.

"About like a burr haircut down there." Duley turned and quietly spoke into Sam's ear without breaking his stare-down for any sign of a gust. "That's exactly what just put the old beast back there at the mercy of Brown Cat."

A long while had passed since Sam let a ball escape into the thicket, though he stayed on top of being cautious. Same thing was true with the water.

"Going to have to get the ball up in the air to get it to stop easy down there, and this stick is feeling like it might be on the slim side of reaching home. Going to need that jar of sand." Sam said as he broke eyes from the green and stepped away for his practice swings.

"Sam, you don't think the old broadstick can give it a go? You said you fixed it." Duley whispered.

"I reckon it has one good shot in it, Duley. We'll worry about that when the time comes." Sam said, barely moving his lips and pausing before another swing.

Sam grabbed the sand from Duley and walked back to the tee marker, where he poured out his first ever sand tee. And, a perfect looking one at that. Duley grabbed the jar and dismissed himself to the side, "Get 'em, Sambo." he said. The golfer placed his savored ball and backed away.

"Ladies and Gentleman, the hometown boy. Everyone in five counties knows his passion and prowess in the game. By the looks of the place, he is a perfectionist." announced Reverend Jessup. The latter sentence at a lower volume level and directly to Sam, with a grin. There were small amounts of laughter from around and then the reverend continued, "From right here at The Judge Merit Golfing Club in Merit, Texas. A young prodigy, they say. Sam Stallings!" Applause came forth for a less-than share of time. Only sparse shouts and yells could be heard from the locals. Hopper Hackman gave out a loud and long whistle and Arwin Rank belted out a deep mumbled up something or other. Daisy Williamson clapped the longest, which caught a look from the corner of her father's eye. In hearing his name, Sam put two fingers on the brim of the fedora and gave a gentle nod as he stepped up to play his game.

The fedora was pulled down tight, followed by the eyes going to the hole and the mind setting off with its part of the work. Holding the unfamiliar JM Special in his right hand, he gave a tug on the right sleeve then switched the golf stick to the left hand and gave a better tuck to the left sleeve. There was a thought to Mr. Fair and hope for needed magic. Ross and Otis's hands went to the air and all fell silent. The world stopped as Sam stepped around to the right and about-faced to the flag that was still hanging undisturbed, down the way.

Hips cocked to the south, the right foot was slightly in front of his left and supported less weight. The shaft of the club hovered just above his right collarbone and the grip rested on his chest. Looking up from the ball, he kept his head still as he strained the eyes to begin a study. He was looking at a Hole N⁰· 1 that was going to play somewhat different today. The lie below, the stillness above, the desired right-curving flight path that would draw a ball close to the hole, and the tool to do it with were all under intense survey. "Give me all you got, Judge." Sam mouthed to himself without breath.

He twisted over the handle of the JM Special as he stepped back left, then mightily assumed his routine and bold statue of a golf stance. Movements were slowed, steady, and with purpose. A warrior under immense self-control and ready to meet the task at hand. Left foot a tick past its normal spot ahead of the right, for hope of even a small boost in distance. Standing tall with a bend at the knee and an easy lean forward at the waist. Back straight. Head perfectly aligned and perfectly focused. Eyes both looking left with an intense, undistracted, piercing stare that was dead on with the right front part of the green. To the collection of observers, Sam's eyes and their fixation, the smooth and well-practiced body movements, the very semblance of his being at that moment in time, cast a dauntless look that spoke to the becoming of a grand act. A champion-like aura was fully displayed, mouths opened, just a bit, and breathing slowed all around while wonderment of what was coming filled the spectator's minds.

The golf stick was clutched with arms extended and held with hands that were away from the body and below his waist. Left hand on top, right on bottom, and about an inch of space in between. Firm, but relaxed. Steadily, he placed the iron head beside the waiting ball. For a slight moment, he lifted his head and, again, sized up the small targeted space. Eyes were stalking like a bird of prey, then fell quickly back to the ball. There was the automatic feeling deep in his muscles and bones, which were now unconsciously controlled. Sam inhaled and breathing stopped.

A hint toward looser with his grip, the head of the golf club retreated as the chin rose a very small tick to his right. The right elbow bent and the left stayed straight, crossing his torso until the latter shoulder met chin height. The JM Special reached parallel to the short grass with the iron now placed off his left side and reaching toward the promised land. A magic blur hovered above the bony shoulders. At a moment of complete stillness, with every muscle in his body acutely enacted in a symphonic mission, Sam knew nothing except a pathway toward a miraculous destiny. All might was present in, and flowing rapidly through, each system of the body as all necessary components of the great game of golf stood ready to fly toward glory.

Abruptly yet smoothly, motion shifted in the opposite direction beginning with a slight jig forward at the hips. A slight nod for power, like that of a judge. The iron launched, in controlled chaos and appearing as though fresh out of forging, into an orbit around the soul of the master at hand. In an instant the air before his body rushed to find space, a whoosh led into the thwack, and a sizzle began as the jolted ball sprung from the sand with the speed and trajectory of a slightly upward bullet. A body twisted and left hurling to the aftermath of the act, effortlessly slowed to a pause near its moveable limits. Now at ease physically, the mind began its emotion-filled journey from that of a landscaper to a weatherman, a mathematician, a commanding general, a reverend. Sam stood as a hopeful bystander. All others in the grounds were judging and gave their opinion via escalating amazement as the ball left on a promising bead.

The sizzle faded and the ball grew darker and smaller as it rose toward the high blue curtain. Eyesight struggled to keep track of the sacred ball as the mighty soar faded right and toward home. Head held high with eyes peeled across the picturesque land, Sam wrestled with the powers that were becoming. The JM Special had dropped and rested on his left shoulder. The toe of his right boot was twisted into the grass as he stared into the distance for a sign of any kind. He relaxed and glanced at Duley to receive a confident and affirmative nod. The crowd from around the green sent up a cheer that went on longer than expected and bestowed a message that went along the lines of a savvy achievement.

As soon as the ball was hit, The Whammer and Munroe started their waltz down the middle of the fairway. Sam tucked his golf stick into the bag with a clank on the Folgers can and pulled out the putter, then began his walk to the first verdict with an underlying grin of a smile. At the hollering insistence of all men playing official roles, the noisy herd finally filtered down the left side rough and, good golly, rained down around the green. Nobody bothered to address the mob of rule breakers that packed the fairway for an over-the-water view of the upcoming drama, there was nowhere else for them to go. "To heck with it." Murchison said, in noticing that Bose and his crew had obviously dipped out and were up to who knows what. Those in the very back of the audience had no chance of catching a glimpse of the putts and chose to early-bird a better watching spot at the next hole.

Sam's ball had curved in and rolled past the hole coming to rest on the last inch of the right side of the green, pin high. After a minute of searching, The Whammer's ball was located a yard into the thicket and three paces left of the hole. Players and caddies began sizing up their next shots.

Sam bent his knees and closed one eye. "Look at that from back here, Duley. Ball is going to draw a hair left wouldn't you say."

"You know it, Sambo."

Sam took a few gentle practice swings, then stood back in the rough to watch with legs crossed at the ankles and weight on the putter. Duley laid down the bag and squatted to get an eye on The Whammer's shot as it made its venture over the putting surface.

Eleven hands surrounding the green went up in a call for silence. Awkwardly crouched and opened up to the target, The Whammer's wedge club hovered above a ball that was situated in a tangled mess. Odds were stacked against him and you could see it in his face. Munroe stood behind the hole grasping the flagstick, ready and alert to pull it. "Munroe, coming your way." The Whammer said, as he shuffled his feet away from the shot and then back into his opened stance. He moved his wad of knuckles down a jig and waggled the iron. Reflexing to a clinch, the arms moved as the wrists forced the back swing. Knees flexed forward and hesitation mounted in an instant. The meek strike sent the ball out, up, quickly back down, and rolling on a direct wire into the flagless hole for a 2. The audience exhausted a roar of whooping & hollering to amazed barks of obscure sounds, told-you-so talk, clapping, laughter, reflection, and finally silence.

Pressure on, Sam bent at the waist for another close look at the task before him. He turned and addressed the ball, though stayed inches back for another quick stint of gentle practice swings. He eyed the ball, then the hole, then the ball, and removed his right hand from the putter. He wiped the sweat from his palm and then used both hands to place the face of the putter beside the ball. Feet were adjusted to comfortable, sturdy, and in-tune. Eyes left the ball and went along the three-foot distance to the hole. Back to the ball. To the hole. To the ball. Arms hung straight and body was still. Ready was achieved and the pendulum moved back, then forth. The ball was sent on a slow, straight, then left-bending roll that dunked beneath the playing surface like a rabbit diving home.

The fedora had been tucked, and Sam was making steps to the hole when an interjection of mediocre acclaim chimed in. Nothing like the all hails that The Whammer's had just received. He snagged his ball, handed the putter to Duley, and was ready for the next one. Reverend Jessup marked a score of 2 for each player on the back of a folded over church bulletin and tucked it back into his shirt pocket, then quick stepped it over to help with corralling everyone to N°· 2.

The nearly enveloped tee box was the beginning of a long, people-lined alley that widened as it stretched south along both sides of the fairway. A group of betting men were spreading out deep along the right side of the fairway, each stepping out with a foot to mark their wager on The Whammer's shot. "Closest without guessing over!" called out a man with a top hat and a fistful of cash. "One dollar per man!" he shouted while walking the line and collecting the pot. A growing crowd already filled the space around the green and Murchison sent Ross on down to, "Keep 'em off!" Most that were under the tree had vacated the shade to creep closer to the activity, only the group of older and elderly folks remained. Not a soul was up by the house.

The Whammer grabbed a humongous-headed driver from Munroe and then teed his ball. "See you when you catch up." he said, laughing and turning back. After chuckles from some of the audience members, calls for silence went out. The chubby jowls hurled a wad of spit as he waggled the big wooden head of his golf club. Then he spit, again, as he stepped around to the ball and had a quick glance down range. In an instant, there was a draw and all hell was unleashed. The beating echoed through the grounds as the golf ball bulleted forward, becoming invisible to the eyes that had, a moment ago, been closest. The ball reappeared as it bounced up on a forceful forward roll that would carry on with shorter and shorter bounces, until it finally came to rest way up on the right side of the fairway. A brash effort from the strong man left something close to child's play for the second shot. Cheers were loud, boisterous, and expressive of stunned amazement. The youngest carney of the bunch won the distance wager and had a hand in the air when he snagged the cash from inside the top hat. Suddenly, all eyes shifted from that celebration and there was no need to quiet the crowd for Sam.

Concentration was at its peak and Sam reiterated in his brain that this was not a contest of which man could hit a ball the hardest, or the furthest. The Whammer could have all his glory with the Hail Mary's. The bothersome fact was that any slack in the tee shot would likely leave too much distance to the green. On Hole N° 1, the JM Special seemed to carry just shy of the broadstick's capabilities, thus requiring a more powerful stroke. Sam eyed his preferred target zone, the left middle of the N° 2 fairway around eighty yards shy of the green, as he took paces forward. The golf ball was spotted. No sand tee, as was typical with Sam. He took a moment, visualized the shot, and released tension with swipes at the air. A deep inhale was apparent as he readied. Routine took over and as a northbound wind gust from over Dead Horse Hill, Sam unleashed his own kind of hell on a golf ball. Lining forward, low but rising, and descending straight at the landing zone, the ball suddenly ran into Mother Nature and flailed left as it quickly dropped and stopped near a hundred yards shy of The Whammer.

Trouble brewed and wasn't finished, and everyone knew it. Those rooting for The Whammer were smiling, laughing, carrying on, and already sewing things up as they walked faster and ahead of everyone else to add to those already surrounding the green. There was soreness in Sam's walk. He and Duley brought up the rear of everything, after Sam had killed time digging around in his bag.

Duley posted the bag feet behind the ball and looked to Sam, who was standing with eyes that had not left the green since they were stepped off the tee. The two were flanked by Reverend Jessup and Sherrod, though stood alone in the openness while pondering the next play. There was no crowd immediately surrounding and a first chance at a peaceful moment was had. Something other than people could be heard, a pair of mockingbirds starting to bicker in the thicket.

After silence and nothing said by Sam, Duley spoke up.

"What do you think here, Sambo? All those people sure make the thing look small up there. Don't it?"

"It's the same old golf holes, Duley. Boy, that wind gutted us though." Sam said.

"Your shiny new one is looking like it will barely cut it. I'm going to tell you the broadstick is the one here." Duley voted.

"That broadstick is not going to be able to go here. We have to play our cards right, Duley. Money in the bank would be nice here, but we're going to hold our ace for now."

Sam reached back to Duley, who handed over the JM Special. He licked a thumb and rubbed it on the face of the golf stick, then the body turned perpendicular to the hole. A proper grip in place and a casual stance, Sam took three easy swings with no pause in between.

"The green was feeling a little soft this morning, Duley. You reckon that ground has hardened up in this sunshine?" Sam inquired.

"Pretty good, I imagine." Duley answered.

"That's what I'm thinking. That ball was fast-moving on the last green. Put this one up in the air too much and it's not going to get there. And, we definitely can't have another gust cost us."

"Don't get yourself caught up in that sand." Duley expressed, without an ounce of acknowledgment coming back to him from Sam.

Sam had moved to address the ball. Eyes had still yet to budge from the target.

"Nail it, Sambo." Duley said.

Sam, seeking calm and the moment of ready, was an impulse away from pulling the trigger when he pulled up and stepped away. In reply came a release of breath from all around, then chatter that never built past a spat of hushes.

"That dadgum wind is going to eat this round alive. When is the last time you saw two breezes come over the ridge?" Sam asked.

"Hell, I ain't never caught even one." Duley replied.

"I've seen a hell of a gust, once. The day I bought the place." Sam looked over his shoulder and had a long gaze around what open ground there was. He looked to the house, at the oak tree, deep into the thicket, then back to the stick in hand as he pulled off the fedora and wiped the sweat from his brow.

"Breeze feels nice, huh Duley?" Sam said, replacing his hat and tucking it tight.

"Knocking one up there in the hole would feel better." Duley replied.

Sam smiled and gave a small laugh as he went through more practice swings, then there was another look back to the caddy. Duley gave a small smile and a nod that tried to steer Sam back to business. Sam took one more swing and then looked ahead. Everyone's eyes, including The Whammer, were glued. Murchison had the most concerning stare. Otis and Ross had their backs to the golfing, hands up to the audience and staring over their shoulders.

"Ol' Otis and Ross are going to rot their arms off keeping 'em up like that all afternoon." Sam said.

Duley snickered and Sam laughed enough for it to be seen by all. The Whammer smarted off something about monkey business, which brought a hardened stare and a step forward from Murchison.

"Everything's going here, Duley." Sam said as he readdressed the ball and stared down the green and flag. He inched up on the balls of his feet and slightly tilted his head to the right. The JM Special cut back and forth through still air, colliding with the ball in a potent manner that sent it upward and appearing to be in harmony with success. "Felt good." Sam barely uttered. "Dern thing, felt good." he said louder, as the ball fell into the tall grass on the front side of the sand bunker.

Cuss words went out from both Sam and Duley. The two spats continued, though the volume levels were dropped to zero, as the two young men walked their way on up the fairway to stand short of The Whammer and his position. Sam made well certain that Reverend Jessup never heard a word of the rant.

Munroe had his finger pointed and wiggling around in the air like he was drawing out a diagram. The Whammer had his wedge in hand and was leaned over at the shoulders, listening to every word, and watching every wisp of the finger like he was being educated. Munroe flattened his palm down and moved it away from his body in a rainbow shape, then pulled six golf clubs up over his shoulder and stepped back. After a spit in Murchison's direction, The Whammer squared up to the ball and both knees moved inward. His body hunched into a slight crouch and the knees dipped when the wedge drew back. The forward movement was flung lazily, howbeit sufficient, and the golf ball looped into the air. Thousands of eyes followed the easy knock as it sank down as fast as it had gone up. A short roll left for the next shot to be just above the hole, with only another two feet of child's play remaining.

The cheers went on and on. Those who didn't know any better might have thought that the ball made it in the hole. Many were calling the contest 'over' and others were, right away, swearing down that notion. The commotion riled up even more as The Whammer followed his shot with Whammer-sized smiles and waves to the crowd. After bending to replace the ball with a shiny penny, pointing and winking at members of his entourage, he then walked behind the green and turned an ugly stare down to the two young men standing near the front-side sand trap.

All fell quiet and Sam pulled the chipper from Duley's hand. Duley stepped back, laid down the bag, then took quick steps up the short slope to the flagstick. Sam stepped way to the side and with an informal, open stance let loose thwacks through the tall grass. He stepped back behind the ball, squinted his left eye, and with his right, eyed a straight line between the ball and the hole. The distance of turf between the ball and the ideal landing spot was memorized and known well. Eyes went to the ball and feet were placed, ball now in line with the back foot. The right hand placed the face of the chipper directly behind the ball and the left hand snugged up a pant leg as the knees were bent. The left hand joined the right. Fingers and knuckles were adjusted and wrists were twisted clockwise a tick and a tock.

The golf stick retreated and a mellow whoosh could be heard as iron brushed through the rough grass. Precision directed the downward swipe that popped the golf ball up and to the exact inside edge of the green. The ball short-hopped, skidded, and continued to roll toward the hole in a veering right manner. Noise was teetering on the brink of a boom. Stillness was locked. Mouths were open. Eyes were big. Revolutions slowed as the shiny ball neared the nest, and a whole bunch of air was sucked out of the place. If you could split a hair, that is about the amount of earth that kept the shot from falling down. Sam's knees broke their lock and the head of the chipper made another swipe through the despised, thick grass.

"Keep with it. The big man walks onto the putting surface and that golf ball is likely to fall." Duley said, with one eye locked on the ball and the other looking around, waiting for any type of force to bless a movement of some kind. Everyone looked to that ball when they saw the big feet of The Whammer step on the green.

Sam stuffed the chipper into the bag and pulled out the putter, then turned back for a quick look at the still-hanging ball before he walked around the sand trap and on the green. Any applause for the effort was apparently forgotten in shock. Sam grimaced with a close look at the miniscule left over, tapped in for a 4, and then moved over to the east side of the green.

The Whammer casually smiled and gave a wave to a group of single women as he walked to his duck soup. Munroe grabbed the flagstick. Ross' and Otis' hands were down. Sherrod and Satterfield raised theirs and waved for silence. Before quiet, The Whammer put all his heavy weight on one foot, barely kicked the other one out behind, leaned, and tapped in for a 3. Loud praise cascaded down to fading noise as the congested crowd began shifting over to No. 3. Reverend Jessup marked the scorecard, put it back in his pocket, and then called out, "The Whammer is one stroke ahead. One hole to play."

Murchison and Sherrod hustled over and cut a pathway for Sam and Duley through the jam that was barreling to the third hole. Folks were trying to get to this side of the tee box and folks were trying to get to that side of the fairway. A jumble of people at the back wised up and went the other way around the oak tree in favor of a close-up spot around the green. On the walk over, it was elbow to elbow. So much so, that neither golfer could be seen in the mix. Not even The Whammer.

Finally, the oversized man found his way onto the tee box and was handed the big driver. There was a frenzy of wind stealing whoofs as the big body swung the golf club back and forth in preparation of a long ball. Sam and Duley were behind, near cheek to cheek, talking quietly, and could both feel the air breaking. Satterfield warned everyone back a step and everybody took one, except for Sam and Duley. Those two didn't budge. People were squished in around the tee and down the inside curve of the No. 3 fairway. The collection of folks along the outside bend kept stringing longer and longer, as more spectators filed down the line for a better view of the landing area and the two second shots.

Hands went up. The Whammer stepped forward, placed his club, turned, then ripped one deep down the right side. Driver pointed up over his right shoulder, he twisted left urging the shot to bend around. The golf ball hopped, skipped, and ran through the fairway like a spooked cottontail, coming to rest a length past the end of the long string of onlookers. Way on down there.

"Blast off!" somebody had called out as the ball was struck.

"Holy shit!" said a drunk carney, as the ball sailed. He was the only one that had stayed caught up, the most rugged looking one out of the bunch, and was unknowingly separated from the others for the moment. The others were just now making their way over from counting up the young one's money at Hole Nᵒ· 2.

Applause broke all around, though dallied to stay more customary than on the previous smash. The Whammer pointed his club upward, urged the crowd on in acknowledging his feat, and stepped back in a direct pathway toward Sam.

Sam kept his head down, sidestepped the man without looking, and grabbed the driver from his bag. The tight gathering of people began to loosen around the tee box, so Murchison called for all to cool it and to be quiet. This was quickly seconded by Sherrod with his deep and bold voice.

Sam looked down the fairway, quiet and still.

Duley lightly spoke out, "Good to go, Sambo?"

Sam moved and placed his golf ball atop a small, fine-looking, fresh patch of green grass. He tapped the bottom of the driver's head on the ground as he raised up, and then gave a quick look down the memorized and pre-chosen pathway. In position and feeling ready to go after it, he went with his swing and sent a nice ball tucked snugly around the inside dogleg. The shot began fading left as it cleared the turn and followed near parallel to the cut line in the grass, on the desirable side. The fruits of the effort came to rest in the fairway, just out of the shadow of the Jackson Oak. By the time Sam arrived to the ball, it was sitting in the shade.

The Whammer's ball was deemed to lie further from the hole, so he lined up with his ball first. Out in the middle of the hot sun, he was surround by twenty or thirty rows of people in every direction except for dead ahead. Satterfield and

Murchison were staying to the middle at this point and were not so prompt in helping to provide any relief from the tight grouping of people. Munroe barked out lines of demanding orders in his gravely old voice. A portion of the gallery may have turned against the duo right then, as there were boos and rants about the spout. Munroe went right back at the hecklers, with choice explicatives, and directly received more smearing. Satterfield tried to shout and wave it all off with no immediate impact. The Whammer was trying to undistractedly keep his attention ahead on the green. A short scuffle of words continued on, but ceased when the big guy turned around. He had elbows up and was scanning the crowd like he was looking for someone to razz and rap on. Then, he leaned into Munroe's ear.

"Gonna be a tough one here, Munroe." The Whammer said quietly. "What do you got for me?"

"Lesss see haar, boss man." Munroe replied, then shunned the smart-remarking and looked down range. "Gunna haf ta seat her down quick der on dis close side of da green, ova dis right side. She trickle down der to da hole."

"How far?" asked The Whammer.

"Ya at niney yawds to da pin, boss man. Looking at sitty-five for da landing spot."

The Whammer, again, selected his wedge from the display that Munroe presented and then received affirmation from the caddy, "Dat'll do, boss." Munroe stepped back and gave an ugly and mean look to a small section of crowd, then waved over to Satterfield. "Hows 'bout some clearance 'round haar, mista official?" he blurted out.

"Folks!" Satterfield called over. The people stepped back in peace and quiet. All eyes went to The Whammer, as he began his physical preparations with a dozen or so repeated swings that were bookended by mouthfuls of saliva being hocked to the ground. The big guy addressed, then backed off the ball and did the same spitting and swinging routine. He pulled a pinch of grass and tossed it in the air, then addressed the ball again. Backing off, again, he came together with Munroe. They were both sweating like a pat of butter on a hot biscuit, and apparently not just because of the Texas heat.

Meanwhile, Sam and Duley stood shoulder to shoulder in the shade of the Jackson Oak, facing The Whammer but mostly looking at the green. Sam had arms and ankles crossed, and seemed unmoved at what was coming up. Duley had one hand tucked in his armpit and was chewing his fingernails on the other. A bigger than fair majority of the gallery had gone around the fairway with The Whammer. The next biggest bunch of people was a stretch that started up around the opposite side of the green and spread on up the slope, nearly all the way to the house. Newspapermen and the photographers shuffled through the heaps and stacked together on the strip of rough between the slough and the green, cameras posted and ready for action. Sherrod cleared the crowd from the small area on the south side of the green, they were blocking Sam's view of the green. Those under the oak tree were allowed to stay. Underneath, the elderly women were sitting in a line of wooden chairs, with husbands standing behind them and grandchildren hopping around. Small groups of rich people held their umbrellas and their ground just inside the shade and on the line of the small area of which they had been asked to vacate. Neither Sherrod nor the Reverend pushed the issue. The carnies, they had met up on the back side of the oak and were still passing and swigging.

"You ever think you'd have this many people out here, Sam?" Duley asked.

Sam looked over to see the small group under the tree, gave a nod to the old folks, then pulled the JM Special from the bag. The golf club was held like a cane, upside down, and the brim of the fedora was lifted. "I never thought any of this would happen, Duley." He looked across the fairway at The Whammer, who was still sizing up his shot, and continued. "Did you ever think you would be working at some golfing grounds? Playing more than working?" he said. They both cut up, and that in turn got the gray-haired men and women laughing, and the grandchildren, and then the carnies. Sherrod gave a smile, as did Reverend Jessup, who eventually laughed after everyone else had stopped. And, none of them even knew what the first laughs were about. The nearby rich people did not laugh, only stared with straight faces like there was nothing to be laughing about. No one else in the entire crowd caught wind of anything and remained waiting patiently on The Whammer, who was still eyeballing the obstacles before him.

Duley got straight-faced fast when he looked down and saw the choice golf stick in Sam's hand. "Sam you ain't going to crack at it with the broadstick? You have to put this one down or else we're done."

"Hold on, Duley. Let's see here." Sam said. He then pulled a toothpick out of his front pocket, snapped it in half, and put part between his teeth.

The Whammer addressed his golf ball and was shaking his hips like he was on the way to a dance floor. The big and round eyes looked up to the hole, then back down. Knees bent and came together. A twist, and the ball was sent up along with a fist-sized chunk of green grass and black earth. The airborne ball carried backspin and was hurtling on line with the hole, though showing like it was deemed to fall short. In the descent, the trajectory picked up a slight and building curve in the moments before touch down. A hop took the golf ball to the right side of the crest, and a slow roll continued it toward the north edge. The roll kept on to be stopped by the strip of fringe, six paces past where it had first hit. The Whammer's shot came to rest twenty feet shy of the hole and wasn't exactly on smooth grass.

Enthusiastic fans had scurried, a rambunctious clique ran trying to keep pace with The Whammer's ball, to swarm around the green like flies on honey. Wrangling all of the commotion back required the efforts of six fellows, and then some. Ainsworth and Mr. Dell chimed in with reprimands from separate locations on the grounds. The playing area had indeed shrunk, yet just inches of it mattered at this point in the game.

Sam turned and gave one nod to Duley. That was all of the further discussion about which stick would be used for the upcoming shot. Duley backed away and shouldered the bag. Feet behind the ball, Sam squared his shoulders to the hole and eyed his best approach. Arms at his side and the JM Special dangling from his right hand, he studied a shot that was not so familiar. This one was shorter and tighter than what was usually routine on N$^{o.}$ 3. Too much roll and the ball would careen off to the side, like The Whammer's did. Not enough meat on it to stay up, and it'd go the other way to die a slow death in the slough. Leaving himself with anything close to a long putt, one that could prove next to impossible to make, meant the competition was all but over and he would be handed a first ever loss on his home grounds. First loss, ever.

The Whammer wasn't sitting on anything for certain with his next shot, though every dog has a day. Players had been known to catch the right line and sink one from right around that same spot. One of the visitors yesterday, Duley, Rev. Oliphint, and a President had all done so. Plenty enough times to fill the pockets on a pair of pants, Sam had sent balls to roll down from the top side of the hill and over into the hole. No matter who had made what, the one stroke lead was insurance for the big guy. In order to keep the game going, Sam knew risk was needed. However, it was death-defying to expect a shot directly at the hole to stick and pay off. Twelve hands went up.

Sam had tuned into an unknown mathematical equation and stood prepared to spit out the answer. The JM Special sliced down, propelling the golf ball up and away. Starting right, the streak came back left as it reached the apex of flight. With thousands of eyes steering the shot one way or another, the curve lapsed and the ball descended sharply. Dink! The ball hit the flagstick, bounced one time to a slow dribble, then to a complete stop one stride from the hole.

An awe, an oh, a gasp, laughter, or applause one, came with a smile from certainly everybody. Sherrod and Reverend Jessup were grinning big. Murchison had the biggest smile out there. Daisy Williamson had the biggest, prettiest smile. Rev Oliphint, who had been watching from afar in the shade by the house with his wife, her parents, and a newborn son, thanked the heavens above and then started into another prayer. Arwin was shaking Lowell's arm and pointing at the ball, saying over and over, "Did you see that?" One of the 'Busy Committee' members stated, "The hometown boy earned a mark for hitting the pole." "I'll be." replied the busiest member and, "My lands." responded the really gossipy one. The rich folks were making it clear who they had bet their money on, most all of the suits that were not churchgoers grew quiet and were looking at each other. Several of the carnies were pointing at one of their own, who had predicted the stab hitting the flagstick, then they all payed cash into his hand. The Whammer winced at Munroe and began his walk.

"Let's see what kind of good we have here, Sambo." Duley said, pulling the putter and trying to instill hope during what had to have been a clutching time.

"That monster has got his work cut out for him, and it ain't over 'til he gets that ball in before you do."

Knowing he didn't hold any kind control over the fate of the contest, Sam placed the JM Special in the bag and snagged the putter from Duley's hand. There might have been a smidgen of devastation, but he remained calm and in a mode of full concentration with the fact that promise was still alive. Sam said nothing in reply to Duley and started his walk up.

The general audience in the area surrounding the golf balls and green was like a flock of birds on a sack of bread. As the two players arrived simultaneously to a raised ruckus of appreciations, two fingers touching the brim of the fedora was the only acknowledgment to the continued deluge of appreciation. Taking position just off the fringe, was concern in The Whammer camp. Towering over the close people, he and Munroe moved frenzily about looking at the options. The big guy was covering every detail and then running it by his golf club man. The crowd had calmed, but only fell to all quiet when Munroe spurred Satterfield. Ross and Otis, distracted in the excitement themselves, hastily returned to their responsibilities due to receiving a look from Murchison that may have well been a kick in the rear end. Sam marked his ball with a nickel, then stepped near the newspapermen and photographers with his mind and eyes stirring over three feet of fine-cut grass.

The Whammer squatted and aimed his eyes down at the hole. Munroe got on his knees and shielded his eyes from the western sun, while trying to find a line from ground level. They both walked up and back down each side of any kind of potential route, then came together for an exchange and drifted apart several times. Munroe walked down by the hole and looked up the slope, then The Whammer did the same. Chatter wanted to ensue during the time, but Ross and

Otis were on it and maintained an assemblance of order. The large, circled-up mass of people inched closer when it became clear that action was drawing near. The big man stopped next to the ball, then went into an ensemble of short practice strokes.

He backed away and engaged in more strategizing with Munroe. Munroe backed away and went to stand at attention with the flagstick. Staring meanly at the chosen line, the giant crept toward the tiny ball and assumed his stance. The Whammer was crouched and looking like a man carrying a childrens golf club. He kept his face parallel to the earth and shifted his front foot ahead, then turned eyes over the slope and down to the hole. Finally, eyes went back to his task. In utter silence, wrists flexed right and punched left. The ball, jolted into a roll that took off onto the upper side of the crest, picked up speed as it cascaded over and began running on down the slope. A rising rumble began to spawn from the crowd as a verdict was nearing. Munroe whisked away the flag and side stepped. An instant later, doop! The ball lipped in and out of the hole, fumbling on down lower than Sam's marked spot. For a brief moment, the wind had been knocked out of a majority of lungs. The Whammer stormed over, took a sighing look at the remaining distance, grimaced at Munroe, then recklessly putted the ball over the yard and a half stint. He was careless and the thing almost lipped out, again, but fell in the hole after a lucky ricochet.

Sighs and gasps, followed by a small helping of giddy excitement, suddenly ceased. No hands in the air necessary, as Sam stepped to the putting surface. He placed his golf ball, snatched up the nickel, and dropped the coin in his pocket. The distance over which the putt would travel was eyed, again and again, during the last minutes. Sam hadn't looked at anything else and did not have another care in the world. In no particular special fashion, he stepped up in a casual stance, evened his feet, and nonchalantly drained the remaining distance with bold and pure confidence. A solid round of big applause was followed by an earful of hollering, then all cheer faded to the sounds of people moving on a mission.

Reverend Jessup marked the scorecard and called the players together, still on the N⁰· 3 green. Sam and The Whammer stood toe to toe. The Whammer looked stunned and kept shifting to various mean and mad faces and foot positions, like he was needing to step off into the thicket for a tree to go behind. Sam was nothing other than ready for more golfing. He looked the reverend in the eye and The Whammer was, every once in a moment, still wincing over to Munroe about the missed putt. "Tie game, gentlemen. Remarkable play by both of you." Reverend Jessup said. "We're going to start playing however many extra holes we need. We'll start at hole one and go in order, until a player achieves a lower total than the other. Any questions?"

"No, sir, Reverend." Sam answered.

The Whammer raised his chin so as to say let's get on with it.

"Okay, let us all head on over and we will start off like new with a coin flip to decide who hits first."

The Whammer stomped his way through a crush and toward the N⁰· 1 tee box. He actually had an easy path, with his bullied-up chest sending out a message to get out of the way. People willingly made space, then took their close-up stare at the surreal giant as he passed. Folks were not saying anything, just aweing. It was like there was almost a fear about him, for the good reason that the beast might snap. Munroe even walked steps further back than the short leash he had been on.

Sam and Duley took their time bringing up the very tail end, only the carnies straggled behind. Between the two young men, there was whispered debate as they each watched the other's feet meander the familiar, this time slower than ever, pathway from N°· 3 to N°· 1. Golfing stick selection was the topic, and they were both quite disregarding of the busy grounds being run amuck.

The carnies had gathered in a small circle on the N°· 3 green and were putting their morning takes against each other on the remainder of the match-up. They all had Sam to win, but the wagers were for it to happen on either Hole 4, 5, 6,7, or 8. Others, mostly the rich folks, were doubling up on their bets as they arrived to their spots. The tall grass on the right and left sides of the N°· 1 fairway was back to being trampled and the old folks had turned and angled their chairs under the Jackson Oak, then stood to see over the crowd before them. A pack of runners took across the fairway and turned west, jumping the water at the fence line, to claim the front spots along the northern side of the green. Other delinquents followed, jumped, and filled in where they could. In the blink of an eye, all space around three sides of the green was taken- shrinking the playing area by a foot along each. Arwin Rank, Jim Ainsworth, and Lowell Fields, all standing on the bridge, hollered for the offenders to back up. A gang of teenage boys had scaled the split-rail fence and were at the edge of the thicket climbing trees for a better view. 'The Busy Committee' welcomed themselves to the shade on the back porch and had already been through nearly every wrong guess there is at the breed of tree in the middle. Two of the women went right to occupying the new rocking chairs. Loose, younger kids were being corralled from their brief run between holes and a gang of older ones snuck around the front side of the house to smoke cigarettes.

A photographer went to the N$^{\text{o.}}$ 1 tee and the two others headed to wrangle a front-row spot at the green. The newspapermen had huddled, parted ways, and all were now walking in different directions while writing on their notepads. After discussion, Satterfield and Murchison moved into position on this and that side of the slough, respectively. Reverend Jessup and Sherrod would be monitoring the players. Ross and Otis took their places, one on each side of the tee box and urged back the pressing assembly that was waiting for the playoff to begin. The Whammer, Munroe in tow, came through the crevasse he'd made in the crowd and stepped to the tee box. The opening had closed, leaving Sam and Duley to navigate through a trove of well-wishers and supporters with plenty of pats on the back and positive words of encouragement. The participants stepped together and the twenty-dollar coin was flipped, once again, to come tumbling down in favor of Sam. Heads. The Whammer was given the honor and Sam stepped off the back of the tee box.

Reverend Jessup gave an all clear after another group of young boys sprinted through a corner of the fairway, then The Whammer stepped up to place his ball on a sand tee. Four hands went up and silence fell across the golfing club. Down the way, Satterfield put his hands up, too. Murchison's stayed down and his fingers were squeezing one another, a side effect of the hopeful, tense, and concerned look he had taken on in the last minutes.

There was a tantrum of spits, swings of the iron, and in the fullness of time a walk up to the ball. And, another spit. He bent, then sent a pinch of grass to the air that fell only as far as it was tossed. The large-size, right, shiny-brown leather shoe was placed and twisted into the short grass below. The Whammer peddled his shoulders as he stared off to the right side, honing in. The left foot was planted into position and big round eyes dropped to the ball. There was a pause and the hack began. As he wound, power was relinquished in favor of finesse and a smooth, yet swift, attempt was launched at a brand-new imprinted golf ball. Eyes strained as the ball flew off from a noisy eruption. All of the sound faded, then made a comeback following the birth of more lauding that reached up from the green. Fans called out, "Come on!", "Get there!", "Hurry!" and so forth. Locals cursed it back toward the slough or into the depths of thicket. The ball landed on the putting surface with a bite and continued its curving northwestward way in steady trickle directly toward the hole. The roll slowed as it drew nearer and nearer, slower and slower. A well concerted and stretched out, "Oh!" rang out from those within close eyesight of the landing area, followed by a round of applause that spread like a lie. No one at the top knew what had happened, until Murchison and Satterfield put both of their hands in the air with approximately one foot of space between. As he stepped off, The Whammer gave a big cocky and self-fulfilling grin to a very mildly talkative group that was sardined around the tee box.

A cluster of enormous white clouds breezed in front of the beating sun, shading all foreground, darkening the grass, and relieving the Texas heat. With the all quiet expectation heeded, the name Sam flew from a half dozen mouths. There were sparse but sharp-willed claps as the young man stepped to place his golf ball on a choice smudge of grass that was a smidge taller and stiffer than any other that could be found. The JM Special was in hand. Sam walked away and turned. He had a long, fierce look to the hole with the ball spotted at the bottom of his vision. The flag hung still and the top branches of the Jackson Oak swayed barely. Ripples interrupted still water in the slough and a pair of dragonflies were orbiting above. The bunch of clouds was drifting high and blades of taller grass surrounding the water waved below. A known landing area was desired, Mother Nature's variables were rolling over, and a dilemma was still churning.

Sam turned to Duley with a peripheral eye and a slight twist of the head. Duley and the golf bag stepped forward to Sam's hip. Both sets of eyes were locked on the green ahead and Sam spoke to Duley's ear. The immediate crowd quieted and leaned in. Many desiring to be a fly on the wall were looking to the Nº 1 tee and making guesses about what was being said between the two young men. Rev. Oliphint and his father-in-law left the family in the shade and walked closer to the action. Moments ago, Rev. stepped away to slide into the congestion and catch Sam's eye with a good and gracious nod of confidence. Now, he was back with his in-law, smiling, pointing to the western sky, leaning in, and telling exactly what Sam was up to.

"What's your brain telling you, Duley?" Sam whispered.

"I'm thinking the green has become about a foot shorter on three sides."

Sam kept from a smile. "Hopefully, we're not going to need that part of the green." he said, "What else are you thinking?"

"I'm thinking you know this hole like the back of your hand, better than anyone. It looks to me like you fixed that broadstick just fine. I've been examining it and feeling around on it the entire round, seems fine to me. Don't know why you haven't swapped 'em out. You have to get this one on, Sambo."

"What else?"

"Well, you want me to hand it to you?"

"No, Duley. This is the one that's got to go here. That last time through, it just slipped off a little. Feels to me like it was made for this hole. It's going to be close. What else?"

"What do you mean, what else? If you got it then knock it there, Sambo."

"I mean, what else are you thinking here?" Sam said, putting a quick eye on Duley. Duley was beginning to look around at the crowd that was looking back for something to happen.

"This wind ain't going to mess with it any more than any other day. Go at it and nail it." Duley said as he began to back away.

Sam turned and gave him an eye that said, "Don't go anywhere."

Duley didn't go anywhere.

"Anything else?" Sam whispered softly.

"Sambo, I don't know anything else I can tell you."

"Okay, making sure." Sam said quietly.

"When you are ready, Sambo." Duley said at a little higher volume level, then started to take a step back.

Sam gave him the eye again and Duley stayed put.

"Look here, watch for a second." Sam said.

Duley looked at Sam to see his face become lit with golden rays of sunshine. There was a small grin from Sam and a big smile from Duley. Duley leaned in and whispered, "Sun is shining, Sambo."

"Here we go. Hopefully, by the time this ball gets there those blades of grass will be reaching up and standing tall."

Duley winked and backed away.

Sam gave a short speech with silent words of gratitude for the JM Special. There was a feeling of wanting to make Murchison, and the town, proud. There was a thought that a big story in the newspaper, one that spelled out a successful take down of the notorious giant, could get around and maybe make its way to long lost family. There were thoughts to Mr. Fair and Miss Ann. Sam wanted to make those two proud but knew he could never. In a last check of the sun and the clouds, a small smile showed when he imagined they were looking down. He saw the great Ellis Fair rolling his sleeves. His heart warmed when Murchison, standing tall on the left side of the green, came into view. There was a feeling that Judge Jackson and Mary Merit were watching over as well. Judge would be getting a kick out of this competition, perhaps be in the middle of it. These thoughts turned the young golfer back to serious business, not that he had ever left. There was no weighing of the Georgia round and no recollections of any nouns on his adventures to Merit. There were no hands up around the green. There was no crowd, no carnies, no officials, no rival. No house and no flagstick. No short grass and no smell of fresh-cut grass. No willow trees and no honey suckle delighting the air. The grass before Sam was tall, knee-high. One hundred and eighty yards away, over the slough, there was a glass jar buried stuck down in a twenty by twenty patch.

There was ease in Sam's manner as he found a plug of grass to his liking. Chin and chest were up and proud, then he bent to place his golf ball. The fedora was cinched, followed by the eyes making another long stare to the green. Holding the JM Special with belief in his right hand and giving a tug on the right sleeve, he then switched to the left hand and gave a better tuck to the left sleeve. Hips cocked south, the right foot was in front of his left and barely supported any weight. The shaft of the favored golf stick hovered just above his right collarbone and the relaxed grip rested on his chest. Looking down at the ball, Sam remained with his head still and raised his eyes back to the hole.

He twisted over, several times, the handle in his right hand as he stepped back left, then mightily assumed his routine and bold statue of a golf stance. Movements were slowed, steady, and with purpose. He was a warrior. The left foot was a tick ahead of the right and just in front of the ball. Tall with the slight bend at the knee, the left one a little more than the right. An easy lean forward and perfectly aligned. Chin was dropped and eyes looked left with an intense, undistracted, piercing stare that was dead on with the right front corner of the nineteen by nineteen patch. To the observers, the eyes, the body, the semblance of his being at that moment in time, cast a dauntless look that spoke to the becoming of something grand. Mouths were open, just a bit, and breathing was slow while the people stood in wonderment of what they were about to witness.

The JM Special was clutched with the same hint of looseness, yet in the hands, the stick was held firmly with faith surmounting over all else. Left hand on top, right on bottom, an inch of space in between. Firm and relaxed. Steadily, he placed the iron head of the heralded golf stick beside the savored golf ball. For a slight moment, Sam lifted his head and took in what lie ahead. Eyes fell quickly back to the ball. He was automatic and unconsciously controlled. A dose of hot summer air and then breathing stopped.

A hint toward looser with his grip, the golf club retreated as Sam's chin did the small tick of a rise to the right. Right elbow bent, left stayed straight and crossed the torso. The wooden stick reached parallel to the tips of grass and, in coming out of the magical blur, the iron was pointing at the promised land. In stillness, a symphonic mission was going at full speed ahead. Nothing present, except the path to a miraculous destiny. Might was there and all necessary components of the great game of golf stood ready for glory.

Motion shifted and the real magic started. Controlled chaos coming from the soul of the master Sam. The air rushed for space. Whoosh! Thwack! The sizzle of a jolted ball sprung from the grass like a bullet. Sam was left hurling and slowed to a pause at the moveable limits of his act. At ease, the bystander's mind was thinking like a landscaper, a weatherman, a mathematician, a commanding general, a reverend.

The sizzle faded and the ball grew darker and smaller as it rose toward the sun, and the blue sky, and the bunch of drifting western white clouds. Eyesight struggled to keep track of the golf ball as the mighty soar faded toward a shining bead of gold. Head held high with eyes hoping and dreaming across the picturesque land, Sam relaxed with confidence in the powers that be. The JM Special had dropped and rested on his left shoulder. The toe of his right boot was twisted into the black earth and he stared into the distance.

The carnies were out of liquor and the first to head down Main Street and into town, Hopper in tow telling stories to the eldest of the fellows. Mayor Abernathy was ahead, he had to watch the last hole from Dead Horse Hill. Mal, too. Arwin was hustling to open the cafe. Mr. Dell, Mr. Kearney, and others rushed to open the doors to their businesses. The only spin on the barber pole was when Lowell turned and headed back with his golf sticks in hand, though there would be no more golf on that day. Umbrellas and other folks off the N$^{o.}$ 56 followed vacated the premises and not long thereafter, smoke blew above the railroad tracks. The largest group, those from the surrounding area, headed back to their horses, wagons, and camps. The elderly slowly made their way out, as did the small groups of locals lingering about, gossiping, and having looks around the quieted and clearing grounds. The 'Busy Committee' left with the idea of purchasing rocking chairs for their get-togethers. Lowell and Ainsworth replaced the ladies chit-chat on back porch with golf talk.

Young children ran in the open area of the southeast part of the grounds and older ones raced ahead of them. A scattering of boys and girls knocked magical golf balls from the N$^{o.}$ 1 fairway, over the water, onto the green, and into the

243

hole- all the while, refusing their parents commands. Murchison waited around to get a word in, though was getting pulled away by Doctor Smith. Same for Daisy Williamson, though her father was doing the pulling. The reverends were walking out together, three of them all dressed alike. Rev. Oliphint was walking out with family and looking back at the grounds. He had pried his way right through the hullabaloo for a quick handshake and to say, "See you next Sunday." "Tomorrow!" replied Sam. Duley was right to watering the N$^{o.}$ 1 green and also had his hand clippers out, then he would be on top of repairing all of the ruts that The Whammer had left.

The sun cast a sliver of shine over the blackness of the thicket and a dark blue Texas sky washed the east. Under the Jackson Oak, a half-dozen newspapermen huddled with notepads to the side of three tripods posting cameras. Sherrod stood close by intently writing on his tablet. When the sun slipped lower, the group disbanded and made their way out the front gate and down Main. Children and adults alike were taking part in games with the drunk carnies. The youngest and newest local carney still had the longest line with his golf hole. The cafe was on a wait list and a line went around the corner at the ice cream shop, on a Sunday. Strangers and locals stood shoulder to shoulder in the bar. The boardwalks and intersection were filled with folks strolling along in one direction or another, and at the south end a three-piece band started into a catchy tune. Bright lights sparkled with bams and pops in the holiday sky above Merit, a town that was laughing, smiling, and filled with joy at the hand of the legendary Sam Stallings.

CHAPTER 9

Prideful was the small population of Merit and for days after, the buzz of the holiday weekend, the golf contest, and the first son's miraculous win lingered in the small town. Sam had captured hearts, minds, and imaginations. Love and loyalty. However many people were in attendance that storied day, is the same number of fans that both he and the game of golf garnered. There were free meals at the cafe, free drinks and toasts at the bar. Free ice cream. Even, flowers and donations that were sent to the golfing club. Sam didn't much walk around smiling during his rare times in town shortly after the showdown, but everyone else did when he was around. A week to the date, Sherrod's article about the thrilling match came out on the front page of the *Times Herald*, a photograph included of all might thrusting into the famed tee shot. *'Young Texas Golf Prodigy Takes Down the Great Whammer in Merit'* read the headline. A train passenger had first brought a day-old edition of the Sunday paper into the cafe, then Murchison made a special trip to Dallas where he was able to round up a stack. A quarter of the issues were saved for good-keeping and the rest went up for sale in the mercantile for twice the advertised cost. A copy was put behind glass and hung on the back wall of the bar and Sam was given a copy, which was never read but folded and placed in the bottom of Mr. Fair's old wooden trunk. By the time the people in Merit read the paper, it seemed old news. From there, the details of the round were only repetitively discussed by the less than handful of golfers still in town.

When the thick of August hit, a dozen more lots were up for sale and a nervous tension was wrecking its way through Merit. The number of trains coming through had been cut to three a week due to a new junction opening up off the northern part of the loop. The stockyard and stable closed down to move closer to Greenville, where more livestock was coming through. Word had it the inn would quickly be running in the red and a sale was looking imminent for Mr. Kearney. J.K. Elliott's shelves were near empty and with vacant houses looming to stifle business, he headed out of town at the drop of a hat with no notice at all. August seemed to have been rough all around on everyone in town. To top things off, and to the dismay of the small enrollment of school children, the ice cream freezer at Dell's quit working. Business melted to a halt, until further notice.

The Bateson Brothers changed to having the office open only one day of the week, and every day but Saturday there was a sign in the barbershop window letting anyone looking for a haircut know that Lowell Fields was at the golfing club. Arwin was playing less and working more, after two of the servers were lost when their husbands were laid off from the railroad. As a result, two more houses went up for sale. Attendance at both churches was down to single digits the last two Sundays and the collection plates held about the same count of dollars. No one in town had died, yet, so Fulton's closed until someone did. Finus was off somewhere, apparently still doing railroad work, and Hopper had not been seen since the early morning hours of July 5th. Murchison had been drinking quite a lot, working hard on luring new residents to town, and watching them leave as quickly as they had arrived. Duley was spending long hard days caring for the grounds and battling the blazing Texas sun. Not a blade of grass was out of place and all signs of The Whammer were repaired and well healed over.

Sam was still at it, golfing round after round every day, and helping Duley in between. He walked humble in these days, more so than before the astounding victory. Doubling down on his game, there became twice as much stubbornness in his pursuit of excellence. Practice held tremendous purpose and his skills had come to be sharp as a tack in their second-nature standing. Most all of the golf balls from that original box were near plum worn out. Not in as bad of shape as the old leather ones, but pretty bad. Thankfully, a week after the article released, a note of congratulations on the phenomenal victory came packed on top of a gross of new gutty balls. The note was signed by Jack Malley and these balls were dimpled all over. They flew further and straighter, Doctor Newman Smith explained the science behind it. On the last day of July, the first time Sam played with one of the new balls, he registered a record for eighteen holes. A remarkable six trips around The Judge Merit Golfing Club in 59 strokes.

Sam came to very well know the ins and outs of the grounds, and really took to playing some good golf during that time after the big win. His favorite way to play the second hole was hitting a dozen drives from the tee, then knocking them all to the green from there with the broadstick. Always easy as pie. If there wasn't one in the hole per twelve, he would play the bunch of balls all over again from the tee box. The drive at N[o.] 2 came to be more challenging when a wide strip of rough was allowed to grow all the way across the fairway, prior to where a great tee shot would land. That space was left alone because a new tree of some type was sprouting up. The others that played during this time had to really up their long game to get over the thick patch, otherwise lie short or else end up in the ankle-high grass. Either of the latter and the golfer was very likely not going to be making their ball to the green on the next shot. Duley played shots that were tangled in the tall grass many a time, before Sam let him cut it back a little.

Perhaps, N°. 3 was the hole that Sam mastered more so than the others. The driver was used like an artist uses a brush when placing an emphatic line, like a fine craftsman uses a tool, and like a writer chooses a first paragraph for a story, to handle the left bending curve of the fairway. The ball was always struck to a sizzle and a hooking pathway, one that launched to high above and then nipped over the thick grass lying off the touches of the shade from the Jackson Oak. The ball would fall and come chopping down to a rest just off the fine-cut grass on the front side of the green. Sam started calling that favored nook of a landing spot, Mrs. Merit's Place. Right next to Judge Jackson Merit's oak tree and you could always smell the scent of honeysuckle blowing over from the front gate.

A lot of putting took place at the charismatic N°. 3 green. 'Green practice', as Sam called it. He very well knew the ups and downs, rolls and punches of the N°. 3 green. Most often, he drained every one of his putts. No matter the hole location, no matter the line. Duley called watching Sam practice putting at N°. 3 more fun than a frog in a glass of milk. Sam would knock sidewinding, slithering, and seemingly magnetized putts into the hole from north to south, east to west, and every direction in between. Many stunned moments of laughs, giggles, smiles, handshakes, and high-fives were shared over the near-impossible shots that rolled up and across, down and along, or steady on the edge of the crowned and sloping green.

The first hole was played repetitively more than the others, especially in the evening hours. Over and over, ball after ball. The challenging beast that laid as N$^{o.}$ 1 was lately most often every time tamed in two, one shot plus a sure tap-in. Since the holiday, there had been a handful more times that Sam stood on the tee and heard a gutty ball send an echo of a rattle through a silent Judge Merit Golfing Club. Because no one else was much ever around when the wood was pluncked, Duley took to the routine of hollering out a big loud, "Sambo" up to the tee from wherever he was working. In the last week of August, the green down at N$^{o.}$ 1 had come to looking like a summer hail storm rolled through and the space desperately needed a break. Aside from placing himself in harm's way of a golf ball or flying iron, Duley couldn't keep up with repairing all of the ball marks on the greens, nor the divots on the tees.

The traditional Sunday afternoon rounds with the boys continued, though Lowell Fields had replaced a busy Arwin Rank in the group. A fourth was going to be needed after next Sunday, Rev. Oliphint had the Methodist Episcopal Church in Celeste added to his charge. All golf stick manufacturing had ceased, though at Sam's request Duley was making up a special set for the minister in hopes that he would continue to come play at least one day of the week. The connections between the game and the almighty universe brought forth by Rev. Oliphint on the walks from shot to shot were too good for the soul to miss.

Though town wasn't bustling, the grandeur of the golfing club steadily grew. People passing through were always saying something about it or wanting to visit, though golfing attendance was lacking at best. Routine was so routine that the two mainstays took to coming up with some wild variations of the game.

251

They played one evening using shovels, rakes, and milk bottles as golf clubs, then another day they used bad peaches as the golf balls. After a surprisingly successful nighttime round, the next morning they played blindfolded just to see if they could beat their tallies from hours ago. They played the holes backward and forward. They played right handed and even switched over imitating The Whammer as they played a round left handed. The dog days had likely drove the buddies to boredom, though they seemed to be having fun and enjoying their game-filled lifestyle to the maximum. All of everything was centered around the game, every day.

One of Sam's favorite pastimes of leaving out for a stint of trail golf still remained. It was in his blood. Most of the time he went by himself off to the south or even a time or so for a battle through the thicket, though on the last two trips Duley had been invited to go along. Both times were less than half-a-day up Katy Trail and on the last one, an overnighter into the prairie was planned for the following Friday. Early that morning, the two young men teed off pointed south on Main Street with two day's supply of dried meat, peaches, and water. Duley chose the first post on the porch of the cafe as Hole N°. 1 and after Sam knocked it with his ball in a record 3 strokes, the pair went inside for a biscuit before continuing. The first tree in the first cluster of elms was called out by Sam as the second hole, and then he let one fly south. Per the rules, Sam would have the honor of calling out the rest of the holes on this trip.

The number of miles into the prairie was unknown and the number of holes and strokes was forgotten. The two had played until well after sundown, made camp that night, and then turned around in the morning. Each man hit one ball headed north at sunrise from the middle of nowhere to start the second round. They played through the hot and dry day, retracing their pathway back to town on a mission to beat yesterday's score over the same stretch. The day was rolling smooth and the play was too. Town could barely be seen in the far-off distance with plenty of light left for a round or two once home. Just south of Merit, while assuming his routine golf stance and peering with eagle eyes to his next target, which was the biggest oak in the last cluster before town, a sorrowful gaze came forth and deep chills shot through Sam's shocked body. The broadstick was dropped in the first lunge north, then a desperate sprint set forth.

There was not a soul around in town and by the time Sam reached Katy Trail the black smoke was billowing into gray as it rapidly expanded on up to the clouds. Below, shots of bright orange flames of fury began peeking over the top of the ridgeline. Duley was a steady clip behind and coming up Main Street when Sam, atop Dead Horse Hill, realized that Hole No.1 and No. 2 were gone and dropped to his knees. The Jackson Oak, $N^{o.}$ 3, then the house followed. There was nothing that could be done. Duley's calls to get to the water wagons were unanswered and then faded with his realization that there was no hope.

Before a small group of witnesses, the fire at The Judge Merit Golfing Club raged into the night. The ridge saved the devastation from sweeping through town and the river contained the blaze to the east. Sam's graceland, and well into Brown Cat Thicket, was left as a smoldering and charred wasteland.

A crushed heart and an aching soul didn't sleep a wink with forehead pressed to the bar that night. No drinks, though Murchison was passed out sitting up, leaning against the wall by the front door, exhausted from all of the trips back and forth between Sam and the fire. The door was left open and the first light, along with the smell of burnt land, awoke Murchison. He gave an unreactive Sam a gentle pat on the back and then walked to the street for a wry look at the white smoke loitering above the distance. He returned moments later carrying an envelope.

"Sam." he said quietly.

The head raised slightly but still hung.

"I think you need to open this up." Murchison said, as he put forth the mail.

The eyes widened as he sat up and glanced back, before moving to a dead stare in the mirror.

"It arrived yesterday. Addressed from the National Golfing Association. Open it up." Murchison urged with a nod and another extension of the letter.

Sam took the letter and placed it on the bar. He was on the cusp of speaking, though did not and the forehead returned to the bar.

"I'm going to leave you be, for now." Murchison said.

Sam stayed put for a short while, then walked to the top of Dead Horse Hill and had a seat for the day. He looked north over the blackness and poured through a range of emotions as afternoon went to evening and into the night. In complete darkness, the letter was opened and read with squinted eyes. Finally, a second break was taken from the stare over the black land and eyes moved to the golfing bag laying by his side.

Sometime in the early morning hours, Sam walked down through the crispy remains and nailed back the singed sign that declared the land as The Judge Merit Golfing Club. At sun up, he said his goodbyes to Duley and then to Murchison, who both sought to deliver any and all reconciliation possible. The elder assured the young man that Merit was there to stay and then offered anything and all that he could muster.

With that, Sam dropped his satchel, placed his trunk in the middle of the intersection, slung the golf bag from his shoulder, and pulled the broadstick before dropping the bag and a brand new dimpled gutty ball to the ground before him. He assumed his routine and statue-like golf stance, then stared east down the railroad tracks. There were no thoughts about anything. None of the past. No thinking of hopping trains or heading out on his own. No thoughts of the controversy in Georgia and no thoughts of the challenging round against and the victory over one of the so-called greats. No thoughts of The Judge Merit Golfing Club, nor of the fire. Sam Stallings eyed his bead and drew the broadstick, then let go a first shot headed toward Riverdale, Illinois, site of the upcoming first ever Grand National Golf Championship.

ABOUT THE AUTHOR

Matt Hargrove, a native Texan, has worked in education, athletics, public relations, and now as an author with the debut of his first novel, The Judge Merit Golfing Club. An avid fan of just about all sports, golf is one of the favorites and, like Sam, he plays as much as time allows. He is a graduate of Texas A&M University – Commerce and resides in Dallas, Texas.

www.ingramcontent.com/pod-product-compliance
Lightning Source LLC
Chambersburg PA
CBHW071457170626
46811CB00007B/2604